PHILIP MARLOWE

'I'm a licensed private investigator and have been for quite a while. I'm a lone wolf, unmarried, getting middle-aged, and not rich. I've been in jail more than once and I don't do divorce business. I like liquor and women and chess and a few other things. The cops don't like me too well, but I know a couple I get along with. I'm a native son, born in Santa Rosa, both parents dead, no brothers or sisters, and when I get knocked off in a dark alley sometime, if it happens, as it could to anyone in my business, nobody will feel that the bottom has dropped out of his or her life.'

RAYMOND CHANDLER was born in Chicago in 1888 and moved to England with his family when he was twelve. He attended Dulwich College, Alma Mater to some of the twentieth century's most renowned writers. Returning to America in 1912, he settled in Calfornia, worked in a number of jobs, and later married. It was during the Depression era that he seriously turned his hand to writing and his first published story appeared in the pulp magazine *Black Mask* in 1933, followed six years later by his first novel. *The Big Sleep* introduced the world to Philip Marlowe, the often-imitated but never-bettered hard-boiled private investigator. It is in Marlowe's long shadow that every fictional detective must stand – and under the influence of Raymond Chandler's addictive prose that every crime author must write.

JONATHAN KELLERMAN is the author of twenty-five consecutive bestselling crime novels, three books on psychology and two volumes for children. He lives with his wife, the novelist Faye Kellerman, in Southern California

The Lady in the Lake

RAYMOND CHANDLER

with an Introduction by Jonathan Kellerman

PENGUIN BOOKS

PENGUIN BOOKS

Published by the Penguin Group
Penguin Books Ltd, 80 Strand, London WC2R ORL, England
Penguin Group (USA) Inc., 375 Hudson Street, New York, New York 10014, USA
Penguin Group (Canada), 90 Eglinton Avenue East, Suite 700, Toronto, Ontario,
Canada M4P 2Y3 (a division of Pearson Penguin Canada Inc.)
Penguin Ireland, 25 St Stephen's Green, Dublin 2, Ireland (a division of Penguin Books Ltd)
Penguin Group (Australia), 250 Camberwell Road, Camberwell, Victoria 3124, Australia
(a division of Pearson Australia Group Pty Ltd)
Penguin Books India Pvt Ltd, 11 Community Centre, Panchsheel Park, New Delhi – 110 017, India
Penguin Group (NZ), 67 Apollo Drive, Rosedale, Auckland 0632, New Zealand
(a division of Pearson New Zealand Ltd)
Penguin Books (South Africa) (Pty) Ltd, 24 Sturdee Avenue,
Rosebank, Johannesburg 2196, South Africa

Penguin Books Ltd, Registered Offices: 80 Strand, London WC2R ORL, England

www.penguin.com

First published by Hamish Hamilton 1944
Published in Penguin Books 1952
Reissued in Penguin Books with a new Introduction 2005
This edition published 2011

001

Copyright 1944 by Raymond Chandler
Introduction copyright © Jonathan Kellerman, 2005
All rights reserved

The moral right of the author has been asserted

Set in 11/13pt Monotype Dante
Typeset by Rowland Phototypesetting Ltd, Bury St Edmunds, Suffolk
Printed in England by Clays Ltd, St Ives plc

ISBN: 978-0-241-98064-4

www.greenpenguin.co.uk

Jonathan Kellerman on
The Lady in the Lake

A Stranger's Eye

Many of the finest American crime novels have been set in Southern California. How could it be otherwise?

Los Angeles, the city where I live and write, is a Third World Nation, marked by waves of ethnic confusion, ostentation as religion, stunning extremes of wealth and poverty, and a diminishing middle class struggling to hold up the centre. As Freud and Machiavelli and Marie Antoinette could all testify, that kind of chaos can lead to psychosocial tension. And tension, when cranky, sometimes nudges the back door open for his reprobate cousin, violence.

L.A.'s a company town. The product's fantasy – both the chronically over-budgeted spectaculars filmed on studio lots and the wrap-in-a-day 'adult entertainment' loops video-cammed hundred of times a week in San Fernando Valley ranch houses.

Then, there's the weather. All that sunshine means more leisure time for those so-inclined to get into mischief. Smog and mudslides and earthquakes can sour a person's mood. Run for your life and reach the ocean and there's nowhere else to go.

And, ah, the Santa Anas.

'. . . those hot dry winds that come down through the mountain passes and curl your hair and make your nerves jump and your skin itch. On nights like that every booze party ends in a fight. Meek little wives feel the edge of the carving knife and study their husbands' necks. Anything can happen.'

That's Raymond Chandler, from his short story, 'Red Wind'.

Chandler was born in Chicago but he grew up in England after his parents' divorce. Sometimes the immigrant's perspective teases out nuance and irony overlooked by the native. Chandler's outsider status, combined with a depressive, lone-wolf's jaundiced eye, contributed to his genius.

Chandler's career trajectory defies cliché: journalist, failed poet, bookkeeper, Canadian army enlistee, petroleum executive, hard-boiled crime novelist. When he began writing seriously, in his forties, he didn't create a new genre. So-called pulp fiction was well-established and Chandler was one of many story-smiths turning out tales of lust, bloodshed and disillusionment.

Some of those guys were hacks, a few were artists. Chandler was the best of the artists and he has endured. Though that appraisal would probably make his lip curl.

Chandler's books hold up structurally, but plotting wasn't his forte. What keeps the reader turning pages are dead-eye observations of hypocrisy, self-delusion and evil, tormented characters about whose fate we come to care and an hypnotic sense of place that has never been surpassed by any other crime writer.

Chandler wasn't prolific. Depression and heartbreak and the writer's affliction – self-medication with alcohol – eroded his productivity.

The Lady in the Lake is the fourth of six novels he completed. It is a dark, evocative, page-turning tale of passion and revulsion and betrayal set in a city too damn sunny for its own good. Set in another time, the book is timeless.

Read and discover.

I

The Treloar Building was, and is, on Olive Street, near Sixth, on the west side. The sidewalk in front of it had been built of black and white rubber blocks. They were taking them up now to give to the government, and a hatless pale man with a face like a building superintendent was watching the work and looking as if it was breaking his heart.

I went past him through an arcade of speciality shops into a vast black and gold lobby. The Gillerlain Company was on the seventh floor, in front, behind swinging double plate-glass doors bound in platinum. Their reception-room had Chinese rugs, dull silver walls, angular but elaborate furniture, sharp shiny bits of abstract sculpture on pedestals and a tall display in a triangular showcase in the corner. On tiers and steps and islands and promontories of shining mirror-glass it seemed to contain every fancy bottle and box that has ever been designed. There were creams and powders and soaps and toilet waters for every season and every occasion. There were perfumes in tall thin bottles that looked as if a breath would blow them over and perfumes in little pastel phials tied with ducky satin bows, like little girls at a dancing class. The cream of the crop seemed to be something very small and simple in a squat amber bottle. It was in the middle at eye height, had a lot of space to itself, and was labelled *Gillerlain Regal, The Champagne of*

Perfumes. It was definitely the stuff to get. One drop of that in the hollow of your throat and the matched pink pearls started falling on you like summer rain.

A neat little blonde sat off in a far corner at a small P.B.X., behind a railing and well out of harm's way. At a flat desk in line with the doors was a tall, lean, dark-haired lovely whose name, according to the titled embossed plaque on her desk, was Miss Adrienne Fromsett.

She wore a steel-grey business suit and under the jacket a dark blue shirt and a man's tie of lighter shade. The edges of the folded handkerchief in the breast pocket looked sharp enough to slice bread. She wore a linked bracelet and no other jewellery. Her dark hair was parted and fell in loose but not unstudied waves. She had a smooth ivory skin and rather severe eyebrows and large dark eyes that looked as if they might warm up at the right time and in the right place.

I put my plain card, the one without the tommy gun in the corner, on her desk and asked to see Mr Derace Kingsley.

She looked at the card and said: 'Have you an appointment?'

'No appointment.'

'It is very difficult to see Mr Kingsley without an appointment.'

That wasn't anything I could argue about.

'What is the nature of your business, Mr Marlowe?'

'Personal.'

'I see. Does Mr Kingsley know you, Mr Marlowe?'

'I don't think so. He may have heard my name. You might say I'm from Lieutenant M'Gee.'

'And does Mr Kingsley know Lieutenant M'Gee?'

She put my card beside a pile of freshly typed letter-heads. She leaned back and put one arm on the desk and tapped lightly with a small gold pencil.

I grinned at her. The little blonde at the PBX cocked a shell-like ear and smiled a small fluffy smile. She looked playful and eager, but not quite sure of herself, like a new kitten in a house where they don't care much about kittens.

'I'm hoping he does,' I said. 'But maybe the best way to find out is to ask him.'

She initialled three letters rapidly, to keep from throwing her pen set at me. She spoke again without looking up.

'Mr Kingsley is in conference. I'll send your card in when I have an opportunity.'

I thanked her and went and sat in a chromium and leather chair that was a lot more comfortable than it looked. Time passed and silence descended on the scene. Nobody came in or went out. Miss Fromsett's elegant hand moved over her papers and the muted peep of the kitten at the P.B.X. was audible at moments, and the little click of the plugs going in and out.

I lit a cigarette and dragged a smoking stand beside the chair. The minutes went by on tiptoe, with their fingers to their lips. I looked the place over. You can't tell anything about an outfit like that. They might be making millions, and they might have the sheriff in the back room, with his chair tilted against the safe.

Half an hour and three or four cigarettes later a door opened behind Miss Fromsett's desk and two men came out backwards, laughing. A third man held the door for them and helped them laugh. They all shook hands heartily and the two men went across the office and out. The third man dropped the grin off his face and looked as if he had never grinned in his life. He was a tall bird in a grey suit and he didn't want any nonsense.

'Any calls?' he asked in a sharp bossy voice.

Miss Fromsett said softly: 'A Mr Marlowe to see you. From Lieutenant M'Gee. His business is personal.'

'Never heard of him,' the tall man barked. He took my card, didn't even glance at me, and went back into his office. His door closed on the pneumatic closer and made a sound like 'phooey'. Miss Fromsett gave me a sweet sad smile and I gave it back to her in the form of an obscene leer. I ate another cigarette and more time staggered by. I was getting to be very fond of the Gillerlain Company.

Ten minutes later the same door opened again and the big shot came out with his hat on and sneered that he was going to get a hair-cut. He started off across the Chinese rug in a swinging athletic stride, made about half the distance to the door and then did a sharp cutback and came over to where I was sitting.

'You want to see me?' he barked.

He was about six feet two and not much of it soft. His eyes were stone grey with flecks of cold light in them. He filled a large size in smooth grey flannel with a narrow chalk stripe, and filled it elegantly. His manner said he was very tough to get along with.

I stood up. 'If you're Mr Derace Kingsley.'

'Who the hell did you think I was?'

I let him have that trick and gave him my other card, the one with the business on it. He clamped it in his paw and scowled down at it.

'Who's M'Gee?' he snapped.

'He's just a fellow I know.'

'I'm fascinated,' he said, glancing back at Miss Fromsett. She liked it. She liked it very much. 'Anything else you would care to let drop about him?'

'Well, they call him Violets M'Gee,' I said. 'On account of he chews little throat pastilles that smell of violets. He's a big man with soft silvery hair and a cute little mouth made to kiss babies with. When last seen he was wearing a neat blue suit, wide-toed brown shoes, grey homburg hat, and he was smoking opium in a short briar pipe.'

'I don't like your manner,' Kingsley said in a voice you could have cracked a brazil nut on.

'That's all right,' I said. 'I'm not selling it.'

He reared back as if I had hung a week-old mackerel under his nose. After a moment he turned his back on me and said over his shoulder:

'I'll give you exactly three minutes. God knows why.'

He burned the carpet back past Miss Fromsett's desk to his door, yanked it open and let it swing to in my face. Miss Fromsett liked that too, but I thought there was a little sly laughter behind her eyes now.

2

The private office was everything a private office should be. It was long and dim and quiet and air-conditioned and its windows were shut and its grey venetian blinds half-closed to keep out the July glare. Grey drapes matched the grey carpeting. There was a large black and silver safe in the corner and a low row of low filing cases that exactly matched it. On the wall there was a huge tinted photograph of an elderly party with a chiselled beak and whiskers and a wing collar. The Adam's apple that edged through his wing collar looked harder than most people's chins. The plate underneath the photograph read: *Mr Matthew Gillerlain, 1860–1934*.

Derace Kingsley marched briskly behind about eight hundred dollars' worth of executive desk and planted his backside in a tall leather chair. He reached himself a panatela out of a copper and mahogany box and trimmed it and lit it with a fat copper desk lighter. He took his time about it. It didn't matter about my time. When he had finished this, he leaned back and blew a little smoke and said:

'I'm a business man. I don't fool around. You're a licensed detective, your card says. Show me something to prove it.'

I got my wallet out and handed him things to prove it. He looked at them and threw them back across the desk. The celluloid holder with the photostat of my licence in it fell to the floor. He didn't bother to apologize.

'I don't know M'Gee,' he said. 'I know Sheriff Petersen. I asked for the name of a reliable man to do a job. I suppose you are the man.'

'M'Gee is in the Hollywood sub-station of the sheriff's office,' I said. 'You can check on that.'

'Not necessary. I guess you might do, but don't get flip with me. And remember when I hire a man he's my man. He does exactly what I tell him and he keeps his mouth shut. Or he goes out fast. Is that clear? I hope I'm not too tough for you.'

'Why not leave that an open question?' I said.

He frowned. He said sharply: 'What do you charge?'

'Twenty-five a day and expenses. Eight cents a mile for my car.'

'Absurd,' he said. 'Far too much. Fifteen a day flat. That's plenty. I'll pay the mileage, within reason, the way things are now. But no joyriding.'

I blew a little grey cloud of cigarette smoke and fanned it with my hand. I said nothing. He seemed a little surprised that I said nothing.

He leaned over the desk and pointed with his cigar. 'I haven't hired you yet,' he said, 'but if I do, the job is absolutely confidential. No talking it over with your cop friends. Is that understood?'

'Just what do you want done, Mr Kingsley?'

'What do you care? You do all kinds of detective work, don't you?'

'Not all kinds. Only the fairly honest kinds.'

He stared at me level-eyed, his jaw tight. His grey eyes had an opaque look.

'For one thing I don't do divorce business,' I said. 'And I get a hundred down as a retainer – from strangers.'

'Well, well,' he said, in a voice suddenly soft. 'Well, well.'

'And as for your being too tough for me,' I said, 'most of the clients start out either by weeping down my shirt or bawling me out to show who's boss. But usually they end up very reasonable – if they're still alive.'

'Well, well,' he said again, in the same soft voice, and went on staring at me. 'Do you lose very many of them?' he asked.

'Not if they treat me right,' I said.

'Have a cigar,' he said.

I took a cigar and put it in my pocket.

'I want you to find my wife,' he said. 'She's been missing for a month.'

'Okay,' I said. 'I'll find your wife.'

He patted his desk with both hands. He stared at me solidly. 'I think you will at that,' he said. Then he grinned. 'I haven't been called down like that in four years,' he said.

I didn't say anything.

'Damn it all,' he said, 'I liked it. I liked it fine.' He ran a hand through his thick dark hair. 'She's been gone a whole month,' he said. 'From a cabin we have in the mountains. Near Puma Point. Do you know Puma Point?'

I said I knew Puma Point.

'Our place is three miles from the village,' he said, 'partly over a private road. It's on a private lake. Little Fawn Lake. There's a dam three of us put up to improve the property. I own the tract with two other men. It's

8

quite large, but undeveloped and won't be developed now for some time, of course. My friends have cabins, I have a cabin and a man named Bill Chess lives with his wife in another cabin rent-free and looks after the place. He's a disabled veteran with a pension. That's all there is up there. My wife went up the middle of May, came down twice for week-ends, was due down the 12th of June for a party and never showed up. I haven't seen her since.'

'What have you done about it?' I asked.

'Nothing. Not a thing. I haven't even been up there.' He waited, wanting me to ask why.

I said: 'Why?'

He pushed his chair back to get a locked drawer open. He took out a folded paper and passed it over. I unfolded it and saw it was a postal telegraph form. The wire had been filed at El Paso on June 14th, at 9.19 a.m. It was addressed to Derace Kingsley, 965 Carson Drive, Beverly Hills, and read:

AM CROSSING TO GET MEXICAN DIVORCE STOP WILL MARRY CHRIS STOP GOOD LUCK AND GOODBYE CRYSTAL

I put this down on my side of the desk and he was handing me a large and very clear snapshot on glazed paper which showed a man and a woman sitting on the sand under a beach umbrella. The man wore trunks and the woman what looked like a very daring sharkskin bathing suit. She was a slim blonde, young and shapely and smiling. The man was a hefty dark handsome lad with fine shoulders and legs, sleek dark hair and white teeth. Six feet of a standard type of home-wrecker. Arms

9

to hold you close and all his brains in his face. He was holding a pair of dark glasses in his hand and smiling at the camera with a practised and easy smile.

'That's Crystal,' Kingsley said, 'and that's Chris Lavery. She can have him and he can have her and to hell with them both.'

I put the photo down on the telegram. 'All right, what's the catch?' I asked him.

'There's no telephone up there,' he said, 'and there was nothing important about the affair she was coming down for. So I got the wire before I gave much thought to it. The wire surprised me only mildly. Crystal and I have been washed up for years. She lives her life and I live mine. She has her own money and plenty of it. About twenty thousand a year from a family holding corporation that owns valuable oil leases in Texas. She plays around and I knew Lavery was one of her playmates. I might have been a little surprised that she would actually marry him, because the man is nothing but a professional chaser. But the picture looked all right so far, you understand?'

'And then?'

'Nothing for two weeks. Then the Prescott Hotel in San Bernardino got in touch with me and said a Packard Clipper registered to Crystal Grace Kingsley at my address was unclaimed in their garage and what about it. I told them to keep it and I sent them a cheque. There was nothing much in that either. I figured she was still out of the state and that if they had gone in a car at all, they had gone in Lavery's car. The day before yesterday, however, I met Lavery in front of the Athletic Club down on the corner here. He said he didn't know where Crystal was.'

Kingsley gave me a quick look and reached a bottle and two tinted glasses up on the desk. He poured a couple of drinks and pushed one over. He held his against the light and said slowly:

'Lavery said he hadn't gone away with her, hadn't seen her in two months, hadn't had any communication with her of any kind.'

I said, 'You believed him?'

He nodded, frowning, and drank his drink and pushed the glass to one side. I tasted mine. It was Scotch. Not very good Scotch.

'If I believed him – ' Kingsley said, 'and I was probably wrong to do it – it wasn't because he's a fellow you have to believe. Far from it. It's because he's a no-good son of a bitch who thinks it is smart to lay his friends' wives and brag about it. I feel he would have been tickled pink to stick it into me and break it off that he had got my wife to run away with him and leave me flat. I know these tomcats and I know this one too well. He rode a route for us for a while and he was in trouble all the time. He couldn't keep his hands off the office help. And apart from all that there was this wire from El Paso and I told him about it, and why would he think it worth while to lie about it?'

'She might have tossed him out on his can,' I said. 'That would have hurt him in his deep place – his Casanova complex.'

Kingsley brightened up a little, but not very much. He shook his head. 'I still more than half-way believe him,' he said. 'You'll have to prove me wrong. That's part of why I wanted you. But there's another and very worrying angle. I have a good job here, but a job is all it is. I can't stand scandal. I'd be out of here in a hurry if my wife got mixed up with the police.'

'Police?'

'Among her other activities,' Kingsley said grimly, 'my wife occasionally finds time to lift things in department stores. I think it's just a sort of delusion of grandeur she gets when she has been hitting the bottle too hard, but it happens, and we have had some pretty nasty scenes in managers' offices. So far I've been able to keep them from filing charges, but if something like that happened in a strange city where nobody knew her' – he lifted his hands and let them fall with a smack on the desk – 'well, it might be a prison matter, mightn't it?'

'Has she ever been finger-printed?'

'She has never been arrested,' he said.

'That's not what I mean. Sometimes in large department stores they make it a condition of dropping shop-lifting charges that you give them your prints. It scares the amateurs and builds up a file of kleptomaniacs in their protective association. When the prints come in a certain number of times they call time on you.'

'Nothing like that has happened to my knowledge,' he said.

'Well, I think we might almost throw the shoplifting angle out of this for the time being,' I said. 'If she got arrested, she would get searched. Even if the cops let her use a Jane Doe name on the police blotter, they would be likely to get in touch with you. Also she would start yelling for help when she found herself in a jam.' I tapped the blue-and-white telegraph form. 'And this is a month old. If what you are thinking about happened around that time, the case would have been settled by now. If it was a first offence, she would get off with a scolding and a suspended sentence.'

He poured himself another drink to help him with his worrying. 'You're making me feel better,' he said.

'There are too many other things that could have happened,' I said. 'That she did go away with Lavery and they split up. That she went away with some other man and the wire is a gag. That she went away alone or with a woman. That she drank herself over the edge and is holed up in some private sanatorium taking a cure. That she got into some jam we have no idea of. That she met with foul play.'

'Good God, don't say that,' Kingsley exclaimed.

'Why not? You've got to consider it. I get a very vague idea of Mrs Kingsley – that she is young, pretty, reckless, and wild. That she drinks and does dangerous things when she drinks. That she is a sucker for the men and might take up with a stranger who might turn out to be a crook. Does that fit?'

He nodded. 'Every word of it.'

'How much money would she have with her?'

'She liked to carry enough. She has her own bank and her own bank account. She could have any amount of money.'

'Any children?'

'No children.'

'Do you have the management of her affairs?'

He shook his head. 'She hasn't any – excepting depositing cheques and drawing out money and spending it. She never invests a nickel. And her money certainly never does me any good, if that's what you are thinking.' He paused and then said: 'Don't think I haven't tried. I'm human and it's not fun to watch twenty thousand a year go down the drain and nothing to show for it but hangovers and boy friends of the class of Chris Lavery.'

'How are you with her bank? Could you get a detail of the cheques she has drawn for the past couple of months?'

'They wouldn't tell me. I tried to get some information of the sort once, when I had an idea she was being blackmailed. All I got was ice.'

'We can get it,' I said, 'and we may have to. It will mean going to the Missing Persons Bureau. You wouldn't like that?'

'If I had liked that, I wouldn't have called you,' he said.

I nodded, gathered my exhibits together and put them away in my pockets. 'There are more angles to this than I can even see now,' I said, 'but I'll start by talking to Lavery and then taking a run up to Little Fawn Lake and asking questions there. I'll need Lavery's address and a note to your man in charge at the mountain place.'

He got a letterhead out of his desk and wrote and passed it over. I read: 'Dear Bill: This will introduce Mr Philip Marlowe who wishes to look over the property. Please show him my cabin and assist him in every way. Yrs Derace Kingsley.'

I folded this up and put it in the envelope he had addressed while I was reading it. 'How about the other cabins up there?' I asked.

'Nobody up this year so far. One man's in government service in Washington and the other is at Fort Leavenworth. Their wives are with them.'

'Now Lavery's address,' I said.

He looked at a point well above the top of my head. 'In Bay City. I could find the house but I forget the address. Miss Fromsett can give it to you, I think. She needn't know why you want it. She probably will. And you want a hundred dollars, you said.'

'That's all right,' I said. 'That's just something I said when you were tramping on me.'

He grinned. I stood up and hesitated by the desk looking at him. After a moment I said: 'You're not holding anything back, are you – anything important?'

He looked at his thumb. 'No. I'm not holding anything back. I'm worried and I want to know where she is. I'm damn worried. If you get anything at all, call me any time, day or night.'

I said I would do that, and we shook hands and I went back down the long cool office and out to where Miss Fromsett sat elegantly at her desk.

'Mr Kingsley thinks you can give me Chris Lavery's address,' I told her and watched her face.

She reached very slowly for a brown leather address book and turned the leaves. Her voice was tight and cold when she spoke.

'The address we have is 623 Altair Street, in Bay City. Telephone Bay City 12523. Mr Lavery has not been with us for more than a year. He may have moved.'

I thanked her and went on to the door. From there I glanced back at her. She was sitting very still, with her hands clasped on her desk, staring into space. A couple of red spots burned in her cheeks. Her eyes were remote and bitter.

I got the impression that Mr Chris Lavery was not a pleasant thought to her.

3

Altair Street lay on the edge of the V forming the inner end of a deep canyon. To the north was the cool blue sweep of the bay out to the point about Malibu. To the south the beach town of Bay City was spread out on a bluff above the coast highway.

It was a short street, not more than three or four blocks, and ended in a tall iron fence enclosing a large estate. Beyond the gilded spikes of the fence I could see trees and shrubs and a glimpse of lawn and part of a curving driveway, but the house was out of sight. On the inland side of Altair Street the houses were well kept and fairly large, but the few scattered bungalows on the edge of the canyon were nothing much. In the short half-block ended by the iron fence were only two houses, on opposite sides of the street and almost directly across from each other. The smaller was number 623.

I drove past it, turned the car in the paved half-circle at the end of the street and came back to park in front of the lot next to Lavery's place. His house was built downwards, one of those clinging vine effects, with the front door a little below street level, the patio on the roof, the bedrooms in the basement, and a garage like the corner pocket on a pool table. A crimson bougain-villea was rustling against the front wall and the flat stones of the front walk were edged with Korean moss. The door was narrow, grilled and topped by a lancet arch. Below the grille there was an iron knocker. I hammered on it.

Nothing happened. I pushed the bell at the side of the door and heard it ring inside not very far off and waited and nothing happened. I worked on the knocker again. Still nothing. I went back up the walk and along to the garage and lifted the door far enough to see that a car with white side-walled tyres was inside. I went back to the front door.

A neat black Cadillac coupé came out of the garage across the way, backed, turned and came along past Lavery's house, slowed, and a thin man in dark glasses looked at me sharply, as if I hadn't any business to be there. I gave him my steely glare and he went on his way.

I went down Lavery's walk again and did some more hammering on his knocker. This time I got results. The judas window opened and I was looking at a handsome bright-eyed number through the bars of the grille.

'You make a hell of a lot of noise,' a voice said.

'Mr Lavery?'

He said he was Mr Lavery and what about it. I poked a card through the grille. A large brown hand took the card. The bright brown eyes came back and the voice said: 'So sorry. Not needing any detectives to-day, please.'

'I'm working for Derace Kingsley.'

'The hell with both of you,' he said, and banged the judas window.

I leaned on the bell beside the door and got a cigarette out with my free hand and had just struck the match on the woodwork beside the door when it was yanked open and a big guy in bathing trunks, beach sandals and a white terrycloth bathrobe started to come out at me.

I took my thumb off the bell and grinned at him. 'What's the matter?' I asked him. 'Scared?'

'Ring that bell again,' he said, 'and I'll throw you clear across the street.'

'Don't be childish,' I told him. 'You know perfectly well I'm going to talk to you and you're going to talk to me.'

I got the blue-and-white telegram out of my pocket and held it in front of his bright brown eyes. He read it morosely, chewed his lips and growled:

'Oh for Chrissake, come on in then.'

He held the door wide and I went in past him, into a dim pleasant room with an apricot Chinese rug that looked expensive, deep-sided chairs, a number of white drum lamps, a big Capehart in the corner, a long and very wide davenport in pale tan mohair shot with dark brown, and a fire place with a copper screen and an overmantel in white wood. A fire was laid behind the screen and partly masked by a large spray of manzanita bloom. The bloom was turning yellow in places but was still pretty. There was a bottle of Vat 69 and glasses on a tray and a copper icebucket on a low round burl walnut table with a glass top. The room went clear to the back of the house and ended in a flat arch through which showed three narrow windows and the top few feet of the white iron railing of the staircase going down.

Lavery swung the door shut and sat on the davenport. He grabbed a cigarette out of a hammered silver box and lit it and looked at me irritably. I sat down opposite him and looked him over. He had everything in the way of good looks the snapshot had indicated. He had a terrific torso and magnificent thighs. His eyes were chestnut brown and the whites of them slightly grey-white. His hair was rather long and curled a little over his temples. His brown skin showed no signs of dissipation. He was a nice piece of beef, but to me that was all he was. I could understand that women would think he was something to yell for.

'Why not tell us where she is?' I said. 'We'll find out eventually anyway, and if you tell us now we won't be bothering you.'

'It would take more than a private dick to bother me,' he said.

'No, it wouldn't. A private dick can bother anybody. He's persistent and used to snubs. He's paid for his time and he would just as soon use it to bother you as any other way.'

'Look,' he said, leaning forward and pointing his cigarette at me. 'I know what that wire says, but it's the bunk. I didn't go to El Paso with Crystal Kingsley. I haven't seen her in a long time – long before the date of that wire. I haven't had any contact with her. I told Kingsley that.'

'He didn't have to believe you.'

'Why would I lie to him?' He looked surprised.

'Why wouldn't you?'

'Look,' he said earnestly, 'it might seem so to you, but you don't know her. Kingsley has no strings on her. If he doesn't like the way she behaves he has a remedy. These proprietary husbands make me sick.'

'If you didn't go to El Paso with her,' I said, 'why did she send this telegram?'

'I haven't the faintest idea.'

'You can do better than that,' I said. I pointed to the spray of manzanita in the fireplace. 'You pick that up at Little Fawn Lake?'

'The hills around here are full of manzanita,' he said contemptuously.

'It doesn't bloom like that down here.'

He laughed. 'I was up there the third week in May. If you have to know. I suppose you can find out. That's the last time I saw her.'

'You didn't have any idea of marrying her?'

He blew smoke and said through it: 'I've thought of it, yes. She has money. Money is always useful. But it would be too tough a way to make it.'

I nodded, but didn't say anything. He looked at the manzanita spray in the fireplace and leaned back to blow smoke in the air and show me the strong brown line of his throat. After a moment, when I still didn't say anything, he began to get restless. He glanced down at the card I had given him and said:

'So you hire yourself out to dig up dirt? Doing well at it?'

'Nothing to brag about. A dollar here, a dollar there.'

'And all of them pretty slimy,' he said.

'Look, Mr Lavery, we don't have to get into a fight. Kingsley thinks you know where his wife is, but won't tell him. Either out of meanness or motives of delicacy.'

'Which way would he like it?' the handsome brown-faced man sneered.

'He doesn't care, as long as he gets the information. He doesn't care a great deal what you and she do together or where you go or whether she divorces him or not.

He just wants to feel sure that everything is all right and that she isn't in trouble of any kind.'

Lavery looked interested. 'Trouble? What kind of trouble?' He licked the word around on his brown lips, tasting it.

'Maybe you won't know the kind of trouble he is thinking of.'

'Tell me,' he pleaded sarcastically. 'I'd just love to hear about some kind of trouble I didn't know about.'

'You're doing fine,' I told him. 'No time to talk business, but always time for a wisecrack. If you think we might try to get a hook into you because you crossed a state line with her, forget it.'

'Go climb up your thumb, wise guy. You'd have to prove I paid the freight, or it wouldn't mean anything.'

'This wire has to mean something,' I said stubbornly. It seemed to me that I had said it before, several times.

'It's probably just a gag. She's full of little tricks like that. All of them silly, and some of them vicious.'

'I don't see any point in this one.'

He flicked cigarette ash carelessly at the glass-top table. He gave me a quick up from under look and immediately looked away.

'I stood her up,' he said slowly. 'It might be her idea of a way to get back at me. I was supposed to run up there one week-end. I didn't go. I was – sick of her.'

I said: 'Uh-huh,' and gave him a long steady stare. 'I don't like that so well. I'd like it better if you did go to El Paso with her and had a fight and split up. Could you tell it that way?'

He flushed solidly behind the sunburn.

'God damn it,' he said, 'I told you I didn't go anywhere with her. Not anywhere. Can't you remember that?'

'I'll remember it when I believe it.'

He leaned over to snub out his cigarette. He stood up with an easy movement, not hurried at all, pulled the belt of his robe tight, and moved out to the end of the davenport.

'All right,' he said in a clear tight voice. 'Out you go. Take the air. I've had enough of your third-degree tripe. You're wasting my time and your own – if it's worth anything.'

I stood up and grinned at him. 'Not a lot, but for what it's worth I'm being paid for it. It couldn't be, for instance, that you ran into a little unpleasantness in some departmental store – say at the stocking or jewellery counter.'

He looked at me very carefully, drawing his eyebrows down at the corners and making his mouth small.

'I don't get it,' he said, but there was thought behind his voice.

'That's all I wanted to know,' I said. 'And thanks for listening. By the way, what line of business are you in – since you left Kingsley?'

'What the hell business is it of yours?'

'None. But of course I can always find out,' I said, and moved a little way towards the door, not very far.

'At the moment I'm not doing anything,' he said coldly. 'I expect a commission in the Navy almost any day.'

'You ought to do well at that,' I said.

'Yeah. So long, snooper. And don't bother to come back. I won't be at home.'

I went over to the door and pulled it open. It stuck on the lower sill, from the beach moisture. When I had it open, I looked back at him. He was standing there narrow-eyed, full of muted thunder.

'I may have to come back,' I said. 'But it won't be just to swop gags. It will be because I find something out that needs talking over.'

'So you still think I'm lying,' he said savagely.

'I think you have something on your mind. I've looked at too many faces not to know. It may not be any of my business. If it is, you're likely to have to throw me out again.'

'A pleasure,' he said. 'And next time bring somebody to drive you home. In case you land on your fanny and knock your brains out.'

Then without any rhyme or reason that I could see, he spat on the rug in front of his feet.

It jarred me. It was like watching the veneer peel off and leave a tough kid in an alley. Or like hearing an apparently refined woman start expressing herself in four-letter words.

'So long, beautiful hunk,' I said, and left him standing there. I closed the door, had to jerk it to get it shut, and went up the path to the street. I stood on the sidewalk looking at the house across the way.

4

It was a wide shallow house with rose stucco walls faded out to a pleasant pastel shade and trimmed with dull green at the window frames. The roof was of green tiles, round rough ones. There was a deeply inset front door framed in a mosaic of multi-coloured pieces of tiling and a small flower garden in front, behind a low stucco wall topped by an iron railing which the beach moisture had begun to corrode. Outside the wall to the left was the three-car garage, with a door opening inside the yard and a concrete path going from there to a side door of the house.

Set into the gate post was a bronze tablet which read: 'Albert S. Admore, M. D.'

While I was standing there staring across the street, the black Cadillac I had already seen came purring around the corner and then down the block. It slowed and started to sweep outwards to get turning space to go into the garage, decided my car was in the way of that, and went on to the end of the road and turned in the widened-out space in front of the ornamental iron railing. It came back slowly and went into the empty third of the garage across the way.

The thin man in sun-glasses went along the sidewalk to the house, carrying a double-handled doctor's bag. Halfway along he slowed down to stare across at me. I went along towards my car. At the house he used a key and as he opened the door he looked across at me again.

I got into the Chrysler and sat there smoking and trying to make up my mind whether it was worth while hiring somebody to pull a tail on Lavery. I decided it wasn't, not the way things looked so far.

Curtains moved at a lower window close to the side door Dr Almore had gone in at. A thin hand held them aside and I caught the glint of light on glasses. They were held aside for quite some time, before they fell together again.

I looked along the street at Lavery's house. From this angle I could see that his service porch gave on a flight of painted wooden steps to a sloping concrete walk and a flight of concrete steps ending in the paved alley below.

I looked across at Dr Almore's house again, wondering idly if he knew Lavery and how well. He probably knew him, since theirs were the only two houses in the block. But being a doctor, he wouldn't tell me anything about him. As I looked, the curtains which had been lifted apart were now completely drawn aside.

The middle segment of the triple window they had masked had no screen. Behind it, Dr Almore stood staring across my way, with a sharp frown on his thin face. I shook cigarette ash out of the window and he turned abruptly and sat down at a desk. His double-handled bag was on the desk in front of him. He sat rigidly, drumming on the desk beside the bag. His hand reached for the telephone, touched it and came away again. He lit a cigarette and shook the match violently, then strode to the window and stared out at me some more.

This was interesting, if at all, only because he was a

26

doctor. Doctors, as a rule, are the least curious of men. While they are still internes they hear enough secrets to last them a lifetime. Dr Almore seemed interested in me. More than interested, bothered.

I reached down to turn the ignition key, then Lavery's front door opened and I took my hand away and leaned back again. Lavery came briskly up the walk of his house, shot a glance down the street and turned to go into his garage. He was dressed as I had seen him. He had a rough towel and a steamer rug over his arm. I heard the garage door lift up, then the car door open and shut, then the grind and cough of the starting car. It backed up the steep incline to the street, white steamy exhaust pouring from its rear end. It was a cute little blue convertible, with the top folded down and Lavery's sleek dark head just rising above it. He was now wearing a natty pair of sun-goggles with very wide white sidebows. The convertible swooped off down the block and danced around the corner.

There was nothing in that for me. Mr Christopher Lavery was bound for the edge of the broad Pacific, to lie in the sun and let the girls see what they didn't necessarily have to go on missing.

I gave my attention back to Dr Almore. He was on the telephone now, not talking, holding it to his ear, smoking and waiting. Then he leaned forward as you do when the voice comes back, listened, hung up and wrote something on a pad in front of him. Then a heavy book with yellow sides appeared on his desk and he opened it just about in the middle. While he was doing this he gave one quick look out of the window, straight at the Chrysler.

He found his place in the book, leaned down over it and quick puffs of smoke appeared in the air over the pages. He wrote something else, put the book away, and grabbed for the telephone again. He dialled, waited, began to speak quickly, pushing his head down and making gestures in the air with his cigarette.

He finished his call and hung up. He leaned back and sat there brooding, staring down at his desk, but not forgetting to look out of the window every half-minute. He was waiting, and I waited with him, for no reason at all. Doctors make many phone calls, talk to many people. Doctors look out of their front windows, doctors frown, doctors show nervousness, doctors have things on their mind and show the strain. Doctors are just people, born to sorrow, fighting the long grim fight like the rest of us.

But there was something about the way this one behaved that intrigued me. I looked at my watch, decided it was time to get something to eat, lit another cigarette and didn't move.

It took about five minutes. Then a green sedan whisked around the corner and bore down the block. It coasted to a stop in front of Dr Almore's house and its tall buggy-whip aerial quivered. A big man with dusty blond hair got out and went up to Dr Almore's front door. He rang the bell and leaned down to strike a match on the step. His head came around and he stared across the street exactly at where I was sitting.

The door opened and he went into the house. An invisible hand gathered the curtains at Dr Almore's study window and blanked the room. I sat there, and stared at the sun-darkened lining of the curtains. More time trickled by.

The front door opened again and the big man loafed casually down the steps and through the gate. He snapped his cigarette end off into the distance and rumpled his hair. He shrugged once, pinched the end of his chin, and walked diagonally across the street. His steps in the quiet were leisurely and distinct. Dr Almore's curtains moved apart again behind him. Dr Almore stood in his window and watched.

A large freckled hand appeared on the sill of the car door at my elbow. A large face, deeply lined, hung above it. The man had eyes of metallic blue. He looked at me solidly and spoke in a deep harsh voice.

'Waiting for somebody?' he asked.

'I don't know,' I said. 'Am I?'

'I'll ask the questions.'

'Well, I'll be damned,' I said. 'So that's the answer to the pantomime.'

'What pantomime?' He gave me a hard level unfriendly stare from his very blue eyes.

I pointed across the street with my cigarette. 'Nervous Nellie and the telephone. Calling the cops, after first getting my name from the Auto Club, probably, then looking it up in the city directory. What goes on?'

'Let me see your driver's licence.'

I gave him back his stare. 'You fellows ever flash a buzzer – or is acting tough all the identification you need?'

'If I have to get tough, fellow, you'll know it.'

I leaned down and turned my ignition key and pressed the starter. The motor caught and idled down.

'Cut that motor,' he said savagely, and put his foot on the running-board.

I cut the motor again and leaned back and looked at him.

'God damn it,' he said, 'do you want me to drag you out of there and bounce you on the pavement?'

I got my wallet out and handed it to him. He drew the celluloid pocket out and looked at my driver's licence, then turned the pocket over and looked at the photostat of my other licence on the back. He rammed it contemptuously back into the wallet and handed me the wallet. I put it away. His hand dipped and came up with a blue-and-gold police badge.

'Degarmo, detective-lieutenant,' he said in his heavy brutal voice.

'Pleased to meet you, lieutenant.'

'Skip it. Now tell why you're down here casing Almore's place.'

'I'm not casing Almore's place, as you put it, lieutenant. I never heard of Dr Almore and I don't know of any reason why I should want to case his house.'

He turned his head to spit. I was meeting the spitting boys to-day.

'What's your grift then? We don't like peepers down here. We don't have one in town.'

'Is that so?'

'Yeah, that's so. So come on, talk it up. Unless you want to ride down to the clubhouse and sweat it out under the bright lights.'

I didn't answer him.

'Her folks hire you?' he asked suddenly.

I shook my head.

'The last boy that tried it ended up on the road gang, sweetheart.'

'I bet it's good,' I said, 'if only I could guess. Tried what?'

'Tried to put the bite on him,' he said thinly.

'Too bad I don't know how,' I said. 'He looks like an easy man to bite.'

'That line of talk don't buy you anything,' he said.

'All right,' I said. 'Let's put it this way. I don't know Dr Almore, never heard of him, and I'm not interested in him. I'm down here visiting a friend and looking at the view. If I'm doing anything else, it doesn't happen to be any of your business. If you don't like that, the best thing to do is to take it down to headquarters and see the day captain.'

He moved a foot heavily on the running-board and looked doubtful. 'Straight goods?' he asked slowly.

'Straight goods.'

'Aw hell, the guy's screwy,' he said suddenly and looked back over his shoulder at the house. 'He ought to see a doctor.' He laughed, without any amusement in the laugh. He took his foot off my running-board and rumpled his wiry hair.

'Go on – beat it,' he said. 'Stay off our reservation, and you won't make any enemies.'

I pressed the starter again. When the motor was idling gently I said: 'How's Al Norgaard these days?'

He stared at me. 'You knew Al?'

'Yeah. He and I worked on a case down here a couple of years ago – when Wax was chief of police.'

'Al's in the military police. Wish I was,' he said bitterly. He started to walk away and then swung sharply on his heel. 'Go on, beat it before I change my mind,' he snapped.

He walked heavily across the street and through Dr Almore's front gate again.

I let the clutch in and drove away. On the way back to the city, I listened to my thoughts. They moved fitfully in and out, like Dr Almore's thin nervous hands pulling at the edges of his curtains.

Back in Los Angeles I ate lunch and went up to my office in the Cahuenga Building to see what mail there was. I called Kingsley from there.

'I saw Lavery,' I told him. 'He told me just enough dirt to sound frank. I tried to needle him a little, but nothing came of it. I still like the idea that they quarrelled and split up and that he hopes to fix it up with her yet.'

'Then he must know where she is,' Kingsley said.

'He might, but it doesn't follow. By the way, a rather curious thing happened to me on Lavery's street. There are only two houses. The other belongs to a Dr Almore.' I told him briefly about the rather curious thing.

He was silent for a moment at the end and then he said: 'Is this Dr Albert Almore?'

'Yes.'

'He was Crystal's doctor for a time. He came to the house several times when she was – well, when she had been overdrinking. I thought him a little too quick with a hypodermic needle. His wife – let me see, there was something about his wife. Oh yes, she committed suicide.'

I said, 'When?'

'I don't remember. Quite a long time now. I never knew them socially. What are you going to do now?'

I told him I was going up to Puma Lake, although it was a little late in the day to start.

He said I would have plenty of time and that they had an hour more of daylight in the mountains.

I said that was fine and we hung up.

5

San Bernardino baked and shimmered in the afternoon heat. The air was hot enough to blister my tongue. I drove through it gasping, stopped long enough to buy a pint of liquor in case I fainted before I got to the mountains, and started up the long grade to Crestline. In fifteen miles the road climbed five thousand feet, but even then it was far from cool. Thirty miles of mountain driving brought me to the tall pines and a place called Bubbling Springs. It had a clapboard store and a gas pump, but it felt like paradise. From there on it was cool all the way.

The Puma Lake dam had an armed sentry at each end and one in the middle. The first one I came to had me close all the windows of the car before crossing over the dam. About a hundred yards from the dam a rope with cork floats barred the pleasure boats from coming any closer. Beyond these details the war did not seem to have done anything much to Puma Lake.

Canoes paddled about on the blue water and rowing-boats with outboard motors put-putted and speedboats showing off like fresh kids made wide swathes of foam and turned on a dime and girls in them shrieked and dragged their hands in the water. Jounced around in the wake of the speedboats people who had paid two dollars for a fishing licence were trying to get a dime of it back in tired-tasting fish.

The road skimmed along a high granite outcrop and

dropped to meadows of coarse grass in which grew what was left of the wild irises and white and purple lupin and bugle flowers and columbine and pennyroyal and desert paint brush. Tall yellow pines probed at the clear blue sky. The road dropped again to lake level and the landscape began to be full of girls in gaudy slacks and snoods and peasant handkerchiefs and rat rolls and fat-soled sandals and fat white thighs. People on bicycles wobbled cautiously over the highway and now and then an anxious-looking bird thumped past on a power-scooter.

A mile from the village the highway was joined by another lesser road which curved back into the mountains. A rough wooden sign under the highway sign said: *Little Fawn Lake 1¾ miles*. I took it. Scattered cabins were perched along the slopes for the first mile and then nothing. Presently another very narrow road debouched from this one and another rough wood sign said: *Little Fawn Lake. Private Road. No Trespassing*.

I turned the Chrysler into this and crawled carefully around huge bare granite rocks and past a little waterfall and through a maze of black oak-trees and ironwood and manzanita and silence. A blue-jay squawked on a branch and a squirrel scolded at me and beat one paw angrily on the pine cone it was holding. A scarlet-topped woodpecker stopped probing in the bark long enough to look at me with one beady eye and then dodge behind the tree trunk to look at me with the other one. I came to a five-barred gate and another sign.

Beyond the gate the road wound for a couple of hundred yards through trees and then suddenly below me was a small oval lake deep in trees and rocks and wild grass, like a drop of dew caught in a curled leaf. At the near end of it was a rough concrete dam with a rope hand-rail across the top and an old millwheel at the side. Near that stood a small cabin of native pine with the bark on it.

Across the lake the long way by the road and the short way by the top of the dam a large redwood cabin overhung the water and farther along, each well separated from the others, were two other cabins. All three were shut up and quiet, with drawn curtains. The big one had orange-yellow venetian blinds and a twelve-paned window facing on the lake.

At the far end of the lake from the dam was what looked like a small pier and band pavilion. A warped wooden sign on it was painted in large white letters: *Camp Kilkare*. I couldn't see any sense in that in these surroundings, so I got out of the car and started down towards the nearest cabin. Somewhere behind it an axe thudded.

I pounded on the cabin door. The axe stopped. A man's voice yelled from somewhere. I sat down on a rock and lit a cigarette. Steps came around the corner of the cabin, uneven steps. A man with a harsh face and a swarthy skin came into view carrying a double-bitted axe.

He was heavily built and not very tall and he limped as he walked, giving his right leg a little kick out with each step and swinging the foot in a shallow arc. He had a dark unshaven chin and steady blue eyes and grizzled hair that curled over his ears and needed cutting badly. He wore blue denim pants and a blue shirt open on a brown muscular neck. A cigarette hung from the corner of his mouth. He spoke in a tight tough city voice.

'Yeah?'

'Mr Bill Chess?'

'That's me.'

I stood up and got Kingsley's note of introduction out of my pocket and handed it to him. He squinted at the note, then clumped into the cabin and came back with glasses perched on his nose. He read the note carefully and then again. He put it in his shirt pocket, buttoned the flap of the pocket and put his hand out.

'Pleased to meet you, Mr Marlowe.'

We shook hands. He had a hand like a wood rasp.

'You want to see Kingsley's cabin, huh? Glad to show you. He ain't selling, for Chrissake?' He eyed me steadily and jerked a thumb across the lake.

'He might,' I said. 'Everything's for sale in California.'

'Ain't that the truth? That's his – the redwood job. Lined with knotty pine, composition roof, stone foundations and porches, full bath and shower, venetian blinds all around, big fireplace, oil-stove in the big bedroom – and brother, you need it in the spring and autumn – Pilgrim combination gas and wood range, everything first class. Cost about eight thousand and that's money for a mountain cabin. And private reservoir in the hills for water.'

'How about electric light and telephone?' I asked, just to be friendly.

'Electric light, sure. No phone. You couldn't get one now. If you could, it would cost plenty to string the lines out here.'

He looked at me with steady blue eyes and I looked at him. In spite of his weathered appearance he looked like a drinker. He had the thickened and glossy skin, the too noticeable veins, the bright glitter in the eyes.

I said: 'Anybody living there now?'

'Nope. Mrs Kingsley was here a few weeks back. She went down the hill. Back any day, I guess. Didn't he say?'

I looked surprised. 'Why? Does she go with the cabin?'

He scowled and then put his head back and burst out laughing. The roar of his laughter was like a tractor backfiring. It blasted the woodland silence to shreds.

'Jesus, if that ain't a kick in the pants!' he gasped. 'Does she go with the –' He put out another bellow and then his mouth shut tight as a trap.

'Yeah, it's a swell cabin,' he said, eyeing me carefully.

'The beds comfortable?' I asked.

He leaned forward and smiled. 'Maybe you'd like a face full of knuckles,' he said.

I stared at him with my mouth open. 'That one went by me too fast,' I said. 'I never laid an eye on it.'

'How would I know if the beds are comfortable?' he snarled, bending down a little so that he could reach me with a hard right, if it worked out that way.

'I don't know why you wouldn't know,' I said. 'I won't press the point. I can find out for myself.'

'Yah,' he said bitterly, 'think I can't smell a dick when I meet one? I played hit and run with them in every state in the Union. Nuts to you, pal. And nuts to Kingsley. So he hires himself a dick to come up here and see am I wearing his pyjamas, huh? Listen, Jack, I might have a stiff leg and all, but the women I could get –'

I put a hand out, hoping he wouldn't pull it off and throw it in the lake.

'You're slipping your clutch,' I told him. 'I didn't come up here to inquire into your love life. I never saw Mrs

Kingsley. I never saw Mr Kingsley until this morning. What the hell's the matter with you?'

He dropped his eyes and rubbed the back of his hand viciously across his mouth, as if he wanted to hurt himself. Then he held the hand in front of his eyes and squeezed it into a hard fist and opened it again and stared at the fingers. They were shaking a little.

'Sorry, Mr Marlowe,' he said slowly. 'I was out on the roof last night and I've got a hangover like seven Swedes. I've been up here alone for a month and it's got me talking to myself. A thing happened to me.'

'Anything a drink would help?'

His eyes focused sharply on me and glinted. 'You got one?'

I pulled the pint of rye out of my pocket and held it so that he could see the green label over the cap.

'I don't deserve it,' he said. 'God damn it, I don't. Wait till I get a couple of glasses or would you come into the cabin?'

'I like it out here. I'm enjoying the view.'

He swung his stiff leg and went into his cabin and came back carrying a couple of small cheese glasses. He sat down on the rock beside me, smelling of dried perspiration.

I tore the metal cap off the bottle and poured him a stiff drink and a light one for myself. We touched glasses and drank. He rolled the liquor on his tongue and a bleak smile put a little sunshine into his face.

'Man, that's from the right bottle,' he said. 'I wonder what made me sound off like that. I guess a guy gets the blues up here all alone. No company, no real friends,

39

no wife.' He paused and added with a sideways look. 'Especially no wife.'

I kept my eyes on the blue water of the tiny lake. Under an overhanging rock a fish surfaced in a lance of light and a circle of widening ripples. A light breeze moved the tops of the pines with a noise like a gentle surf.

'She left me,' he said slowly. 'She left me a month ago. Friday the 12th of June. A day I'll remember.'

I stiffened, but not too much to pour more whisky into his empty glass. Friday the 12th of June was the day Mrs Crystal Kingsley was supposed to have come into town for a party.

'But you don't want to hear about that,' he said. And in his faded blue eyes was the deep yearning to talk about it, as plain as anything could possibly be.

'It's none of my business,' I said. 'But if it would make you feel any better – '

He nodded sharply. 'Two guys will meet on a park bench,' he said, 'and start talking about God. Did you ever notice that? Guys that wouldn't talk about God to their best friend.'

'I know that,' I said.

He drank and looked across the lake. 'She was one swell kid,' he said softly. 'A little sharp in the tongue sometimes, but one swell kid. It was love at first sight with me and Muriel. I met her in a joint in Riverside, a year and three months ago. Not the kind of joint where a guy would expect to meet a girl like Muriel, but that's how it happened. We got married. I loved her. I knew I was well off. And I was too much of a skunk to play ball with her.'

I moved a little to show him I was still there, but I didn't say anything for fear of breaking the spell. I sat with my drink untouched in my hand. I like to drink, but not when people are using me for a diary.

He went on sadly: 'But you know how it is with marriage – any marriage. After a while a guy like me, a common no-good guy like me, he wants to feel a leg. Some other leg. Maybe it's lousy, but that's the way it is.'

He looked at me and I said I had heard the idea expressed.

He tossed his second drink off. I passed him the bottle. A blue-jay went up a pine-tree hopping from branch to branch without moving his wings or even pausing to balance.

'Yeah,' Bill Chess said. 'All these hillbillies are half-crazy and I'm getting that way too. Here I am sitting pretty, no rent to pay, a good pension cheque every month, half my bonus money in war bonds, I'm married to as neat a little blonde as ever you clapped an eye on and all the time I'm nuts and I don't know it. I go for *that*.' He pointed hard at the redwood cabin across the lake. It was turning the colour of ox blood in the late afternoon light. 'Right in the front yard,' he said, 'right under the windows, and a showy little tart that means no more to me than a blade of grass. Jesus, what a sap a guy can be.'

He drank his third drink and steadied the bottle on a rock. He fished a cigarette out of his shirt, fired a match on his thumb-nail and puffed rapidly. I breathed with my mouth open, as silent as a burglar behind a curtain.

'Hell,' he said at last, 'you'd think if I had to jump off

the dock I'd go a little ways from home and pick me a change in types at least. But little roundheels over there ain't even that. She's a blonde like Muriel, same size and weight, same type, almost the same colour eyes. But, brother, how different from then on in. Pretty, sure, but no prettier to anybody and not half so pretty to me. Well, I'm over there burning trash that morning and minding my own business, as much as I ever mind it. And she comes to the back door of the cabin in peekaboo pyjamas so thin you can see the pink of her nipples against the cloth. And she says in her lazy, no-good voice: "Have a drink, Bill. Don't work so hard on such a beautiful morning." And me, I like a drink too well and I go to the kitchen door and take it. And then I take another and then I take another and then I'm in the house. And the closer I get to her the more bedroom her eyes are.'

He paused and swept me with a hard level look.

'You asked me if the beds over there were comfortable and I got sore. You didn't mean a thing. I was just too full of remembering. Yeah – the bed I was in was comfortable.'

He stopped talking and I let his words hang in the air. They fell slowly and after them was silence. He leaned to pick the bottle off the rock and stare at it. He seemed to fight with it in his mind. The whisky won the fight, as it always does. He took a long savage drink out of the bottle and then screwed the cap on tightly, as if that meant something. He picked up a stone and flicked it into the water.

'I came back across the dam,' he said slowly, in a voice already thick with alcohol. 'I'm as smooth as a new piston head. I'm getting away with something. Us boys can be so wrong about those little things, can't we? I'm not getting away with anything at all. Not anything at all. I listen to Muriel telling me and she don't even raise her voice. But she tells me things about myself I didn't even imagine. Oh yeah, I'm getting away with it lovely.'

'So she left you,' I said, when he fell silent.

'That night. I wasn't even here. I felt too mean to stay even half-sober. I hopped into my Ford and went over to the north side of the lake and holed up with a couple of no-goods like myself and got good and stinking. Not that it did me any good. Along about 4 a.m. I got back home and Muriel had gone, packed up and gone, nothing left but a note on the bureau and some cold cream on the pillow.'

He pulled a dog-eared piece of paper out of a shabby old wallet and passed it over. It was written in pencil on blue-lined paper from a note-book. It read:

'I'm sorry, Bill, but I'd rather be dead than live with you any longer. Muriel.'

I handed it back. 'What about over there?' I asked, pointing across the lake with a glance.

Bill Chess picked up a flat stone and tried to skip it across the water, but it refused to skip.

'Nothing over there,' he said. 'She packed up and went down the same night. I didn't see her again. I don't want to see her again. I haven't heard a word from Muriel in the whole month, not a single word. I don't have any idea at all where she's at. With some other guy, maybe. I hope he treats her better than I did.'

He stood up and took keys out of his pocket and shook them. 'So if you want to go across and look at

43

Kingsley's cabin, there isn't a thing to stop you. And thanks for listening to the soap opera. And thanks for the liquor. Here.' He picked the bottle up and handed me what was left of the pint.

6

We went down the slope to the bank of the lake and the narrow top of the dam. Bill Chess swung his stiff leg in front of me, holding on to the rope hand-rail set in iron stanchions. At one point water washed over the concrete in a lazy swirl.

'I'll let some out through the wheel in the morning,' he said over his shoulder. 'That's all the darn thing is good for. Some movie outfit put it up three years ago. They made a picture up here. That little pier down at the other end is some more of their work. Most of what they built is torn down and hauled away, but Kingsley had them leave the pier and the millwheel. Kind of gives the place a touch of colour.'

I followed him up a flight of heavy wooden steps to the porch of the Kingsley cabin. He unlocked the door and we went into hushed warmth. The closed-up room was almost hot. The light filtering through the slatted blinds made narrow bars across the floor. The living-room was long and cheerful and had Indian rugs, padded mountain furniture with metal-strapped joints, chintz curtains, a plain hardwood floor, plenty of lamps and a little built-in bar with round stools in one corner. The room was neat and clean and had no look of having been left at short notice.

We went into the bedrooms. Two of them had twin beds and one a large double bed with a cream-coloured spread having a design in plum-coloured wool stitched over it. This was the master bedroom, Bill Chess said. On a dresser of varnished wood there were toilet articles and accessories in jade-green enamel and stainless steel, and an assortment of cosmetic oddments. A couple of cold cream jars had the wavy gold brand of the Gillerlain Company on them. One whole side of the room consisted of closets with sliding doors. I slid one open and peeked inside. It seemed to be full of women's clothes of the sort they wear at resorts. Bill Chess watched me sourly while I pawed them over. I slid the door shut and pulled open a deep shoe drawer underneath. It contained at least half a dozen pairs of new-looking shoes. I heaved the drawer shut and straightened up.

Bill Chess was planted squarely in front of me, with his chin pushed out and his hard hands in knots on his hips.

'So what did you want to look at the lady's clothes for?' he asked in an angry voice.

'Reasons,' I said. 'For instance, Mrs Kingsley didn't go home when she left here. Her husband hasn't seen her since. He does not know where she is.'

He dropped his fists and twisted them slowly at his sides. 'Dick it is,' he snarled. 'The first guess is always right. I had myself about talked out of it. Boy, did I open up to you. Nellie with her hair in her lap. Boy, am I a smart little egg!'

'I can respect a confidence as well as the next fellow,' I said, and walked around him into the kitchen.

There was a big green-and-white combination range, a sink of lacquered yellow pine, an automatic water-heater in the service porch, and opening off the other side of the kitchen a cheerful breakfast-room with many windows and an expansive plastic breakfast set. The shelves were gay with coloured dishes and glasses and a set of pewter serving-dishes.

Everything was in apple-pie order. There were no dirty cups or plates on the drain-board, no smeared glasses or empty liquor bottles hanging around. There were no ants and no flies. Whatever loose living Mrs Derace Kingsley indulged in she managed without leaving the usual Greenwich Village slop behind her.

I went back to the living-room and out on the front porch again and waited for Bill Chess to lock up. When he had done that and turned to me with his scowl well in place I said:

'I didn't ask you to take your heart out and squeeze it for me, but I didn't try to stop you either. Kingsley doesn't have to know his wife made a pass at you, unless there's a lot more behind all this than I can see now.'

'The hell with you,' he said, and the scowl stayed right where it was.

'All right, the hell with me. Would there be any chance your wife and Kingsley's wife went away together?'

'I don't get it,' he said.

'After you went to drown your troubles they could have had a fight and made up and cried down each other's necks. Then Mrs Kingsley might have taken your wife down the hill. She had to have something to ride in, didn't she?'

It sounded silly, but he took it seriously enough.

'Nope. Muriel didn't cry down anybody's neck. They left the weeps out of Muriel. And if she did want to cry on a shoulder, she wouldn't have picked little roundheels. And as for transportation, she has a Ford of her own. She couldn't drive mine easily on account of the way the controls are switched over for my stiff leg.'

'It was just a passing thought,' I said.

'If any more like it pass you, let them go right on,' he said.

'For a guy that takes his long wavy hair down in front of complete strangers, you're pretty damn touchy,' I said.

He took a step towards me. 'Want to make something of it?'

'Look, pal,' I said. 'I'm working hard to think you are a fundamentally good egg. Help me out a little, can't you?'

He breathed hard for a moment and then dropped his hands and spread them helplessly.

'Boy, can I brighten up anybody's afternoon,' he sighed. 'Want to walk back around the lake?'

'Sure, if your leg will stand it.'

'Stood it plenty of times before.'

We started off side by side, as friendly as puppies again. It would probably last all of fifty yards. The road-way, barely wide enough to pass a car, hung above the level of the lake and dodged between high rocks. About half-way to the far end another smaller cabin was built on a rock foundation. The third was well beyond the end of the lake, on a patch of almost level ground. Both were closed up and had that long-empty look.

Bill Chess said after a minute or two: 'That straight, good little roundheels lammed off ?'

'So it seems.'

'You are a real dick or just a shamus?'

'Just a shamus.'

'She go with some guy?'

'I should think it likely.'

'Sure she did. It's a cinch. Kingsley ought to be able to guess that. She had plenty of friends.'

'Up here?'

He didn't answer me.

'Was one of them named Lavery?'

'I wouldn't know,' he said.

'There's no secret about this one,' I said. 'She sent a wire from El Paso saying she and Lavery were going to Mexico.' I dug the wire out of my pocket and held it out. He fumbled his glasses loose from his shirt and stopped to read it. He handed the paper back and put his glasses away again and stared out over the blue water.

'That's a little confidence for you to hold against some of what you gave me,' I said.

'Lavery was up here once,' he said slowly.

'He admits he saw her a couple of months ago, probably up here. He claims he hasn't seen her since. We don't know whether to believe him. There's no reason why we should and no reason why we shouldn't.'

'She isn't with him now, then?'

'He says not.'

'I wouldn't think she would fuss with little details like getting married,' he said soberly. 'A Florida honeymoon would be more in her line.'

'But you can't give me any positive information? You didn't see her go or hear anything that sounded authentic?'

'Nope,' he said. 'And if I did, I doubt if I would tell. I'm dirty, but not that kind of dirty.'

'Well, thanks for trying,' I said.

49

'I don't owe you any favours,' he said. 'The hell with you and every other God-damn snooper.'

'Here we go again,' I said.

We had come to the end of the lake now. I left him standing there and walked out on the little pier. I leaned on the wooden railing at the end of it and saw that what had looked like a band pavilion was nothing but two pieces of propped-up wall meeting at a flat angle towards the dam. About two feet deep of overhanging roof was stuck on the wall, like a coping. Bill Chess came up behind me and leaned on the railing at my side.

'Not that I don't thank you for the liquor,' he said.

'Yeah. Any fish in the lake?'

'Some smart old bastards of trout. No fresh stock. I don't go for fish much myself. I don't bother with them. Sorry I got tough again.'

I grinned and leaned on the railing and stared down into the deep, still water. It was green when you looked down into it. There was a swirl of movement down there and a swift greenish form moved in the water.

'There's Granpa,' Bill Chess said. 'Look at the size of that old bastard. He ought to be ashamed of himself getting so fat.'

Down below the water there was what looked like an underwater flooring. I couldn't see the sense of that. I asked him.

'Used to be a boat landing before the dam was raised. That lifted the water level so far the old landing was six feet under.'

A flat-bottomed boat dangled on a frayed rope tied to a post of the pier. It lay in the water almost without motion, but not quite. The air was peaceful and calm and sunny and held a quiet you don't get in cities. I could have stayed there for hours doing nothing but forgetting all about Derace Kingsley and his wife and her boy friends.

There was a hard movement at my side and Bill Chess said, 'Look there!' in a voice that growled like mountain thunder.

His hard fingers dug into the flesh of my arm until I started to get mad. He was bending far out over the railing, staring down like a loon, his face as white as the weather tan would let it get. I looked down with him into the water at the edge of the submerged staging.

Languidly at the edge of this green and sunken shelf of wood something waved out from the darkness, hesitated, waved back again out of sight under the flooring.

The something had looked far too much like a human arm.

Bill Chess straightened his body rigidly. He turned without a sound and clumped back along the pier. He bent to a loose pile of stones and heaved. His panting breath reached me. He got a big one free and lifted it breast high and started back out on the pier with it. It must have weighed a hundred pounds. His neck muscles stood out like ropes under canvas under his taut brown skin. His teeth were clamped tight and his breath hissed between them.

He reached the end of the pier and steadied himself and lifted the rock high. He held it a moment poised, his eyes staring down now, measuring. His mouth made a vague, distressful sound and his body lurched forward hard against the quivering rail and the heavy stone smashed down into the water.

The splash it made went over both of us. The rock fell straight and true and struck on the edge of the submerged planking, almost exactly where we had seen the thing wave in and out.

For a moment the water was a confused boiling, then the ripples widened off into the distance, coming smaller and smaller with a trace of froth at the middle, and there was a dim sound as of wood breaking under water, a sound that seemed to come to us a long time after it should have been audible. An ancient rotted plank popped suddenly through the surface, stuck out a full foot of its jagged end, and fell back with a flat slap and floated off.

The depths cleared again. Something moved in them that was not a board. It rose slowly, with an infinitely careless languor, a long dark twisted something that rolled lazily in the water as it rose. It broke surface casually, lightly, without haste. I saw wool, sodden and black, a leather jerkin blacker than ink, a pair of slacks. I saw shoes and something that bulged nastily between the shoes and the cuffs of the slacks. I saw a wave of dark blonde hair straighten out in the water and hold still for a brief instant as if with a calculated effect, and then swirl into a tangle again.

The thing rolled over once more and an arm flapped up barely above the skin of the water and the arm ended in a bloated hand that was the hand of a freak. Then the face came. A swollen pulpy grey white mass without features, without eyes, without mouth. A blotch of grey dough, a nightmare with human hair on it.

A heavy necklace of green stones showed on what had been a neck, half-embedded, large rough green stones with something that glittered joining them together.

Bill Chess held the hand-rail and his knuckles were polished bones.

'Muriel!' his voice said croakingly. 'Sweet Christ, it's Muriel!'

His voice seemed to come to me from a long way off, over a hill, through a thick silent growth of trees.

7

Behind the window of the board shack one end of a counter was piled with dusty folders. The glass upper half of the door was lettered in flaked black paint. *Chief of Police. Fire Chief. Town Constable. Chamber of Commerce.* In the lower corners a U.S.O. card and a Red Cross emblem were fastened to the glass.

I went in. There was a pot-bellied stove in the corner and a roll-top desk in the other corner behind the counter. There was a large blue print map of the district on the wall and beside that a board with four hooks on it, one of which supported a frayed and much-mended mackinaw. On the counter beside the dusty folders lay the usual sprung pen, exhausted blotter and smeared bottle of gummy ink. The end wall beside the desk was covered with telephone numbers written in hard-bitten figures that would last as long as the wood and looked as if they had been written by a child.

A man sat at the desk in a wooden armchair whose legs were anchored to flat boards, fore and aft, like skis. A spittoon big enough to coil a hose in was leaning against the man's right leg. He had a sweat-stained Stetson on the back of his head and his large hairless hands were clasped comfortably over his stomach, above the waistband of a pair of khaki pants that had been scrubbed thin years ago. His shirt matched the pants except that it was even more faded. It was buttoned tight to the man's thick neck and undecorated by a tie. His hair was mousy-brown except at the temples, where it was the colour of old snow. He sat more on his left hip than his right, because there was a hip holster down inside his right hip pocket, and a half-foot of forty-five gun reared up and bored into his solid back. The star on his left breast had a bent point.

He had large ears and friendly eyes and his jaws munched slowly and he looked as dangerous as a squirrel and much less nervous. I liked everything about him. I leaned on the counter and looked at him and he looked at me and nodded and loosed half a pint of tobacco juice down his right leg into the spittoon. It made a nasty sound of something falling into water.

I lit a cigarette and looked round for an ash-tray.

'Try the floor, son,' the large friendly man said.

'Are you Sheriff Patton?'

'Constable and deputy-sheriff. What law we got to have around here I'm it. Come election anyways. There's a couple of good boys running against me this time and I might get whupped. Job pays eighty a month, cabin, firewood and electricity. That ain't hay in these little old mountains.'

'Nobody's going to whip you,' I said. 'You're going to get a lot of publicity.'

'That so?' he asked indifferently and ruined the spittoon again.

'That is, if your jurisdiction extends over to Little Fawn Lake.'

'Kingsley's place. Sure. Something bothering over there, son?'

'There's a dead woman in the lake.'

That shook him to the core. He unclasped his hands and scratched one ear. He got to his feet by grasping the arms of his chair and deftly kicking it back from under him. Standing up he was a big man and hard. The fat was just cheerfulness.

'Anybody I know?' he inquired uneasily.

'Muriel Chess. I guess you know her. Bill Chess's wife.'

'Yep, I know Bill Chess.' His voice hardened a little.

'Looks like suicide. She left a note which sounded as if she was just going away. But it could be a suicide note just as well. She's not nice to look at. Been in the water a long time, about a month judging by the circumstances.'

He scratched his other ear. 'What circumstances would that be?' His eyes were searching my face now, slowly and calmly, but searching. He didn't seem in any hurry to blow his whistle.

'They had a fight a month ago. Bill went over to the north shore of the lake and was gone some hours. When he got home she was gone. He never saw her again.'

'I see. Who are you, son?'

'My name is Marlowe. I'm up from L.A. to look at the property. I had a note from Kingsley to Bill Chess. He took me around the lake and we went out on that little pier the movie people built. We were leaning on the rail and looking down into the water and something that looked like an arm waved out under the submerged flooring, the old boat landing. Bill dropped a heavy rock in and the body popped up.'

Patton looked at me without moving a muscle.

'Look, sheriff, hadn't we better run over there? The man's half-crazy with shock and he's there all alone.'

'How much liquor has he got?'

'Very little when I left. I had a pint, but we drank most of it talking.'

He moved over to the roll-top desk and unlocked a drawer. He brought up three or four bottles and held them against the light.

'This baby's near full,' he said, patting one of them. 'Mount Vernon. That ought to hold him. County don't allow me no money for emergency liquor, so I just have to seize a little here and there. Don't use it myself. Never could understand folks letting theirselves get gummed up with it.'

He put the bottle on his left hip and locked the desk up and lifted the flap in the counter. He fixed a card against the inside of the glass door panel. I looked at the card as we went out. It read: *Back in Twenty Minutes – Maybe*.

'I'll run down and get Doc Hollis,' he said. 'Be right back and pick you up. That your car?'

'Yes.'

'You can follow along then, as I come back by.'

He got into a car which had a siren on it, two red spotlights, two fog-lights, a red and white fire plate, a new air-raid horn on top, three axes, two heavy coils of rope and a fire-extinguisher in the back seat, extra petrol and oil and water-cans in a frame on the running-board, an extra spare tyre roped to the one on the rack, the stuffing coming out of the upholstery in dingy wads, and half an inch of dust over what was left of the paint.

Behind the right-hand lower corner of the windshield there was a white card printed in block capitals. It read:

VOTERS, ATTENTION! KEEP JIM PATTON CONSTABLE. HE IS TOO
OLD TO GO TO WORK

He turned the car and went off down the street in a
swirl of white dust.

8

He stopped in front of a white frame building across the road from the stage depot. He went into the white building and presently came out with a man who got into the back seat with the axes and the rope. The official car came back up the street and I fell in behind it. We sifted along the main stem through the slacks and shorts and French sailor jerseys and knotted bandannas and knobby knees and scarlet lips. Beyond the village we went up a dusty hill and stopped at a cabin. Patton touched the siren gently and a man in faded blue overalls opened the cabin door.

'Get in, Andy. Business.'

The man in blue overalls nodded morosely and ducked back into the cabin. He came back out wearing an oyster-grey lion-hunter's hat and got in under the wheel of Patton's car while Patton slid over. He was about thirty, dark, lithe, and had the slightly dirty and slightly underfed look of the native.

We drove out to Little Fawn Lake with me eating enough dust to make a batch of mud pies. At the five-barred gate Patton got out and let us through and we went on down to the lake. Patton got out again and went to the edge of the water and looked along towards the little pier. Bill Chess was sitting naked on the floor of the pier, with his head in his hands. There was something stretched out on the wet planks beside him.

'We can ride a ways more,' Patton said.

The two cars went on to the end of the lake and all four of us trooped down to the pier behind Bill Chess's back. The doctor stopped to cough rackingly into a handkerchief and then look thoughtfully at the handkerchief. He was an angular bug-eyed man with a sad sick face.

The thing that had been a woman lay face down on the boards with a rope under the arms. Bill Chess's clothes lay to one side. His stiff leg, flat and scarred at the knee, was stretched out in front of him, the other leg bent up and his forehead resting against it. He didn't move or look up as we came down behind him.

Patton took the pint bottle of Mount Vernon off his hip and unscrewed the top and handed it.

'Drink hearty, Bill.'

There was a horrible, sickening smell in the air. Bill Chess didn't seem to notice it, nor Patton nor the doctor. The man called Andy got a dusty brown blanket out of the car and threw it over the body. Then without a word he went and vomited under a pine-tree.

Bill Chess drank a long drink and sat holding the bottle against his bare bent knee. He began to talk in a stiff wooden voice, not looking at anybody, not talking to anybody in particular. He told about the quarrel and what happened after it, but not why it had happened. He didn't mention Mrs Kingsley even in the most casual way. He said that after I left him he had got a rope and stripped and gone down into the water and got the thing out. He had dragged it ashore and then got it up on his back and carried it out on the pier. He didn't know why. He had gone back into the water again then. He didn't have to tell us why.

Patton put a cut of tobacco into his mouth and chewed on it silently, his calm eyes full of nothing. Then he shut his teeth tight and leaned down to pull the blanket off the body. He turned the body over carefully, as if it might come to pieces. The late afternoon sun winked on the necklace of large green stones that were partly embedded in the swollen neck. They were roughly carved and lustreless, like soapstone or false jade. A gilt chain with an eagle clasp set with small brilliants joined the ends. Patton straightened his broad back and blew his nose on a tan handkerchief.

'What you say, Doc?'

'About what?' the bug-eyed man snarled.

'Cause and time of death.'

'Don't be a damn fool, Jim Patton.'

'Can't tell nothing, huh?'

'By looking at that? Good God!'

Patton sighed. 'Looks drowned all right,' he admitted. 'But you can't always tell. There's been cases where a victim would be knifed or poisoned or something, and they would soak him in the water to make things look different.'

'You get many like that up here?' the doctor inquired nastily.

'Only honest to God murder I ever had up here,' Patton said, watching Bill Chess out of the corner of his eye, 'was old Dad Meacham over on the north shore. He had a shack in Sheedy Canyon, did a little panning in summer on an old placer claim he had back in the valley near Belltop. Folks didn't see him around for a while in late fall, then come a heavy snow and his roof caved in to one side. So we was over there trying to prop her up a bit, figuring Dad had gone down the hill for the winter without telling anybody, the way them old prospectors do things. Well by gum, old Dad never went down the hill at all. There he was in bed with most of a kindling axe in the back of his head. We never did find out who done it. Somebody figured he had a little bag of gold hid away from the summer's panning.'

He looked thoughtfully at Andy. The man in the lion-hunter's hat was feeling a tooth in his mouth. He said:

''Course we know who done it. Guy Pope done it. Only Guy was dead nine days of pneumonia before we found Dad Meacham.'

'Eleven days,' Patton said.

'Nine,' the man in the lion-hunter's hat said.

'Was all of six years ago, Andy. Have it your own way, son. How you figure Guy Pope done it?'

'We found about three ounces of small nuggets in Guy's cabin along with some dust. Never was anything bigger'n sand on Guy's claim. Dad had nuggets all of a pennyweight, plenty of times.'

'Well, that's the way it goes,' Patton said, and smiled at me in a vague manner. 'Fellow always forgets something, don't he? No matter how careful he is.'

'Cop stuff,' Bill Chess said disgustedly and put his pants on and sat down again to put on his shoes and shirt. When he had them on he stood up and reached down for the bottle and took a good drink and laid the bottle carefully on the planks. He thrust his hairy wrists out towards Patton.

'That's the way you guys feel about it, put the cuffs on and get it over,' he said in a savage voice.

Patton ignored him and went over to the railing and

looked down. 'Funny place for a body to be,' he said. 'No current here to mention, but what there is would be towards the dam.'

Bill Chess lowered his wrists and said quietly: 'She did it herself, you darn fool. Muriel was a fine swimmer. She dived down in and swum under the boards there and just breathed water in. Had to. No other way.'

'I wouldn't quite say that, Bill,' Patton answered him mildly. His eyes were as blank as new plates.

Andy shook his head. Patton looked at him with a sly grin. 'Crabbin' again, Andy?'

'Was nine days, I tell you. I just counted back,' the man in the lion-hunter's hat said morosely.

The doctor threw his arms up and walked away, with one hand to his head. He coughed into his handkerchief again, and again looked into the handkerchief with passionate attention.

Patton winked at me and spat over the railing. 'Let's get on to this one, Andy.'

'You ever try to drag a body six feet under water?'

'Nope, can't say I ever did, Andy. Any reason it couldn't be done with a rope?'

Andy shrugged. 'If a rope was used, it will show on the corpse. If you got to give yourself away like that, why bother to cover up at all?'

'Question of time,' Patton said. 'Fellow has his arrangements to make.'

Bill Chess snarled at them and reached down for the whisky. Looking at their solemn mountain faces I couldn't tell what they were really thinking.

Patton said absently: 'Something was said about a note.'

Bill Chess rummaged in his wallet and drew the folded piece of ruled paper loose. Patton took it and read it slowly.

'Don't seem to have any date,' he observed.

Bill Chess shook his head sombrely. 'No. She left a month ago. June 12th.'

'Left you once before, didn't she?'

'Yeah.' Bill Chess stared at him fixedly. 'I got drunk and stayed with a chippy. Just before the first snow last December. She was gone a week and came back all prettied up. Said she just had to get away for a while and had been staying with a girl she used to work with in L.A.'

'What was the name of this party?' Patton asked.

'Never told me and I never asked her. What Muriel did was all silk with me.'

'Sure. Note left that time. Bill?' Patton asked smoothly.

'No.'

'This note here looks middling old,' Patton said, holding it up.

'I carried it a month,' Bill Chess growled. 'Who told you she left me before?'

'I forget,' Patton said. 'You know how it is in a place like this. Not much folks don't notice. Except maybe in summer time where there's a lot of strangers about.'

Nobody said anything for a while and then Patton said absently: 'June 12th you say she left? Or you thought she left? Did you say the folks across the lake were up here then?'

Bill Chess looked at me and his face darkened again. 'Ask this snoopy guy – if he didn't already spill his guts to you.'

Patton didn't look at me at all. He looked at the line of mountains far beyond the lake. He said gently: 'Mr Marlowe here didn't tell me anything at all, Bill, except how the body come up out of the water and who it was. And that Muriel went away, as you thought, and left a note you showed him. I don't guess there's anything wrong in that, is there?'

There was another silence and Bill Chess stared down at the blanket-covered corpse a few feet away from him. He clenched his hands and a thick tear ran down his cheek.

'Mrs Kingsley was here,' he said. 'She went down the hill that same day. Nobody was in the other cabins. Perrys and Farquhars ain't been up at all this year.'

Patton nodded and was silent. A kind of charged emptiness hung in the air, as if something that had not been said was plain to all of them and didn't need saying.

Then Bill Chess said wildly: 'Take me in, you sons of bitches! Sure I did it! I drowned her. She was my girl and I loved her. I'm a heel, always was a heel, always will be a heel, but just the same I loved her. Maybe you guys wouldn't understand that. Just don't bother to try. Take me in, damn you!'

Nobody said anything at all.

Bill Chess looked down at his hard brown fist. He swung it up viciously and hit himself in the face with all his strength.

'You rotten son of a bitch,' he breathed in a harsh whisper.

His nose began to bleed slowly. He stood and the blood ran down his lip, down the side of his mouth, to the point of his chin. A drop fell sluggishly to his shirt.

Patton said quietly: 'Got to take you down the hill for questioning, Bill. You know that. We ain't accusing you of anything, but the folks down there have got to talk to you.'

Bill Chess said heavily: 'Can I change my clothes?'

'Sure. You go with him, Andy. And see what you can find to kind of wrap up what he got here.'

They went off along the path at the edge of the lake. The doctor cleared his throat and looked out over the water and sighed.

'You'll want to send the corpse down in my ambulance, Jim, won't you?'

Patton shook his head. 'Nope. This is a poor county, Doc. I figure the lady can ride cheaper than what you get for that ambulance.'

The doctor walked away from him angrily, saying over his shoulder: 'Let me know if you want me to pay for the funeral.'

'That ain't no way to talk,' Patton sighed.

9

The Indian Head Hotel was a brown building on a corner across from the new dance hall. I parked in front of it and used its rest-room to wash my face and hands and comb the pine needles out of my hair, before I went into the dining-drinking parlour that adjoined the lobby. The whole place was full to overflowing with males in leisure jackets and liquor breaths and females in high-pitched laughs, ox-blood finger-nails and dirty knuckles. The manager of the joint, a low budget tough guy in shirt sleeves and a mangled cigar, was prowling the room with watchful eyes. At the cash desk a pale-haired man was fighting to get the war news on a small radio that was as full of static as the mashed potatoes were full of water. In the deep back corner of the room, a hillbilly orchestra of five pieces, dressed in ill-fitting white jackets and purple shirts, was trying to make itself heard above the brawl at the bar and smiling glassily into the fog of cigarette smoke and the blur of alcoholic voices. At Puma Point summer, that lovely season, was in full swing.

I gobbled what they called the regular dinner, drank a brandy to sit on its chest and hold it down, and went out on to the main street. It was still broad daylight but some of the neon signs had been turned on, and the evening reeled with the cheerful din of motor horns, children screaming, bowls rattling, skeeballs clunking, .22s snapping merrily in shooting-galleries, juke boxes playing like crazy, and behind all this out on the lake the hard barking roar of the speedboats going nowhere at all and acting as though they were racing with death.

In my Chrysler a thin, serious-looking, brown-haired girl in dark slacks was sitting smoking a cigarette and talking to a dude ranch cowboy who sat on my running-board. I walked around the car and got into it. The cowboy strolled away hitching his jeans up. The girl didn't move.

'I'm Birdie Keppel,' she said cheerfully. 'I'm the beautician here daytimes and evenings I work on the *Puma Point Banner*. Excuse me sitting in your car.'

'That's all right,' I said. 'You want to just sit or you want me to drive you somewhere?'

'You can drive down the road a piece where it's quieter, Mr Marlowe. If you're obliging enough to talk to me.'

'Pretty good grapevine you've got up here,' I said and started the car.

I drove down past the post office to a corner where a blue-and-white arrow marked *Telephone* pointed down a narrow road towards the lake. I turned down that, drove down past the telephone office, which was a log cabin with a tiny railed lawn in front of it, passed another small cabin and pulled up in front of a huge oak-tree that flung its branches all the way across the road and a good fifty feet beyond it.

'This do, Miss Keppel?'

'Mrs But just call me Birdie. Everybody does. This is fine. Pleased to meet you, Mr Marlowe. I see you come from Hollywood, that sinful city.'

She put a firm brown hand out and I shook it. Clamping bobbie pins into fat blondes had given her a grip like a pair of iceman's tongs.

'I was talking to Doc Hollis,' she said, 'about poor Muriel Chess. I thought you could give me some details. I understand you found the body.'

'Bill Chess found it really. I was just with him. You talk to Jim Patton?'

'Not yet. He went down the hill. Anyway, I don't think Jim would tell me much.'

'He's up for re-election,' I said. 'And you're a newspaper woman.'

'Jim's no politician, Mr Marlowe, and I could hardly call myself a newspaper woman. This little paper we get out up here is a pretty amateurish proposition.'

'Well, what do you want to know?' I offered her a cigarette and lit it for her.

'You might just tell me the story.'

'I came up here with a letter from Derace Kingsley to look at his property. Bill Chess showed me around, got talking to me, told me his wife had moved out on him and showed me the note she left. I had a bottle along and he punished it. He was feeling pretty blue. The liquor loosened him up, but he was lonely and aching to talk anyway. That's how it happened. I didn't know him. Coming back around the end of the lake we went out on the pier and Bill spotted an arm waving out from under the planking down in the water. It turned out to belong to what was left of Muriel Chess. I guess that's all.'

'I understand from Doc Hollis she had been in the water a long time. Pretty badly decomposed and all that.'

'Yes. Probably the whole month he thought she had

been gone. There's no reason to think otherwise. The note's a suicide note.'

'Any doubt about that, Mr Marlowe?'

I looked at her sideways. Thoughtful dark eyes looked out at me under fluffed-out brown hair. The dusk had begun to fall now, very slowly. It was no more than a slight change in the quality of the light.

'I guess the police always have doubts in these cases,' I said.

'How about you?'

'My opinion doesn't go for anything.'

'But for what it's worth?'

'I only met Bill Chess this afternoon,' I said. 'He struck me as a quick-tempered lad and from his own account he's no saint. But he seems to have been in love with his wife. And I can't see him hanging around there for a month knowing she was rotting down in the water under that pier. Coming out of his cabin in the sunlight and looking along that soft blue water and seeing in his mind what was under it and what was happening to it. And knowing he put it there.'

'No more can I,' Birdie Keppel said softly. 'No more could anybody. And yet we know in our minds that such things have happened and will happen again. Are you in the real-estate business, Mr Marlowe?'

'No.'

'What line of business are you in, if I may ask?'

'I'd rather not say.'

'That's almost as good as saying,' she said. 'Besides, Doc Hollis heard you tell Jim Patton your full name. And we have an L.A. city directory in our office. I haven't mentioned it to anyone.'

'That's nice of you,' I said.

'And what's more, I won't,' she said. 'If you don't want me to.'

'What does it cost me?'

'Nothing,' she said. 'Nothing at all. I don't claim to be a very good newspaper woman. And we wouldn't print anything that would embarrass Jim Patton. Jim's the salt of the earth. But it does open up, doesn't it?'

'Don't draw any wrong conclusions,' I said. 'I had no interest in Bill Chess whatever.'

'No interest in Muriel Chess?'

'Why should I have any interest in Muriel Chess?'

She snuffed her cigarette out carefully into the ash-tray under the dashboard. 'Have it your own way,' she said. 'But here's a little item you might like to think about, if you don't know it already. There was a Los Angeles copper named De Soto up here about six weeks back, a big rough-neck with damn poor manners. We didn't like him and we didn't open up to him much. I mean the three of us in the *Banner* office didn't. He had a photograph with him and he was looking for a woman called Mildred Haviland, he said. On police business. It was an ordinary photograph, an enlarged snapshot, not a police photo. He said he had information the woman was staying up here. The photo looked a good deal like Muriel Chess. The hair seemed to be reddish and in a very different style than she has worn it here, and the eyebrows were all plucked to narrow arches, and that changes a woman a good deal. But it did look a good deal like Bill Chess's wife.'

I drummed on the door of the car and after a moment I said, 'What did you tell him?'

'We didn't tell him anything. First off, we couldn't be sure. Second, we didn't like his manner. Third, even if we had been sure and had liked his manner, we likely would not have sicked him on to her. Why would we? Everybody's done something to be sorry for. Take me. I was married once – to a professor of classical languages at Redlands University.' She laughed lightly.

'You might have got yourself a story,' I said.

'Sure. But up here we're just people.'

'Did this man De Soto see Jim Patton?'

'Sure, he must have. Jim didn't mention it.'

'Did he show you his badge?'

She thought and then shook her head. 'I don't recall that he did. We just took him for granted, from what he said. He certainly acted like a tough city cop.'

'To me that's a little against his being one. Did anybody tell Muriel about this guy?'

She hesitated, looking quietly out through the windshield for a long moment before she turned her head and nodded.

'I did. Wasn't any of my damn business, was it?'

'What did she say?'

'She didn't say anything. She gave a funny little embarrassed laugh, as if I had been making a bad joke. Then she walked away. But I did get the impression that there was a queer look in her eyes, just for an instant. You still not interested in Muriel Chess, Mr Marlowe?'

'Why should I be? I never heard of her until I came up here this afternoon. Honest. And I never heard of anybody named Mildred Haviland either. Drive you back to town?'

'Oh no, thanks. I'll walk. It's only a few steps. Much

obliged to you. I kind of hope Bill doesn't get into a jam. Especially a nasty jam like this.'

She got out of the car and hung on one foot, then tossed her head and laughed. 'They say I'm a pretty good beauty operator,' she said. 'I hope I am. As an interviewer I'm terrible. Good night.'

I said good night and she walked off into the evening. I sat there watching her until she reached the main street and turned out of sight. Then I got out of the Chrysler and went over towards the telephone company's little rustic building.

10

A tame doe deer with a leather dog collar on wandered across the road in front of me. I patted her rough hairy neck and went into the telephone office. A small girl in slacks sat at a small desk working on the books. She got me the rate to Beverly Hills and the change for the coin box. The booth was outside, against the front wall of the building.

'I hope you like it up here,' she said. 'It's very quiet, very restful.'

I shut myself into the booth. For ninety cents I could talk to Derace Kingsley for five minutes. He was at home and the call came through quickly but the connexion was full of mountain static.

'Find anything up there?' he asked me in a three-highball voice. He sounded tough and confident again.

'I've found too much,' I said. 'And not at all what we want. Are you alone?'

'What does that matter?'

'It doesn't matter to me. But I know what I'm going to say. You don't.'

'Well, get on with it, whatever it is,' he said.

'I had a long talk with Bill Chess. He was lonely. His wife had left him – a month ago. They had a fight and he went out and got drunk and when he came back she was gone. She left a note saying she would rather be dead than live with him any more.'

'I guess Bill drinks too much,' Kingsley's voice said from very far off.

'When he got back, both the women had gone. He has no idea where Mrs Kingsley went. Lavery was up here in May, but not since. Lavery admitted that much himself. Lavery could, of course, have come up again while Bill was out getting drunk, but there wouldn't be a lot of point to that and there would be two cars to drive down the hill. And I thought that possibly Mrs K. and Muriel Chess might have gone away together, only Muriel also had a car of her own. But that idea, little as it was worth, has been thrown out by another development. Muriel Chess didn't go away at all. She went down into your little private lake. She came back up to-day. I was there.'

'Good God!' Kingsley sounded properly horrified. 'You mean she drowned herself?'

'Perhaps. The note she left could be a suicide note. It would read as well that way as the other. The body was stuck down under that old submerged landing below the pier. Bill was the one who spotted an arm moving down there while we were standing on the pier looking down into the water. He got her out. They've arrested him. The poor guy's pretty badly broken up.'

'Good God!' Kingsley said again. 'I should think he would be. Does it look as if he –' He paused as the operator came in on the line and demanded another forty-five cents, I put in two quarters and the line cleared.

'Look as if he what?'

Suddenly very clear, Kingsley's voice said: 'Look as if he murdered her?'

I said: 'Very much. Jim Patton, the constable up here,

doesn't like the note not being dated. It seems she left him once before over some woman. Patton sort of suspects Bill might have saved up an old note. Anyhow they've taken Bill down to San Bernardino for questioning and they've taken the body down to be post-mortemed.'

'And what do you think?' he asked slowly.

'Well, Bill found the body himself. He didn't have to take me around by that pier. She might have stayed down in the water very much longer, or for ever. The note could be old because Bill had carried it in his wallet and handled it from time to time, brooding over it. It could just as easily be undated this time as another time. I'd say notes like that are undated more often than not. The people who write them are apt to be in a hurry and not concerned with dates.'

'The body must be pretty far gone. What can they find out now?'

'I don't know how well equipped they are. They can find out if she died by drowning, I guess. And whether there are any marks of violence that wouldn't be erased by water and decomposition. They could tell if she had been shot or stabbed. If the hyoid bone in the throat was broken, they could assume she was throttled. The main thing for us is that I'll have to tell why I came up here. I'll have to testify at an inquest.'

'That's bad,' Kingsley growled. 'Very bad. What do you plan to do now?'

'On my way home I'll stop at the Prescott Hotel and see if I can pick up anything there. Were your wife and Muriel Chess friendly?'

'I guess so. Crystal's easy enough to get along with most of the time. I hardly knew Muriel Chess.'

'Did you ever know anybody named Mildred Haviland?'

'What?'

I repeated the name.

'No,' he said. 'Is there any reason why I should?'

'Every question I ask you ask another right back,' I said. 'No, there isn't any reason why you should know Mildred Haviland. Especially if you hardly knew Muriel Chess. I'll call you in the morning.'

'Do that,' he said, and hesitated. 'I'm sorry you had to walk into such a mess,' he added, and then hesitated again and said good night and hung up.

The bell rang again immediately and the long-distance operator told me sharply I had put in five cents too much money. I said the sort of thing I would be likely to put into an opening like that. She didn't like it.

I stepped out of the booth and gathered some air into my lungs. The tame doe with the leather collar was standing in the gap in the fence at the end of the walk. I tried to push her out of the way, but she just leaned against me and wouldn't push. So I stepped over the fence and went back to the Chrysler and drove back to the village.

There was a hanging light in Patton's headquarters but the shack was empty and his 'Back in Twenty Minutes' sign was still against the inside of the glass part of the door. I kept on going down to the boat-landing and beyond to the edge of a deserted swimming-beach. A few put-puts and speedboats were still fooling around on the silky water. Across the lake tiny yellow lights began to show in toy cabins perched on miniature slopes. A single bright star glowed low in the north-east above the ridge of the mountains. A robin sat on the spike top of a hundred-foot pine and waited for it to be dark enough for him to sing his good-night song.

In a little while it was dark enough and he sang and went away into the invisible depths of sky. I snapped my cigarette into the motionless water a few feet away and climbed back into the car and started back in the direction of Little Fawn Lake.

II

The gate across the private road was padlocked. I put the Chrysler between two pine-trees and climbed the gate and pussy-footed along the side of the road until the glimmer of the little lake bloomed suddenly at my feet. Bill Chess's cabin was dark. The three cabins on the other side were abrupt shadows against the pale granite outcrop. Water gleamed white where it trickled across the top of the dam, and fell almost soundlessly along the sloping outer face to the brook below. I listened, and heard no other sound at all.

The front door of the Chess cabin was locked. I padded along to the back and found a brute of a padlock hanging at that. I went along the walls feeling window screens. They were all fastened. One window higher up was screenless, a small double cottage window half-way down the north wall. This was locked too. I stood still and did some more listening. There was no breeze and the trees were as quiet as their shadows.

I tried a knife blade between the two halves of the small window. No soap. The catch refused to budge. I leaned against the wall and thought and then suddenly I picked up a large stone and smacked it against the place where the two frames met in the middle. The catch pulled out of dry wood with a tearing noise. The window swung back into darkness. I heaved up on the sill and wangled a cramped leg over and edged through the opening. I rolled and let myself down into the room. I turned, grunting a little from the exertion at that altitude, and listened again.

A blazing flash beam hit me square in the eyes.

A very calm voice said: 'I'd rest right there, son. You must be all tuckered out.'

The flash pinned me against the wall like a squashed fly. Then a light switch clicked and a table lamp glowed. The flash went out. Jim Patton was sitting in an old brown Morris chair beside the table. A fringed brown scarf hung over the end of the table and touched his thick knee. He wore the same clothes he had worn that afternoon, with the addition of a leather jerkin which must have been new once, say about the time of Grover Cleveland's first term. His hands were empty except for the flash. His eyes were empty. His jaws moved in gentle rhythm.

'What's on your mind, son – besides breaking and entering?'

I poked a chair out and straddled it and leaned my arms on the back and looked around the cabin.

'I had an idea,' I said. 'It looked pretty good for a while, but I guess I can learn to forget it.'

The cabin was larger than it had seemed from outside. The part I was in was the living-room. It contained a few articles of modest furniture, a rag rug on the pineboard floor, a round table against the end wall and two chairs set against it. Through an open door the corner of a big black cookstove showed.

Patton nodded and his eyes studied me without rancour. 'I heard a car coming,' he said. 'I knew it had to be coming here. You walk right nice though. I didn't hear you walk worth a darn. I've been a mite curious about you, son.'

I said nothing.

'I hope you don't mind me callin' you "son", ' he said. 'I hadn't ought to be so familiar, but I got myself into the habit and I can't seem to shake it. Anybody that don't have a long white beard and arthritis is "son" to me.'

I said he could call me anything that came to mind. I wasn't sensitive.

He grinned. 'There's a mess of detectives in the L.A. phone book,' he said. 'But only one of them is called Marlowe.'

'What made you look?'

'I guess you might call it lowdown curiosity. Added to which Bill Chess told me you was some sort of dick. You didn't bother to tell me yourself.'

'I'd have got around to it,' I said. 'I'm sorry it bothered you.'

'It didn't bother me none. I don't bother at all easy. You got any identification with you?'

I got my wallet out and showed him this and that.

'Well, you got a good build on you for the work,' he said, satisfied. 'And your face don't tell a lot of stories. I guess you was aiming to search the cabin.'

'Yeah.'

'I already pawed around considerable myself. Just got back and come straight here. That is, I stopped by my shack a minute and then come. I don't figure I could let you search the place, though.' He scratched his ear. 'That is, dum if I know whether I could or not. You telling who hired you?'

'Derace Kingsley. To trace his wife. She skipped out

on him a month ago. She started from here. So I started from here. She's supposed to have gone away with a man. The man denies it. I thought maybe something up here might give me a lead.'

'And did anything?'

'No. She's traced pretty definitely as far as San Bernardino and then El Paso. There the trail ends. But I've only just started.'

Patton stood up and unlocked the cabin door. The spicy smell of the pines surged in. He spat outdoors and sat down again and rumpled the mousy brown hair under his Stetson. His head with the hat off had the indecent look of heads that are seldom without hats.

'You didn't have no interest in Bill Chess at all?'

'None whatever.'

'I guess you fellows do a lot of divorce business,' he said. 'Kind of smelly work, to my notion.'

I let that ride.

'Kingsley wouldn't have asked help from the police to find his wife, would he?'

'Hardly,' I said. 'He knows her too well.'

'None of what you've been saying don't hardly explain your wanting to search Bill's cabin,' he said judiciously.

'I'm just a great guy to poke around.'

'Hell,' he said, 'you can do better than that.'

'Say I am interested in Bill Chess then. But only because he's in trouble and rather a pathetic case – in spite of being a good deal of a heel. If he murdered his wife, there's something here to point that way. If he didn't, there's something to point that way too.'

He held his head sideways, like a watchful bird. 'As for instance what kind of thing?'

'Clothes, personal jewellery, toilet articles, whatever a woman takes with her when she goes away, not intending to come back.'

He leaned back slowly. 'But she didn't go away, son.'

'Then the stuff should be still here. But if it was still here, Bill would have noticed she hadn't taken it. He would know she hadn't gone away.'

'By gum, I don't like it either way,' he said.

'But if he murdered her,' I said, 'then he would have to get rid of the things she ought to have taken with her, if she had gone away.'

'And how do you figure he would do that, son?' The yellow lamplight made bronze of one side of his face.

'I understand she had a Ford car of her own. Except for that I'd expect him to burn what he could burn and bury what he could not burn out in the woods. Sinking it in the lake might be dangerous. But he couldn't burn or bury her car. Could he drive it?'

Patton looked surprised. 'Sure. He can't bend his right leg at the knee, so he couldn't use the foot-brake very handy. But he could get by with the hand-brake. All that's different on Bill's own Ford is the brake pedal is set over on the left side of the post, close to the clutch, so he can shove them both down with one foot.'

I shook ash from my cigarette into a small blue jar that had once contained a pound of orange honey, according to the small gilt label on it.

'Getting rid of the car would be his big problem,' I said. 'Wherever he took it he would have to get back, and he would rather not be seen coming back. And if he simply abandoned it on a street, say, down in San Bernardino, it would be found and identified very quickly. He wouldn't want that either. The best stunt would be to unload it on a hot car dealer, but he probably doesn't know one. So the chances are he hid it in the woods within walking distance of here. And walking distance for him would not be very far.'

'For a fellow that claims not to be interested, you're doing some pretty close figuring on all this,' Patton said dryly. 'So now you've got the car hid out in the woods. What then?'

'He has to consider the possibility of its being found. The woods are lonely, but rangers and woodcutters get around in them from time to time. If the car is found, it would be better for Muriel's stuff to be found in it. That would give him a couple of outs – neither one very brilliant but both at least possible. One, that she was murdered by some unknown party who fixed things to implicate Bill when and if the murder was discovered. Two, that Muriel did actually commit suicide, but fixed things so that he would be blamed. A revenge suicide.'

Patton thought all this over with calm and care. He went to the door to unload again. He sat down and rumpled his hair again. He looked at me with solid scepticism.

'The first one's possible like you say,' he admitted. 'But only just, and I don't have anybody in mind for the job. There's that little matter of the note to be got over.'

I shook my head. 'Say Bill already had the note from another time. Say she went away, as he thought, without leaving a note. After a month had gone by without any word from her he might be just worried and uncertain enough to show the note, feeling it might be some protection to him in case anything had happened to her.

He didn't say any of this, but he could have had it in his mind.'

Patton shook his head. He didn't like it. Neither did I. He said slowly: 'As to your other notion, it's just plain crazy. Killing yourself and fixing things so as somebody else would get accused of murdering you don't fit in with my simple ideas of human nature at all.'

'Then your ideas of human nature are too simple,' I said. 'Because it has been done, and when it has been done, it has nearly always been done by a woman.'

'Nope,' he said, 'I'm a man fifty-seven years old and I've seen a lot of crazy people, but I don't go for that worth a peanut shell. What I like is that she did plan to go away and did write the note, but he caught her before she got clear and saw red and finished her off. Then he would have to do all them things we been talking about.'

'I never met her,' I said. 'So I wouldn't have any idea what she would be likely to do. Bill said he met her in a place in Riverside something over a year ago. She may have had a long and complicated history before that. What kind of girl was she?'

'A mighty cute little blonde when she fixed herself up. She kind of let herself go with Bill. A quiet girl, with a face that kept its secrets. Bill says she had a temper, but I never seen any of it. I seen plenty of nasty temper in him.'

'And did you think she looked like the photo of somebody called Mildred Haviland?'

His jaws stopped munching and his mouth became almost primly tight. Very slowly he started chewing again.

'By gum,' he said, 'I'll be mighty careful to look under

the bed before I crawl in to-night. To make sure you ain't there. Where did you get that information?'

'A nice little girl called Birdie Keppel told me. She was interviewing me in the course of her spare-time newspaper job. She happened to mention that an L.A. cop named De Soto was showing the photo around.'

Patton smacked his thick knee and hunched his shoulders forward.

'I done wrong there,' he said soberly. 'I made one of my mistakes. This big bruiser showed his picture to darn near everybody in town before he showed it to me. That made me kind of sore. It looked some like Muriel, but not enough to be sure by any manner of means. I asked him what she was wanted for. He said it was police business. I said I was in that way of business myself, in an ignorant countrified kind of way. He said his instructions were to locate the lady and that was all he knew. Maybe he did wrong to take me up short like that. So I guess I done wrong to tell him I didn't know anybody that looked like his little picture.'

The big calm man smiled vaguely at the corner of the ceiling, then brought his eyes down and looked at me steadily.

'I'll thank you to respect this confidence, Mr Marlowe. You done right nicely in your figuring too. You ever happen to go over to Coon Lake?'

'Never heard of it.'

'Back about a mile,' he said, pointing over his shoulder with a thumb, 'there's a little narrow wood road turns over west. You can just drive in and miss the trees. It climbs about five hundred feet in another mile and comes out by Coon Lake. Pretty little place. Folks go up there to picnic once in a while, but not often. It's hard on tyres. There's two three small shallow lakes full of reeds. There's snow up there even now in the shady places. There's a bunch of old hand-hewn log cabins that's been falling down ever since I recall, and there's a big broken-down frame building that Montclair University used to use for a summer camp maybe years back. They ain't used it in a very long time. This building sits back from the lakes in heavy timber. Round at the back of it there's a wash-house with an old rusty boiler and along of that there's a big woodshed with a sliding door hung on rollers. It was built for a garage, but they kept their wood in it and they locked it up out of season. Wood's one of the few things people will steal up here, but folks who might steal it off a pile wouldn't break a lock to get it. I guess you know what I found in that woodshed.'

'I thought you went down to San Bernardino.'

'Changed my mind. Didn't seem right to let Bill ride down there with his wife's body in the back of the car. So I sent it down in Doc's ambulance and I sent Andy down with Bill. I figured I kind of ought to look around a little more before I put things up to the sheriff and the coroner.'

'Muriel's car was in the woodshed?'

'Yep. And two unlocked suit-cases in the car. Packed with clothes and packed kind of hasty, I thought. Women's clothes. The point is, son, no stranger would have known about that place.'

I agreed with him. He put his hand into the slanting side pocket of his jerkin and brought out a small twist of tissue paper. He opened it up on his palm and held the hand out flat.

'Take a look at this.'

I went over and looked. What lay on the tissue was a thin gold chain with a tiny lock hardly larger than a link of the chain. The gold had been snipped through, leaving the lock intact. The chain seemed to be about seven inches long. There was white powder sticking to both chain and paper.

'Where would you guess I found that?' Patton asked.

I picked the chain up and tried to fit the cut ends together. They didn't fit. I made no comment on that, but moistened a finger and touched the powder and tasted it.

'In a can or box of confectioner's sugar,' I said. 'The chain is an anklet. Some women never take them off, like wedding-rings. Whoever took this one off didn't have the key.'

'What do you make of it?'

'Nothing much,' I said. 'There wouldn't be any point in Bill cutting it off Muriel's ankle and leaving that green necklace on her neck. There wouldn't be any point in Muriel cutting it off herself – assuming she had lost the key – and hiding it to be found. A search thorough enough to find it wouldn't be made unless her body was found first. If Bill cut it off, he would have thrown it into the lake. But if Muriel wanted to keep it and yet hide it from Bill, there's some sense in the place where it was hidden.'

Patton looked puzzled this time. 'Why is that?'

'Because it's a woman's hiding-place. Confectioner's sugar is used to make cake icing. A man would never look there. Pretty clever of you to find it, sheriff.'

He grinned a little sheepishly. 'Hell, I knocked the box over and some of the sugar spilled,' he said. 'Without that I don't guess I ever would have found it.' He rolled the paper up again and slipped it back into his pocket. He stood up with an air of finality.

'You staying up here or going back to town, Mr Marlowe?'

'Back to town. Until you want me for the inquest. I suppose you will.'

'That's up to the coroner, of course. If you'll kind of shut that window you bust in, I'll put this lamp out and lock up.'

I did what he said and he snapped his flash on and put out the lamp. We went out and he felt the cabin door to make sure the lock had caught. He closed the screen softly and stood looking across the moonlit lake.

'I don't figure Bill meant to kill her,' he said sadly. 'He could choke a girl to death without meaning to at all. He has mighty strong hands. Once done, he has to use what brains God gave him to cover up what he done. I feel real bad about it, but that don't alter the facts and the probabilities. It's simple and natural and the simple and natural things usually turn out to be right.'

I said: 'I should think he would have run away. I don't see how he could stand it to stay here.'

Patton spat into the black velvet shadow of a manzanita bush. He said slowly: 'He had a government pension and he would have to run away from that too. And most men can stand what they've got to stand, when it steps up and looks them straight in the eye. Like they're doing all over the world right now. Well, good night to you. I'm going to walk down to that little pier again and stand there awhile in the moonlight and feel bad. A night like this, and we got to think about murders.'

He moved quietly off into the shadows and became one of them himself. I stood there until he was out of sight and then went back to the locked gate and climbed over it. I got into the car and drove back down the road looking for a place to hide.

12

Three hundred yards from the gate a narrow track, sifted over with brown oak leaves from last autumn, curved around a granite boulder and disappeared. I followed it around and bumped along the stones of the outcrop for fifty or sixty feet, then swung the car around a tree and set it pointing back the way it had come. I cut the lights and switched off the motor and sat there waiting.

Half an hour passed. Without tobacco it seemed a long time. Then far off I heard a car motor start up and grow louder and the white beam of headlights passed below me on the road. The sound faded into the distance and a faint dry tang of dust hung in the air for a while after it was gone.

I got out of my car and walked back to the gate and to the Chess cabin. A hard push opened the sprung window this time. I climbed in again and let myself down to the floor and poked the flash I had brought across the room to the table lamp. I switched the lamp on and listened a moment, heard nothing and went out to the kitchen. I switched on a hanging bulb over the sink.

The wood-box beside the stove was neatly piled with split wood. There were no dirty dishes in the sink, no foul-smelling pots on the stove. Bill Chess, lonely or not, kept his house in good order. A door opened from the kitchen into the bedroom, and from that a very narrow door led into a tiny bathroom which had evidently been built on to the cabin fairly recently. The clean celotex lining showed that. The bathroom told me nothing.

The bedroom contained a double bed, a pinewood dresser with a round mirror on the wall above it, a bureau, two straight chairs and a tin waste-basket. There were two oval rag rugs on the floor, one on each side of the bed. On the walls Bill Chess had tacked up a set of war maps from the *National Geographic*. There was a silly-looking red-and-white flounce on the dressing-table.

I poked around in the drawers. An imitation leather trinket-box with an assortment of gaudy costume jewellery had not been taken away. There was the usual stuff women use on their faces and finger-nails and eyebrows, and it seemed to me that there was too much of it. But that was just guessing. The bureau contained both man's and woman's clothes, not a great deal of either. Bill Chess had a very noisy check shirt with starched matching collar, among other things. Underneath a sheet of blue tissue paper in one corner I found something I didn't like. A seemingly brand-new peach-coloured silk slip trimmed with lace. Silk slips were not being left behind that year, not by any woman in her senses.

This looked bad for Bill Chess. I wondered what Patton had thought of it.

I went back to the kitchen and prowled the open shelves above and beside the sink. They were thick with cans and jars of household staples. The confectioner's sugar was in a square brown box with a torn corner. Patton had made an attempt to clean up what was spilled. Near the sugar were salt, borax, baking-soda, cornstarch, brown sugar and so on. Something might be hidden in any of them.

Something that had been clipped from a chain anklet whose cut ends did not fit together.

I shut my eyes and poked a finger out at random and it came to rest on the baking-soda. I got a newspaper from the back of the wood-box and spread it out and dumped the soda out of the box. I stirred it around with a spoon. There seemed to be an indecent lot of baking-soda, but that was all there was. I funnelled it back into the box and tried the borax. Nothing but borax. Third time lucky. I tried the cornstarch. It made too much fine dust, and there was nothing but cornstarch.

The sound of distant steps froze me to the ankles. I reached up and yanked the light out and dodged back into the living-room and reached for the lamp switch. Much too late to be of any use, of course. The steps sounded again, soft and cautious. The hackles rose on my neck.

I waited in the dark, with the flash in my left hand. A deadly long two minutes crept by. I spent some of the time breathing, but not all.

It wouldn't be Patton. He would walk up to the door and open it and tell me off. The careful quiet steps seemed to move this way and that, a movement, a long pause, another movement, another long pause. I sneaked across to the door and twisted the knob silently. I yanked the door wide and stabbed out with the flash.

It made golden lamps of a pair of eyes. There was a leaping movement and a quick thudding of hoofs back among the trees. It was only an inquisitive deer.

I closed the door again and followed my flashlight beam back into the kitchen. The small round glow rested squarely on the box of confectioner's sugar.

I put the light on again, lifted the box down and emptied it on the newspaper.

Patton hadn't gone deep enough. Having found one thing by accident he had assumed that was all there was. He hadn't seemed to notice that there ought to be something else.

Another twist of white tissue showed in the fine white powdered sugar. I shook it clean and unwound it. It contained a tiny gold heart, no larger than a woman's little finger-nail.

I spooned the sugar back into the box and put the box back on the shelf and crumpled the piece of newspaper into the stove. I went back to the living-room and turned the table lamp on. Under that brighter light the tiny engraving on the back of the little gold heart could just be read without a magnifying-glass.

It was in script. It read: 'Al to Mildred. June 28th, 1938. With all my love.'

Al to Mildred. Al somebody to Mildred Haviland. Mildred Haviland was Muriel Chess. Muriel Chess was dead – two weeks after a cop named De Soto had been looking for her.

I stood there, holding it, wondering what it had to do with me. Wondering, and not having the faintest glimmer of an idea.

I wrapped it up again and left the cabin and drove back to the village.

Patton was in his office telephoning when I got around there. The door was locked. I had to wait while he talked. After a while he hung up and came to unlock the door.

I walked in past him and put the twist of tissue paper on his counter and opened it up.

'You didn't go deep enough into the powdered sugar,' I said.

He looked at the little gold heart, looked at me, went around behind the counter and got a cheap magnifying-glass off his desk. He studied the back of the heart. He put the glass down and frowned at me.

'Might have known if you wanted to search that cabin, you was going to do it,' he said gruffly. 'I ain't going to have trouble with you, am I, son?'

'You ought to have noticed that the cut ends of the chain didn't fit,' I told him.

He looked at me sadly. 'Son, I don't have your eyes.' He pushed the little heart around with his square blunt finger. He stared at me and said nothing.

I said: 'If you were thinking that anklet meant something Bill could have been jealous about, so was I – provided he ever saw it. But strictly on the cuff I'm willing to bet he never did see it and that he never heard of Mildred Haviland.'

Patton said slowly: 'Looks like maybe I owe this De Soto party an apology, don't it?'

'If you ever see him,' I said.

He gave me another long empty stare and I gave it right back to him. 'Don't tell me, son,' he said. 'Let me guess all for myself that you got a brand-new idea about it.'

'Yeah. Bill didn't murder his wife.'

'No?'

'No. She was murdered by somebody out of her past. Somebody who had lost track of her and then found it again and found her married to another man and didn't like it. Somebody who knew the country up here – as hundreds of people do who don't live here – and knew a good place to hide the car and the clothes. Somebody who hated and could dissimulate. Who persuaded her to go away with him and when everything was ready and the note was written, took her around the throat and gave her what he thought was coming to her and put her in the lake and went his way. Like it?'

'Well,' he said judiciously, 'it does make things kind of complicated, don't you think? But there ain't anything impossible about it. Not one bit impossible.'

'When you get tired of it, let me know. I'll have something else,' I said.

'I'll just be doggone sure you will,' he said, and for the first time since I had met him he laughed.

I said good night again and went out, leaving him there moving his mind around with the ponderous energy of a homesteader digging up a stump.

13

At somewhere around eleven I got down to the bottom of the grade and parked in one of the diagonal slots at the side of the Prescott Hotel in San Bernardino. I pulled an overnight bag out of the boot and had taken three steps with it when a bellhop in braided pants and a white shirt and black bow-tie yanked it out of my hand.

The clerk on duty was an egg-headed man with no interest in me or in anything else. He wore parts of a white linen suit and he yawned as he handed me the desk pen and looked off into the distance as if remembering his childhood.

The hop and I rode a four by four elevator to the second floor and walked a couple of blocks around corners. As we walked it got hotter and hotter. The hop unlocked a door into a boy's-size room with one window on an air-shaft. The air-conditioner inlet up in the corner of the ceiling was about the size of a woman's handkerchief. The bit of ribbon tied to it fluttered weakly, just to show that something was moving.

The hop was tall and thin and yellow and not young and as cool as a slice of chicken in aspic. He moved his gum around in his face, put my bag on a chair, looked up at the grating and then stood looking at me. He had eyes the colour of a drink of water.

'Maybe I ought to have asked for one of the dollar rooms,' I said. 'This one seems a mite close-fitting.'

'I reckon you're lucky to get one at all. This town's fair bulgin' at the seams.'

'Bring us up some ginger ale and glasses and ice,' I said.

'Us?'

'That is, if you happen to be a drinking man.'

'I reckon I might take a chance this late.'

He went out. I took off my coat, tie, shirt and undershirt and walked around in the warm draught from the open door. The draught smelled of hot iron. I went into the bathroom sideways – it was that kind of bathroom – and doused myself with tepid cold water. I was breathing a little more freely when the tall languid hop returned with a tray. He shut the door and I brought out a bottle of rye. He mixed a couple of drinks and we made the usual insincere smiles over them and drank. The perspiration started from the back of my neck down my spine and was halfway to my socks before I put the glass down. But I felt better all the same. I sat on the bed and looked at the hop.

'How long can you stay?'

'Doing what?'

'Remembering.'

'I ain't a damn bit of use at it,' he said.

'I have money to spend,' I said, 'in my own peculiar way.' I got my wallet unstuck from the lower part of my back and spread tired-looking dollar bills along the bed.

'I beg yore pardon,' the hop said. 'I reckon you might be a dick.'

'Don't be silly,' I said. 'You never saw a dick playing solitaire with his own money. You might call me investigator.'

'I'm interested,' he said. 'The likker makes my mind work.'

I gave him a dollar bill. 'Try that on your mind. And can I call you Big Tex from Houston?'

'Amarillo,' he said. 'Not that it matters. And how do you like my Texas drawl? It makes me sick, but I find people go for it.'

'Stay with it,' I said. 'It never lost anybody a dollar yet.'

He grinned and tucked the folded dollar neatly into the watch pocket of his pants.

'What were you doing on Friday, June 12th?' I asked him. 'Late afternoon or evening. It was a Friday.'

He sipped his drink and thought, shaking the ice around gently and drinking past his gum. 'I was right here, six to twelve shift,' he said.

'A woman, slim, pretty blonde, checked in here and stayed until time for the night train to El Paso. I think she must have taken that because she was in El Paso Sunday morning. She came here driving a Packard Clipper registered to Crystal Grace Kingsley, 965 Carson Drive, Beverly Hills. She may have registered as that, or under some other name, and she may not have registered at all. Her car is still in the hotel garage. I'd like to talk to the boys that checked her in and out. That wins another dollar – just thinking about it.'

I separated another dollar from my exhibit and it went into his pocket with a sound like caterpillars fighting.

'Can do,' he said calmly.

He put his glass down and left the room, closing the door. I finished my drink and made another. I went into the bathroom and used some more warm water on my torso. While I was doing this the telephone on the wall tinkled and I wedged myself into the minute space between the bathroom door and the bed to answer it.

The Texas voice said: 'That was Sonny. He was inducted last week. Another boy we call Les checked her out. He's here.'

'Okay. Shoot him up, will you?'

I was playing with my second drink and thinking about the third when a knock came and I opened the door to a small, green-eyed rat with a tight, girlish mouth.

He came in almost dancing and stood looking at me with a faint sneer.

'Drink?'

'Sure,' he said coldly. He poured himself a large one, and added a whisper of ginger ale, put the mixture down in one long swallow, tucked a cigarette between his smooth little lips and snapped a match alight while it was coming up from his pocket. He blew smoke and went on staring at me. The corner of his eye caught the money on the bed, without looking directly at it. Over the pocket of his shirt, instead of a number, the word *Captain* was stitched.

'You Les?' I asked him.

'No.' He paused. 'We don't like dicks here,' he added. 'We don't have one of our own and we don't care to bother with dicks that are working for other people.'

'Thanks,' I said. 'That will be all.'

'Huh?' The small mouth twisted unpleasantly.

'Beat it,' I said.

'I thought you wanted to see me,' he sneered.

'You're the bell captain?'

'Check.'

'I wanted to buy you a drink. I wanted to give you a buck. Here.' I held it out to him. 'Thanks for coming up.'

He took the dollar and pocketed it, without a word of thanks. He hung there, smoke trailing from his nose, his eyes tight and mean.

'What I say here goes,' he said.

'It goes as far as you can push it,' I said. 'And that couldn't be very far. You had your drink and you had your graft. Now you can scram out.'

He turned with a swift tight shrug and slipped out of the room noiselessly.

Four minutes passed, then another knock, very light. The tall boy came in grinning. I walked away from him and sat on the bed again.

'You didn't take to Les, I reckon?'

'Not a great deal. Is he satisfied?'

'I reckon so. You know what captains are. They have to have their cut. Maybe you better call me Les, Mr Marlowe.'

'So you checked her out.'

'No, that was all a stall. She never checked in at the desk. But I remember the Packard. She gave me a dollar to put it away for her and to look after her stuff until train time. She ate dinner here. A dollar gets you remembered in this town. And there's been talk about the car bein' left so long.'

'What was she like to look at?'

'She wore a black and white outfit, mostly white, and a panama hat with a black and white band. She was a neat blonde lady like you said. Later on she took a hack to the station. I put her bags into it for her. They had initials on them but I'm sorry I can't remember the initials.'

'I'm glad you can't,' I said. 'It would be too good. Have a drink. How old would she be?'

He rinsed the other glass and mixed a civilized drink for himself.

'It's mighty hard to tell a woman's age these days,' he said. 'I reckon she was about thirty, or a little more or a little less.'

I dug in my coat for the snapshot of Crystal and Lavery on the beach and handed it to him.

He looked at it steadily and held it away from his eyes, then close.

'You won't have to swear to it in court,' I said.

He nodded. 'I wouldn't want to. These small blondes are so much of a pattern that a change of clothes or light or make-up makes them all alike or all different.' He hesitated, staring at the snapshot.

'What's worrying you?' I asked.

'I'm thinking about the gent in this snap. He enter into it at all?'

'Go on with that,' I said.

'I think this fellow spoke to her in the lobby, and had dinner with her. A tall good-lookin' jasper, built like a fast light-heavy. He went in the hack with her too.'

'Quite sure about that?'

He looked at the money on the bed.

'Okay, how much does it cost?' I asked wearily.

He stiffened, laid the snapshot down and drew the two folded bills from his pocket and tossed them on the bed.

'I thank you for the drink,' he said, 'and to hell with you.' He started for the door.

'Oh, sit down and don't be so touchy,' I growled.

He sat down and looked at me stiff-eyed.

'And don't be so damn southern,' I said. 'I've been knee-deep in hotel hops for a lot of years. If I've met one who wouldn't pull a gag, that's fine. But you can't expect me to expect to meet one that wouldn't pull a gag.'

He grinned slowly and nodded quickly. He picked the snapshot up again and looked at me over it.

'This gent takes a solid photo,' he said. 'Much more so than the lady. But there was another little item that made me remember him. I got the impression the lady didn't quite like him walking up to her so openly in the lobby.'

I thought that over and decided it didn't mean anything much. He might have been late or have missed some earlier appointment. I said:

'There's a reason for that. Did you notice what jewellery the lady was wearing? Rings, ear-pendants, anything that looked conspicuous or valuable?'

He hadn't noticed, he said.

'Was her hair long or short, straight or waved or curly, natural blonde or bleached?'

He laughed. 'Hell, you can't tell that last point, Mr Marlowe. Even when it's natural they want it lighter. As to the rest, my recollection is it was rather long, like they're wearing it now and turned in a little at the bottom and rather straight. But I could be wrong.' He looked at the snapshot again. 'She has it bound back here. You can't tell a thing.'

'That's right,' I said. 'And the only reason I asked you

was to make sure that you didn't over-observe. The guy that sees too much detail is just as unreliable a witness as the guy that doesn't see any. He's nearly always making half of it up. You check just about right, considering the circumstances. Thanks very much.'

I gave him back his two dollars and a five to keep them company. He thanked me, finished his drink and left softly. I finished mine and washed off again and decided I would rather drive home than sleep in that hole. I put my shirt and coat on again and went downstairs with my bag.

The red-headed rat of a captain was the only hop in the lobby. I carried my bag over to the desk and he didn't move to take it off my hands. The egg-headed clerk separated me from two dollars without even looking at me.

'Two bucks to spend the night in this manhole,' I said, 'when for free I could have a nice airy ashcan.'

The clerk yawned, got a delayed reaction and said brightly: 'It gets quite cool here about three in the morning. From then on until eight, or even nine, it's quite pleasant.'

I wiped the back of my neck and staggered out to the car. Even the seat of the car was hot at midnight.

I got home about two-forty-five and Hollywood was an ice-box. Even Pasadena had felt cool.

14

I dreamed I was far down in the depths of icy green water with a corpse under my arm. The corpse had long blonde hair that kept floating around in front of my face. An enormous fish with bulging eyes and a bloated body and scales shining with putrescence swam around leering like an elderly roué. Just as I was about to burst from lack of the air, the corpse came alive under my arm and got away from me and then I was fighting with the fish and the corpse was rolling over and over in the water, spinning its long hair.

I woke up with a mouth full of sheet and both hands hooked on the head-frame of the bed and pulling hard. The muscles ached when I let go and lowered them. I got up and walked the room and lit a cigarette, feeling the carpet with bare toes. When I had finished the cigarette, I went back to bed.

It was nine o'clock when I woke up again. The sun was on my face. The room was hot. I showered and shaved and partly dressed and made the morning toast and eggs and coffee in the dinette. While I was finishing up there was a knock at the apartment door.

I went to open it with my mouth full of toast. It was a lean serious-looking man in a severe grey suit.

'Floyd Greer, lieutenant, Central Detective Bureau,' he said and walked into the room.

He put out a dry hand and I shook it. He sat down on

the edge of a chair, the way they do, and turned his hat in his hands and looked at me with the quiet stare they have.

'We got a call from San Bernardino about that business up at Puma Lake. Drowned woman. Seems you were on hand when the body was discovered.'

I nodded and said, 'Have some coffee?'

'No, thanks. I had breakfast two hours ago.'

I got my coffee and sat down across the room from him.

'They asked us to look you up,' he said. 'Give them a line on you.'

'Sure.'

'So we did that. Seems like you have a clean bill of health so far as we are concerned. Kind of coincidence a man in your line would be around when the body was found.'

'I'm like that,' I said. 'Lucky.'

'So I just thought I'd drop around and say howdy.'

'That's fine. Glad to know you, lieutenant.'

'Kind of a coincidence,' he said again, nodding. 'You up there on business, so to speak?'

'If I was,' I said, 'my business had nothing to do with the girl who was drowned, so far as I know.'

'But you couldn't be sure?'

'Until you've finished with a case, you can't ever be quite sure what its ramifications are, can you?'

'That's right.' He circled his hat brim through his fingers again, like a bashful cowboy. There was nothing bashful about his eyes. 'I'd like to feel sure that if these ramifications you speak of happened to take in this drowned woman's affairs, you would put us wise.'

'I hope you can rely on that,' I said.

He bulged his lower lip with his tongue. 'We'd like a little more than a hope. At the present time you don't care to say?'

'At the present time I don't know anything that Patton doesn't know.'

'Who's he?'

'The constable up at Puma Point.'

The lean serious man smiled tolerantly. He cracked a knuckle and after a pause said: 'The San Berdoo D. A. will likely want to talk to you – before the inquest. But that won't be very soon. Right now they're trying to get a set of prints. We lent them a technical man.'

'That will be tough. The body's pretty far gone.'

'It's done all the time,' he said. 'They worked out the system back in New York where they're all the time pulling in floaters. They cut patches of skin off the fingers and harden them in a tanning solution and make stamps. It works well enough as a rule.'

'You think this woman had a record of some kind?'

'Why, we always take prints of a corpse,' he said. 'You ought to know that.'

I said: 'I didn't know the lady. If you thought I did and that was why I was up there, there's nothing in it.'

'But you wouldn't care to say just why you *were* up there,' he persisted.

'So you think I'm lying to you,' I said.

He spun his hat on a bony forefinger. 'You got me wrong, Mr Marlowe. We don't think anything at all. What we do is investigate and find out. This stuff is just routine. You ought to know that. You been around long enough.' He stood up and put his hat on. 'You might let me know if you have to leave town. I'd be obliged.'

I said I would and went to the door with him. He went out with a duck of his head and a sad half-smile. I watched him drift languidly down the hall and punch the elevator button.

I went back out to the dinette to see if there was any more coffee. There was about two-thirds of a cup. I added cream and sugar and carried my cup over to the telephone. I dialled Police Headquarters downtown and asked for the Detective Bureau and then for Lieutenant Floyd Greer.

The voice said: 'Lieutenant Greer is not in the office. Anybody else do?'

'De Soto in?'

'Who?'

I repeated the name.

'What's his rank and department?'

'Plain clothes something or other.'

'Hold the line.'

I waited. The burring male voice came back after a while and said: 'What's the gag? We don't have a De Soto on the roster. Who's this talking?'

I hung up, finished my coffee and dialled the number of Derace Kingsley's office. The smooth and cool Miss Fromsett said he had just come in and put me through without a murmur.

'Well,' he said, loud and forceful at the beginning of a fresh day, 'what did you find out at the hotel?'

'She was there all right. And Lavery met her there. The hop who gave me the dope brought Lavery into it himself, without any prompting from me. He had dinner with her and went with her in a cab to the railroad station.'

'Well, I ought to have known he was lying,' Kingsley said slowly. 'I got the impression he was surprised when I told him about the telegram from El Paso. I was just letting my impressions get too sharp. Anything else?'

'Not there. I had a cop calling on me this morning, giving me the usual looking over and warning not to leave town without letting him know. Trying to find out why I went to Puma Point. I didn't tell him as he wasn't even aware of Jim Patton's existence, it's evident that Patton didn't tell anybody.'

'Jim would do his best to be decent about it,' Kingsley said. 'Why were you asking me last night about some name – Mildred something or other?'

I told him, making it brief. I told him about Muriel Chess's car and clothes being found and where.

'That looks bad for Bill,' he said. 'I know Coon Lake myself, but it would never have occurred to me to use that old woodshed – or even that there was an old woodshed. It not only looks bad, it looks premeditated.'

'I disagree with that. Assuming he knew the country well enough it wouldn't take him any time to search his mind for a likely hiding-place. He was very restricted as to distance.'

'Maybe. What do you plan to do now?' he asked.

'Go up against Lavery again, of course.'

He agreed that that was the thing to do. He added: 'This other, tragic as it is, is really no business of ours, is it?'

'Not unless your wife knew something about it.'

His voice sounded sharply, saying: 'Look here, Marlowe, I think I can understand your detective instinct to tie everything that happens into one compact knot, but don't let it run away with you. Life isn't like that at all – not life as I have known it. Better leave the affairs of the Chess family to the police and keep your brains working on the Kingsley family.'

'Okay,' I said.

'I don't mean to be domineering,' he said.

I laughed heartily, said good-bye, and hung up. I finished dressing and went down to the basement for the Chrysler. I started for Bay City again.

15

I drove past the intersection of Altair Street to where the cross street continued to the edge of the canyon and ended in a semicircular parking place with a sidewalk and a white wooden guard fence around it. I sat there in the car a little while, thinking, looking out to sea and admiring the blue-grey fall of the foothills towards the ocean. I was trying to make up my mind whether to try handling Lavery with a feather or go on using the back of my hand and the edge of my tongue. I decided I could lose nothing by the soft approach. If that didn't produce for me – and I didn't think it would – nature could take its course and we could bust up the furniture.

The paved alley that ran along half-way down the hill below the houses on the outer edge was empty. Below that, on the next hillside street, a couple of kids were throwing a boomerang up the slope and chasing it with the usual amount of elbowing and mutual insult. Farther down still a house was enclosed in trees and a red brick wall. There was a glimpse of washing on the line in the backyard and two pigeons strutted along the slope of the roof bobbing their heads. A blue and tan bus trundled along the street in front of the brick house and stopped and a very old man got off with slow care and settled himself firmly on the ground and tapped with a heavy cane before he started to crawl back up the slope.

The air was clearer than yesterday. The morning was

full of peace. I left the car where it was and walked along Altair Street to No. 623.

The venetian blinds were down across the front windows and the place had a sleepy look. I stepped down over the Korean moss and punched the bell and saw that the door was not quite shut. It had dropped in its frame, as most of our doors do, and the spring bolt hung a little on the lower edge of the lock plate. I remembered that it had wanted to stick the day before, when I was leaving.

I gave the door a little push and it moved inward with a light click. The room beyond was dim, but there was some light from west windows. Nobody answered my ring. I didn't ring again. I pushed the door a little wider and stepped inside.

The room had a hushed warm smell, the smell of late morning in a house not yet opened up. The bottle of Vat 69 on the round table by the davenport was almost empty and another full bottle waited beside it. The copper ice-bucket had a little water in the bottom. Two glasses had been used, and half a siphon of carbonated water.

I fixed the door about as I had found it and stood there and listened. If Lavery was away I thought I would take a chance and frisk the joint. I didn't have anything much on him, but it was probably enough to keep him from calling the cops.

In the silence time passed. It passed in the dry whirr of the electric clock on the mantel, in the far-off toot of an auto horn on Aster Drive, in the hornet drone of a plane over the foothills across the canyon, in the sudden lurch and growl of the electric refrigerator in the kitchen.

I went farther into the room and stood peering around

and listening and hearing nothing except those fixed sounds belonging to the house and having nothing to do with the humans in it. I started along the rug towards the archway at the back.

A hand in a glove appeared on the slope of the white metal railing, at the edge of the archway, where the stairs went down. It appeared and stopped.

It moved and a woman's hat showed, then her head. The woman came quietly up the stairs. She came all the way up, turned through the arch and still didn't seem to see me. She was a slender woman of uncertain age, with untidy brown hair, a scarlet mess of a mouth, too much rouge on her cheekbones, shadowed eyes. She wore a blue tweed suit that looked like the dickens with a purple hat that was doing its best to hang on to the side of her head.

She saw me and didn't stop or change expression in the slightest degree. She came slowly on into the room, holding her right hand away from her body. Her left hand wore the brown glove I had seen on the railing. The right-hand glove that matched it was wrapped around the butt of a small automatic.

She stopped then and her body arched back and a quick distressful sound came out of her mouth. Then she giggled, a high nervous giggle. She pointed the gun at me, and came steadily on.

I kept on looking at the gun and not screaming.

The woman came close. When she was close enough to be confidential she pointed the gun at my stomach and said:

'All I wanted was my rent. The place seems well taken care of. Nothing broken. He has always been a good tidy careful tenant. I just didn't want him to get too far behind in the rent.'

A fellow with a kind of strained and unhappy voice said politely: 'How far behind is he?'

'Three months,' she said. 'Two hundred and forty dollars. Eighty dollars is very reasonable for a place as well furnished as this. I've had a little trouble collecting before, but it always came out very well. He promised me a cheque this morning. Over the telephone. I mean he promised to give it to me this morning.'

'Over the telephone,' I said. 'This morning.'

I shuffled around a bit in an inconspicuous sort of way. The idea was to get close enough to make a side swipe at the gun, knock it outwards and then jump in fast before she could bring it back in line. I've never had a lot of luck with the technique, but you have to try it once in a while. This looked like the time to try it.

I made about six inches, but not nearly enough for a first down. I said: 'And you're the owner?' I didn't look at the gun directly. I had a faint, a very faint hope that she didn't know she was pointing it at me.

'Why, certainly. I'm Mrs Fallbrook. Who did you think I was?'

'Well, I thought you might be the owner,' I said. 'You talking about the rent and all. But I didn't know your name.' Another eight inches. Nice smooth work. It would be a shame to have it wasted.

'And who are you, if I may inquire?'

'I just came about the car payment,' I said. 'The door was open just a teeny weensy bit and I kind of shoved in. I don't know why.'

I made a face like a man from the finance company

coming about the car payment. Kind of tough, but ready to break into a sunny smile.

'You mean Mr Lavery is behind in his car payments?' she asked, looking worried.

'A little. Not a great deal,' I said soothingly.

I was all set now. I had the reach and I ought to have the speed. All it needed was a clean sharp sweep inside the gun and outward. I started to take my left foot out of the rug.

'You know,' she said, 'it's funny about this gun. I found it on the stairs. Nasty oily things, aren't they? And the stair carpet is a very nice grey chenille. Quite expensive.'

And she handed me the gun.

My hand went out for it, as stiff as an eggshell, almost as brittle. I took the gun. She sniffed with distaste at the glove which had been wrapped around the butt. She went on talking in exactly the same tone of cockeyed reasonableness. My knees cracked, relaxing.

'Well, of course, it's much easier for you,' she said. 'About the car, I mean. You can just take it away, if you have to. But taking a house with nice furniture in it isn't so easy. It takes time and money to evict a tenant. There is apt to be bitterness and things get damaged, sometimes on purpose. The rug on this floor cost over two hundred dollars, second-hand. It's only a jute rug, but it has a lovely colouring, don't you think? You'd never know it was only jute, second-hand. But that's silly too because they're always second-hand after you've used them. And I walked over here too, to save my tyres for the government. I could have taken a bus part way, but the darn things never come along except going in the wrong direction.'

I hardly heard what she said. It was like surf breaking beyond a point, out of sight. The gun had my interest.

I broke the magazine out. It was empty. I turned the gun and looked into the breech. That was empty too. I sniffed the muzzle. It reeked.

I dropped the gun into my pocket. A six-shot ·25-calibre automatic. Emptied out. Shot empty, and not too long ago. But not in the last half-hour either.

'Has it been fired?' Mrs Fallbrook inquired pleasantly. 'I certainly hope not.'

'Any reason why it should have been fired?' I asked her. The voice was steady, but the brain was still bouncing.

'Well, it was lying on the stairs,' she said. 'After all, people do fire them.'

'How true that is,' I said. 'But Mr Lavery probably had a hole in his pocket. He isn't home, is he?'

'Oh no.' She shook her head and looked disappointed. 'And I don't think it's very nice of him. He promised me the cheque and I walked over –'

'When was it you phoned him?' I asked.

'Why, yesterday evening.' She frowned, not liking so many questions.

'He must have been called away,' I said.

She stared at a spot between my big brown eyes.

'Look, Mrs Fallbrook,' I said. 'Let's not kid around any more, Mrs Fallbrook. Not that I don't love it. And not that I like to say this. But you didn't shoot him, did you – on account of he owed you three months' rent?'

She sat down very slowly on the edge of a chair and worked the tip of her tongue along the scarlet slash of her mouth.

'Why, what a perfectly horrid suggestion,' she said angrily. 'I don't think you are nice at all. Didn't you say the gun had not been fired?'

'All guns have been fired sometime. All guns have been loaded sometime. This one is not loaded now.'

'Well, then –' she made an impatient gesture and sniffed at her oily glove.

'Okay, my idea was wrong. Just a gag anyway. Mr Lavery was out and you went through the house. Being the owner, you have a key. Is that correct?'

'I didn't mean to be interfering,' she said, biting a finger. 'Perhaps I ought not to have done it. But I have a right to see how things are kept.'

'Well, you looked. And you're sure he's not here?'

'I didn't look under the beds or in the icebox,' she said coldly. 'I called out from the top of the stairs when he didn't answer my ring. Then I went down to the lower hall and called out again. I even peeped into the bedroom.' She lowered her eyes as if bashfully and twisted a hand on her knee.

'Well, that's that,' I said.

She nodded brightly. 'Yes, that's that. And what did you say your name was?'

'Vance,' I said. 'Philo Vance.'

'And what company are you employed with, Mr Vance?'

'I'm out of work right now,' I said. 'Until the police commissioner gets in a jam again.'

She looked startled. 'But you said you came about a car payment.'

'That's just part-time work,' I said. 'A fill-in job.'

She rose to her feet and looked at me steadily. Her

voice was cold saying: 'Then in that case I think you had better leave now.'

I said: 'I thought I might take a look around first, if you don't mind. There might be something you missed.'

'I don't think that is necessary,' she said. 'This is my house. I'll thank you to leave now, Mr Vance.'

I said: 'And if I don't leave, you'll get somebody who will. Take a chair again, Mrs Fallbrook. I'll just glance through. This gun, you know, is kind of queer.'

'But I told you I found it lying on the stairs,' she said angrily. 'I don't know anything else about it. I don't know anything about guns at all. I – I never shot one in my life.' She opened a large blue bag and pulled a handkerchief out of it and sniffled.

'That's your story,' I said. 'I don't have to get stuck with it.'

She put her left hand to me with a pathetic gesture, like the erring wife in *East Lynne*.

'Oh, I shouldn't have done!' she cried. 'It was horrid of me. I know it was. Mr Lavery will be furious.'

'What you shouldn't have done,' I said, 'was let me find out the gun was empty. Up to then you were holding everything in the deck.'

She stamped her foot. That was all the scene lacked. That made it perfect.

'Why, you perfectly loathsome man,' she squawked. 'Don't you dare touch me! Don't you take a single step towards me! I won't stay in this house another minute with you. How *dare* you be so insulting –'

She caught her voice and snapped it in mid-air like a rubber band. Then she put her head down, purple hat and all, and ran for the door. As she passed me she put a hand out as if to stiff-arm me, but she wasn't near enough and I didn't move. She jerked the door wide and charged out through it and up the walk to the street. The door came slowly shut and I heard her rapid steps above the sound of its closing.

I ran a finger-nail along my teeth and punched the point of my jaw with a knuckle, listening. I didn't hear anything anywhere to listen to. A six-shot automatic, fired empty.

'Something,' I said out loud, 'is all wrong with this scene.'

The house seemed now to be abnormally still. I went along the apricot rug and through the archway to the head of the stairs. I stood there for another moment and listened again.

I shrugged and went quietly down the stairs.

16

The lower hall had a door at each end and two in the middle side by side. One of these was a linen closet and the other was locked. I went along to the end and looked in at a spare bedroom with drawn blinds and no sign of being used. I went back to the other end of the hall and stepped into a second bedroom with a wide bed, a café-au-lait rug, angular furniture in light wood, a box mirror over the dressing-table and a long fluorescent lamp over the mirror. In the corner a crystal greyhound stood on a mirror-top table and beside him a crystal box with cigarettes in it.

Face powder was spilled around on the dressing-table. There was a smear of dark lipstick on a towel hanging over the waste basket. On the bed were pillows side by side, with depressions in them that could have been made by heads. A woman's handkerchief peeped from under one pillow. A pair of sheer black pyjamas lay across the foot of the bed. A rather too emphatic trace of chypre hung in the air.

I wondered what Mrs Fallbrook had thought of all this.

I turned around and looked at myself in the long mirror of a closet door. The door was painted white and had a crystal knob. I turned the knob in my handkerchief and looked inside. The cedar-lined closet was fairly full of man's clothes. There was a nice friendly smell of tweed. The closet was not entirely full of man's clothes.

There was also a woman's black and white tailored suit, mostly white, black and white shoes under it, a panama with a black and white rolled band on a shelf above it. There were other woman's clothes, but I didn't examine them.

I shut the closet door and went out of the bedroom, holding my handkerchief ready for more doorknobs.

The door next the linen closet, the locked door, had to be the bathroom. I shook it, but it went on being locked. I bent down and saw there was a short, slit-shaped opening in the middle of the knob. I knew then that the door was fastened by pushing a button in the middle of the knob inside, and that the slit-like opening was for a metal key without wards that would spring the lock open in case somebody fainted in the bathroom, or the kids locked themselves in and got sassy.

The key for this ought to be kept on the top shelf of the linen closet but it wasn't. I tried my knife blade, but that was too thin. I went back to the bedroom and got a flat nail-file off the dresser. That worked. I opened the bathroom door.

A man's sand-coloured pyjamas were tossed over a painted hamper. A pair of heelless green slippers lay on the floor. There was a safety-razor on the edge of the washbowl and a tube of cream with the cap off. The bathroom window was shut, and there was a pungent smell in the air that was not quite like any other smell.

Three empty shells lay bright and coppery on the nile-green tiles of the bathroom floor, and there was a nice clean hole in the frosted pane of the window. To the left and a little above the window were two scarred places in the plaster where the white showed behind the paint and where something, such as a bullet, had gone in.

The shower curtain was green and white oiled silk and it hung on shiny chromium rings and it was drawn across the shower opening. I slid it aside, the rings making a thin scraping noise, which for some reason sounded indecently loud.

I felt my neck creak a little as I bent down. He was there all right – there wasn't anywhere else for him to be. He was huddled in the corner under the two shining faucets, and water dripped slowly on his chest from the chromium showerhead.

His knees were drawn up but slack. The two holes in his naked chest were dark blue and both of them were close enough to his heart to have killed him. The blood seemed to have been washed away.

His eyes had a curiously bright and expectant look, as if he smelled the morning coffee and would be coming right out.

Nice efficient work. You have just finished shaving and stripped for the shower and you are leaning in against the shower curtain and adjusting the temperature of the water. The door opens behind you and somebody comes in. The somebody appears to have been a woman. She has a gun. You look at the gun and she shoots it.

She misses with three shots. It seems impossible, at such short range, but there it is. Maybe it happens all the time. I've been around so little.

You haven't anywhere to go. You could lunge at her and take a chance, if you were that kind of fellow, and if you were braced for it. But leaning in over the shower faucets, holding the curtains closed, you are off balance. Also you are apt to be somewhat petrified with panic, if you are at all like other people.

That is where you go. You go into it as far as you can, but a shower stall is a small place and the tiled wall stops you. You are backed up against the last wall there is now. You are all out of space, and you are all out of living. And then there are two more shots, possibly three, and you slide down the wall, and your eyes are not even frightened any more now. They are just the empty eyes of the dead.

She reaches in and turns the shower off. She sets the lock of the bathroom door. On her way out of the house she throws the empty gun on the stair carpet. She should worry. It is probably your gun.

Is that right? It had better be right.

I bent and pulled at his arm. Ice couldn't have been any colder or any stiffer. I went out of the bathroom, leaving it unlocked. No need to lock it now. It only makes work for the cops.

I went into the bedroom and pulled the handkerchief out from under the pillow. It was a minute piece of linen rag with a scalloped edge embroidered in red. Two small initials were stitched in the corner, in red. *A.F.*

'Adrienne Fromsett,' I said. I laughed. It was a rather ghoulish laugh.

I shook the handkerchief to get some of the chypre out of it and folded it up in a tissue and put it in a pocket. I went back upstairs to the living-room and poked around in the desk against the wall. The desk contained no interesting letters, phone numbers or provocative match-folders. Or if it did, I didn't find them.

I looked at the phone. It was on a small table against the wall beside the fireplace. It had a long cord so that Mr Lavery could be lying on his back on the davenport, a cigarette between his smooth brown lips, a tall cool one at the table at his side, and plenty of time for a nice long cosy conversation with a lady friend. An easy, languid, flirtatious, kidding, not too subtle and not too blunt conversation, of the sort he would be apt to enjoy.

All that wasted too. I went away from the telephone to the door and set the lock so I could come in again and shut the door tight, pulling it hard over the sill until the lock clicked. I went up the walk and stood in the sunlight looking across the street at Dr Almore's house.

Nobody yelled or ran out of the door. Nobody blew a police whistle. Everything was quiet and sunny and calm. No cause for excitement whatever. It's only Marlowe, finding another body. He does it rather well by now. Murder-a-day Marlowe, they call him. They have the meat wagon following him around to follow up on the business he finds.

A nice enough fellow, in an ingenious sort of way.

I walked back to the intersection and got into my car and started it and backed it and drove away from there.

17

The bellhop at the Athletic Club was back in three minutes with a nod for me to come with him. We rode up to the fourth floor and went around a corner and he showed me a half-open door.

'Around to the left, sir. As quietly as you can. A few of the members are sleeping.'

I went into the club library. It contained books behind glass doors and magazines on a long central table and a lighted portrait of the club's founder. But its real business seemed to be sleeping. Outward-jutting bookcases cut the room into a number of small alcoves and in the alcoves were high-backed leather chairs of an incredible size and softness. In a number of the chairs old boys were snoozing peacefully, their faces violet with high blood pressure, thin racking snores coming out of their pinched noses.

I climbed over a few feet and stole around to the left. Derace Kingsley was in the very last alcove in the far end of the room. He had two chairs arranged side by side, facing into the corner. His big dark head just showed over the top of one of them. I slipped into the empty one and gave him a quick nod.

'Keep your voice down,' he said. 'This room is for after-luncheon naps. Now what is it? When I employed you it was to save me trouble, not to add trouble to what I already had. You made me break an important engagement.'

'I know,' I said, and put my face close to his. He smelled of highballs, in a nice way. 'She shot him.'

His eyebrows jumped and his face got that stony look. His teeth clamped tight. He breathed softly and twisted a large hand on his kneecap.

'Go on,' he said, in a voice the size of a marble.

I looked back over the top of my chair. The nearest old geezer was sound asleep and blowing the dusty fuzz in his nostrils back and forth as he breathed.

'No answer at Lavery's place,' I said. 'Door slightly open. But I noticed yesterday it sticks on the sill. Pushed it open. Room dark, two glasses with drinks having been in them. House very still. In a moment a slim dark woman calling herself Mrs Fallbrook, landlady, came up the stairs with her glove wrapped around a gun. Said she had found it on the stairs. Said she came to collect her three months' back rent. Used her key to get in. Inference is she took the chance to snoop around and look the house over. Took the gun from her and found it had been fired recently, but didn't tell her so. She said Lavery was not home. Got rid of her by making her mad and she departed in high dudgeon. She may call the police, but it's much more likely she will just go out and hunt butterflies and forget the whole thing – except the rent.'

I paused. Kingsley's head was turned towards me and his jaw muscles bulged with the way his teeth were clamped. His eyes looked sick.

'I went downstairs. Signs of a woman having spent the night. Pyjamas, face powder, perfume, and so on. Bathroom locked, but got it open. Three empty shells on the floor, two shots in the wall, one in the window. Lavery in the shower stall, naked and dead.'

'My God!' Kingsley whispered. 'Do you mean to say he had a woman with him last night and she shot him this morning in the bathroom?'

'Just what did you think I was trying to say?' I asked.

'Keep your voice down,' he groaned. 'It's a shock, naturally. Why in the bathroom?'

'Keep your own voice down,' I said. 'Why not in the bathroom? Could you think of a place where a man would be more completely off guard?'

He said: 'You don't know that a woman shot him. I mean, you're not sure, are you?'

'No,' I said. 'That's true. It might have been somebody who used a small gun and emptied it carelessly to look like a woman's work. The bathroom is downhill, facing outwards on space and I don't think shots down there would be easily heard by anyone not in the house. The woman who spent the night might have left – or there need not have been any woman at all. The appearances could have been faked. *You* might have shot him.'

'What would I want to shoot him for?' he almost bleated, squeezing both kneecaps hard. 'I'm a civilized man.'

That didn't seem to be worth an argument either. I said: 'Does your wife own a gun?'

He turned a drawn miserable face to me and said hollowly: 'Good God, man, you can't really think that!'

'Well, does she?'

He got the words out in small gritty pieces. 'Yes – she does. A small automatic.'

'You buy it locally?'

'I – I didn't buy it at all. I took it away from a drunk at a party in San Francisco a couple of years ago. He was waving it around, with an idea that that was very funny. I never gave it back to him.' He pinched his jaw hard until his knuckles whitened. 'He probably doesn't even remember how or when he lost it. He was that kind of a drunk.'

'This is working out almost too neatly,' I said. 'Could you recognize this gun?'

He thought hard, pushing his jaw out and half-closing his eyes. I looked back over the chairs again. One of the elderly snoozers had waked himself up with a snort that almost blew him out of his chair. He coughed, scratched his nose with a thin dried-up hand, and fumbled a gold watch out of his vest. He peered at it bleakly, put it away, and went to sleep again.

I reached in my pocket and put the gun in Kingsley's hand. He stared down at it miserably.

'I don't know,' he said slowly. 'It's like it, but I can't tell.'

'There's a serial number on the side,' I said.

'Nobody remembers the serial numbers of guns.'

'I was hoping you wouldn't,' I said. 'It would have worried me very much.'

His hand closed around the gun and he put it down beside him in the chair.

'The dirty rat,' he said softly. 'I suppose he ditched her.'

'I don't get it,' I said. 'The motive was inadequate for you, on account of you're a civilized man. But it was adequate for her.'

'It's not the same motive,' he snapped. 'And women are more impetuous than men.'

'Like cats are more impetuous than dogs.'

'How?'

'Some women are more impetuous than some men. That's all that means. We'll have to have a better motive, if you want your wife to have done it.'

He turned his head enough to give me a level stare in which there was no amusement. White crescents were bitten into the corners of his mouth.

'This doesn't seem to me a very good spot for the light touch,' he said. 'We can't let the police have this gun. Crystal had a permit and the gun was registered. So they will know the number, even if I don't. We can't let them have it.'

'But Mrs Fallbrook knows I had the gun.'

He shook his head stubbornly. 'We'll have to chance that. Yes, I know you're taking a risk. I intend to make it worth your while. If the set-up were possible for suicide, I'd say put the gun back. But the way you tell it, it isn't.'

'No. He'd have to have missed himself with the first three shots. But I can't cover up a murder, even for a ten-dollar bonus. The gun will have to go back.'

'I was thinking of more money than that,' he said quietly. 'I was thinking of five hundred dollars.'

'Just what did you expect to buy with it?'

He leaned close to me. His eyes were serious and bleak, but not hard. 'Is there anything in Lavery's place, apart from the gun, that might indicate Crystal has been there lately?'

'A black and white dress and a hat like the bellhop in Bernardino described on her. There may be a dozen things I don't know about. There almost certainly will be fingerprints. You say she was never printed, but that doesn't mean they won't get her prints to check. Her bedroom at home will be full of them. So will the cabin at Little Fawn Lake. And her car.'

'We ought to get the car –' he started to say. I stopped him.

'No use. Too many other places. What kind of perfume does she use?'

He looked blank for an instant. 'Oh – Gillerlain Regal, the Champagne of Perfumes,' he said woodenly. 'A Chanel number once in a while.'

'What's this stuff of yours like?'

'A kind of chypre. Sandalwood chypre.'

'The bedroom reeks with it,' I said. 'It smelled like cheap stuff to me. But I'm no judge.'

'Cheap?' he said, stung to the quick. 'My God, cheap? We get thirty dollars an ounce for it.'

'Well, this stuff smelled more like three dollars a gallon.'

He put his hands down hard on his knees and shook his head.

'I'm talking about money,' he said. 'Five hundred dollars. A cheque for it right now.'

I let the remark fall to the ground, eddying like a soiled feather. One of the old boys behind us stumbled to his feet and groped his way wearily out of the room.

Kingsley said gravely: 'I hired you to protect me from scandal, and, of course, to protect my wife, if she needed it. Through no fault of yours the chance to avoid scandal is pretty well shot. It's a question of my wife's neck now. I don't believe she shot Lavery. I have no reason for that belief. None at all. I just feel the conviction. She may even have been there last night, this gun may even be her gun. It doesn't prove she killed him. She would be as careless with the gun as with anything else. Anybody could have got hold of it.'

'The cops down there won't work very hard to believe that,' I said. 'If the one I met is a fair specimen, they'll just pick the first head they see and start swinging with their blackjacks. And hers will certainly be the first head they see when they look the situation over.'

He ground the heels of his hands together. His misery had a theatrical flavour, as real misery so often has.

'I'll go along with you up to a point,' I said. 'The set-up down there is almost too good, at first sight. She leaves clothes there she has been seen wearing and which can probably be traced. She leaves the gun on the stairs. It's hard to think she would be as dumb as that.'

'You give me a little heart,' Kingsley said wearily.

'But none of that means anything,' I said. 'Because we are looking at it from the angle of calculation, and people who commit crimes of passion or hatred just commit them and walk out. Everything I have heard indicates that she is a reckless, foolish woman. There's no sign of planning in any of the scene down there. There's every sign of a complete lack of planning. But even if there wasn't a thing down there to point to your wife, the cops would tie her up to Lavery. They will investigate his background, his friends, his women. Her name is bound to crop up somewhere along the line, and when it does, the fact that she has been out of sight for a month will make them sit up and rub their horny palms with glee. And of course they'll trace the gun, and if it's her gun –'

His hand dived for the gun in the chair beside him.

'Nope,' I said. 'They'll have to have the gun. Marlowe may be a very smart guy and very fond of you personally, but he can't risk the suppression of such vital evidence as the gun that killed a man. Whatever I do has to be on the basis that your wife is an obvious suspect, but that the obviousness can be wrong.'

He groaned and put his big hand out with the gun in it. I took it and put it away. Then I took it out again and said: 'Lend me your handkerchief. I don't want to use mine. I might be searched.'

He handed me a stiff white handkerchief and I wiped the gun off carefully all over and dropped it into my pocket. I handed him back the handkerchief.

'My prints are all right,' I said. 'But I don't want yours on it. Here's the only thing I can do. Go back down there and replace the gun and call the law. Ride it out with them and let the chips fall where they have to. The story will have to come out. What I was doing down there and why. At the worst they'll find her and prove she killed him. At the best they'll find her a lot quicker than I can and let me use my energies proving that she didn't kill him, which means, in effect, proving that someone else did. Are you game for that?'

He nodded slowly. He said: 'Yes – and the five hundred stands. For showing Crystal didn't kill him.'

'I don't expect to earn it,' I said. 'You may as well understand that now. How well did Miss Fromsett know Lavery? Out of office hours?'

His face tightened up like a charleyhorse. His fists went into hard lumps on his thighs. He said nothing.

'She looked kind of queer when I asked her for his address yesterday morning,' I said.

He let a breath out slowly.

'Like a bad taste in the mouth,' I said. 'Like a romance that fouled out. Am I too blunt?'

His nostrils quivered a little and his breath made noise in them for a moment. Then he relaxed and said quietly:

'She – she knew him rather well – at one time. She's a girl who would do about what she pleased in that way. Lavery was, I guess, a fascinating bird – to women.'

'I'll have to talk to her,' I said.

'Why?' he asked shortly. Red patches showed in his cheeks.

'Never mind why. It's my business to ask all sorts of questions of all sorts of people.'

'Talk to her then,' he said tightly. 'As a matter of fact she knew the Almores. She knew Almore's wife, the one who killed herself. Lavery knew her too. Could that have any possible connexion with this business?

'I don't know. You're in love with her, aren't you?'

'I'd marry her to-morrow if I could,' he said stiffly.

I nodded and stood up. I looked back along the room. It was almost empty now. At the far end a couple of elderly relics were still blowing bubbles. The rest of the soft-chair boys had staggered back to whatever it was they did when they were conscious.

'There's just one thing,' I said, looking down at Kingsley. 'Cops get very hostile when there is a delay in calling them after a murder. There's been delay this time and there will be more. I'd like to go down there as if it was the first visit to-day. I think I can make it that way, if I leave the Fallbrook woman out.'

'Fallbrook?' He hardly knew what I was talking about. 'Who the hell – oh yes, I remember.'

'Well, don't remember. I'm almost certain they'll never hear a peep from her. She's not the kind to have anything to do with the police of her own free will.'

'I understand,' he said.

'Be sure you handle it right then. Questions will be asked you *before* you are told Lavery is dead, before I'm allowed to get in touch with you – so far as they know. Don't fall into any traps. If you do, I won't be able to find anything out. I'll be in the clink.'

'You could call me from the house down there – before you call the police,' he said reasonably.

'I know. But the fact that I don't will be in my favour. And they'll check the phone calls one of the first things they do. And if I call you from anywhere else, I might just as well admit that I came up here to see you.'

'I understand,' he said again. 'You can trust me to handle it.'

We shook hands and I left him standing there.

18

The Athletic Club was on a corner across the street and half a block down from the Treloar Building. I crossed and walked north to the entrance. They had finished laying rose-coloured concrete where the rubber sidewalk had been. It was fenced around, leaving a narrow gangway in and out of the building. The space was clotted with office help going in from lunch.

The Gillerlain Company's reception-room looked even emptier than the day before. The same fluffy little blonde was tucked in behind the P.B.X. in the corner. She gave me a quick smile and I gave her the gunman's salute, a stiff forefinger pointing at her, the three lower fingers tucked back under it, and the thumb wiggling up and down like a western gun-fighter fanning his hammer. She laughed heartily, without making a sound. This was more fun than she had had in a week.

I pointed to Miss Fromsett's empty desk and the little blonde nodded and pushed a plug in and spoke. A door opened and Miss Fromsett swayed elegantly out to her desk and sat down and gave me her cool expectant eyes.

'Yes, Mr Marlowe? Mr Kingsley is not in, I'm afraid.'

'I just came from him. Where do we talk?'

'Talk?'

'I have something to show you.'

'Oh, yes?' She looked me over thoughtfully. A lot of guys had probably tried to show her things, including etchings. At another time I wouldn't have been above taking a flutter at it myself.

'Business,' I said. 'Mr Kingsley's business.'

She stood up and opened the gate in the railing. 'We may as well go into his office then.'

We went in. She held the door for me. As I passed her I sniffed. Sandalwood. I said:

'Gillerlain Regal, the Champagne of Perfumes?'

She smiled faintly, holding the door. 'On my salary?'

'I didn't say anything about your salary. You don't look like a girl who has to buy her own perfume.'

'Yes, that's what it is,' she said. 'And if you want to know, I detest wearing perfume in the office. He makes me.'

We went down the long dim office and she took a chair at the end of the desk. I sat where I had sat the day before. We looked at each other. She was wearing tan to-day, with a ruffled jabot at her throat. She looked a little warmer, but still no prairie fire.

I offered her one of Kingsley's cigarettes. She took it, took a light from his lighter, and leaned back.

'We needn't waste time being cagey,' I said. 'You know by now who I am and what I am doing. If you didn't know yesterday morning, it's only because he loves to play big shot.'

She looked down at the hand that lay on her knee, then lifted her eyes and smiled almost shyly.

'He's a great guy,' she said. 'In spite of the heavy executive act he likes to put on. He's the only guy that gets fooled by it after all. And if you only knew what he has stood from that little tramp –' She waved her cigarette. 'Well, perhaps I'd better leave that out. What was it you wanted to see me about?'

'Kingsley said you knew the Almores.'

'I knew Mrs Almore. That is, I met her a couple of times.'

'Where?'

'At a friend's house. Why?'

'At Lavery's house?'

'You're not going to be insolent, are you, Mr Marlowe?'

'I don't know what your definition of that would be. I'm going to talk business as if it was business, not international diplomacy.'

'Very well.' She nodded slightly. 'At Chris Lavery's house, yes. I used to go there – once in a while. He had cocktail parties.'

'Then Lavery knew the Almores – or Mrs Almore.'

She flushed very slightly. 'Yes. Quite well.'

'And a lot of other women – quite well, too. I don't doubt that. Did Mrs Kingsley know her too?'

'Yes, better than I did. They called each other by their first names. Mrs Almore is dead, you know. She committed suicide, about a year and a half ago.'

'Any doubt about that?'

She raised her eyebrows, but the expression looked artificial to me, as if it just went with the question I asked, as a matter of form.

She said: 'Have you any particular reason for asking that question in that particular way? I mean, has it anything to do with – with what you are doing?'

'I didn't think so. I still don't know that it has. But yesterday Dr Almore called a cop just because I looked at his house. After he had found out from my car licence who I was. The cop got pretty tough with me, just for being there. He didn't know what I was doing and I didn't tell him I had been calling on Lavery. But Dr Almore must have known that. He had seen me in front of Lavery's house. Now why would he think it necessary to call a cop? And why would the cop think it smart to say that the last fellow who tried to put the bite on Almore ended up on the road gang? And why would the cop ask me if her folks – meaning Mrs Almore's folks, I suppose – had hired me? If you can answer any of those questions, I might know whether it's any of my business.'

She thought about it for a moment, giving me one quick glance while she was thinking, and then looking away again.

'I only met Mrs Almore twice,' she said slowly. 'But I think I can answer your questions – all of them. The last time I met her was at Lavery's place, as I said, and there were quite a lot of people there. There was a lot of drinking and loud talk. The women were not with their husbands and the men were not with their wives, if any. There was a man there named Brownwell who was very tight. He's in the Navy now, I heard. He was ribbing Mrs Almore about her husband's practice. The idea seemed to be that he was one of those doctors who run around all night with a case of loaded hypodermic needles, keeping the local fast set from having pink elephants for breakfast. Florence Almore said she didn't care how her husband got his money as long as he got plenty of it and she had the spending of it. She was tight too, and not a very nice person sober, I should imagine. One of these slinky glittering females who laugh too much and sprawl all over their chairs, showing a great deal of leg. A very light blonde with high colour and indecently large baby-blue eyes. Well, Brownwell told her not to worry, it would always be a good racket. In and out of the patient's house in fifteen minutes and anywhere from ten to fifty bucks a trip. But one thing bothered him, he said, however a doctor could get hold of so much dope without underworld contacts. He asked Mrs Almore if they had many nice gangsters to dinner at their house. She threw a glass of liquor in his face.'

I grinned, but Miss Fromsett didn't. She crushed her cigarette out in Kingsley's big copper and glass tray and looked at me soberly.

'Fair enough,' I said. 'Who wouldn't, unless he had a large hard fist to throw?'

'Yes. A few weeks later, Florence Almore was found dead in the garage late at night. The door of the garage was shut and the car motor was running.' She stopped and moistened her lips slightly. 'It was Chris Lavery who found her. Coming home at God knows what o'clock in the morning. She was lying on the concrete floor in pyjamas, with her head under a blanket which was also over the exhaust pipe of the car. Dr Almore was out. There was nothing about the affair in the papers, except that she had died suddenly. It was well hushed up.'

She lifted her clasped hands a little and then let them fall slowly into her lap again. I said:

'Was something wrong with it, then?'

'People thought so, but they always do. Some time later I heard what purported to be the lowdown. I meet this man Brownwell on Vine Street and he asked me to have a drink with him. I didn't like him, but I had half an hour to kill. We sat at the back of Levy's bar and he asked me if I remembered the babe who threw the drink in his face. I said I did. The conversation then went something very like this. I remember it very well.

'Brownwell said: "Our pal Chris Lavery is sitting pretty, if he ever runs out of girl friends he can touch for dough."

'I said: "I don't think I understand."

'He said: "Hell, maybe you don't want to. The night the Almore woman died she was over at Lou Condy's place losing her shirt at roulette. She got into a tantrum and said the wheels were crooked and made a scene. Condy practically had to drag her into his office. He got hold of Dr Almore through the Physicians' Exchange and after a while the doc came over. He shot her with one of his busy little needles. Then he went away, leaving Condy to get her home. It seems he had a very urgent case. So Condy took her home and the doc's office nurse showed up, having been called by the doc, and Condy carried her upstairs and the nurse put her to bed. Condy went back to his chips. So she had to be carried to bed and yet the same night she got up and walked down to the family garage and finished herself off with monoxide. What do you think of that?" Brownwell was asking me.

'I said: "I don't know anything about it. How do you?"

'He said: "I know a reporter on the rag they call a newspaper down there. There was no inquest and no autopsy. If any tests were made, nothing was told about them. They don't have a regular coroner down there. The undertakers take turns at being acting coroner, a week at a time. They're pretty well subservient to the political gang naturally. It's easy to fix a thing like that in a small town, if anybody with any pull wants it fixed. And Condy had plenty at that time. He didn't want the publicity of an investigation and neither did the doctor." '

Miss Fromsett stopped talking and waited for me to say something. When I didn't, she went on: 'I suppose you know what all this means to Brownwell?'

'Sure. Almore finished her off and then he and Condy between them bought a fix. It has been done in cleaner little cities than Bay City ever tried to be. But that isn't all the story, is it?'

'No. It seems Mrs Almore's parents hired a private detective. He was a man who ran a night watchman service down there and he was actually the second man on the scene that night, after Chris Brownwell said he must have had something in the way of information, but he never got a chance to use it. They arrested him for drunk driving and he got a jail sentence.'

I said: 'Is that all?'

She nodded. 'And if you think I remember it too well, it's part of my job to remember conversations.'

'What I was thinking was that it doesn't have to add up to very much. I don't see where it has to touch Lavery, even if he was the one who found her. Your gossipy friend Brownwell seems to think what happened gave somebody a chance to blackmail the doctor. But there would have to be some evidence, especially when you're trying to put the bite on a man who has already cleared himself with the law.'

Miss Fromsett said: 'I think so too. And I'd like to think blackmail was one of the nasty little tricks Chris Lavery didn't quite run to. I think that's all I can tell you, Mr Marlowe. And I ought to be outside.'

She started to get up. I said: 'It's not quite all. I have something to show you.'

I got the little perfumed rag that had been under Lavery's pillow out of my pocket and leaned over to drop it on the desk in front of her.

19

She looked at the handkerchief, looked at me, picked up a pencil and pushed the little piece of linen around with the eraser end.

'What's on it?' she asked. 'Flyspray?'

'Some kind of sandalwood, I thought.'

'A cheap synthetic. Repulsive is a mild word for it. And why did you want me to look at this handkerchief, Mr Marlowe?' She leaned back again and stared at me with level cool eyes.

'I found it in Chris Lavery's house, under the pillow on his bed. It has initials on it.'

She unfolded the handkerchief without touching it by using the rubber tip of the pencil. Her face got a little grim and taut.

'It has two letters embroidered on it,' she said in a cold angry voice. 'They happen to be the same letters as my initials. Is that what you mean?'

'Right,' I said. 'He probably knows half a dozen women with the same initials.'

'So you're going to be nasty after all,' she said quietly.

'Is it your handkerchief – or isn't it?'

She hesitated. She reached out to the desk and very quietly got herself another cigarette and lit it with a match. She shook the match slowly, watching the small flame creep along the wood.

'Yes, it's mine,' she said, 'I must have dropped it there.

It's a long time ago. And I assure you I didn't put it under a pillow on his bed. Is that what you wanted to know?'

I didn't say anything, and she added: 'He must have lent it to some woman who – who would like this kind of perfume.'

'I get a mental picture of the woman,' I said. 'And she doesn't quite go with Lavery.'

Her upper lip curled a little. It was a long upper lip. I like long upper lips.

'I think,' she said, 'you ought to do a little more work on your mental picture of Chris Lavery. Any touch of refinement you may have noticed is purely coincidental.'

'That's not a nice thing to say about a dead man,' I said.

For a moment she just sat there and looked at me as if I hadn't said anything and she was waiting for me to say something. Then a slow shudder started at her throat and passed over her whole body. Her hands clenched and the cigarette bent into a crook. She looked down at it and threw it into the ash-tray with a quick jerk of her arm.

'He was shot in his shower,' I said. 'And it looks as if it was done by some woman who spent the night there. He had just been shaving. The woman left a gun on the stairs and this handkerchief on the bed.'

She moved very slightly in her chair. Her eyes were perfectly empty now. Her face was as cold as a carving.

'And did you expect me to be able to give you information about that?' she asked me bitterly.

'Look, Miss Fromsett, I'd like to be smooth and distant and subtle about all this too. I'd like to play this sort of game just once the way somebody like you would like it to be played. But nobody will let me – not the clients, nor the cops, nor the people I play against. However hard I try to be nice I always end up with my nose in the dirt and my thumb feeling for somebody's eye.'

She nodded as if she had only just barely heard me. 'When was he shot?' she asked, and then shuddered slightly again.

'This morning, I suppose. Not long after he got up. I said he had just shaved and was going to take a shower.'

'That,' she said, 'would probably have been quite late. I've been here since eight-thirty.'

'I didn't think you shot him.'

'Awfully kind of you,' she said. 'But it is my hand-kerchief, isn't it? Although not my perfume. But I don't suppose policemen are very sensitive to quality in perfume – or in anything else.'

'No – and that goes for private detectives too,' I said. 'Are you enjoying this a lot?'

'God,' she said, and put the back of her hand hard against her mouth.

'He was shot at five or six times,' I said. 'And missed all but twice. He was cornered in the shower-stall. It was a pretty grim scene, I should think. There was a lot of hate on one side of it. Or a pretty cold-blooded mind.'

'He was quite easy to hate,' she said emptily. 'And poisonously easy to love. Women – even decent women – make such ghastly mistakes about men.'

'All you're telling me is that you once thought you loved him, but not any more, and that you didn't shoot him.'

'Yes.' Her voice was light and dry now, like the per-fume she didn't like to wear at the office. 'I'm sure you'll respect the confidence.' She laughed shortly and bitterly. 'Dead,' she said. 'The poor, egotistical, cheap, nasty, handsome, treacherous guy. Dead and cold and done with. No, Mr Marlowe, I didn't shoot him.'

I waited, letting her work it out of her. After a moment she said quietly: 'Does Mr Kingsley know?'

I nodded.

'And the police, of course.'

'Not yet. At least not from me. I found him. The house door wasn't quite shut. I went in. I found him.'

She picked the pencil up and poked at the handkerchief again. 'Does Mr Kingsley know about this scented rag?'

'Nobody knows about that, except you and me, and whoever put it there.'

'Nice of you,' she said dryly. 'And nice of you to think what you thought.'

'You have a certain quality of aloofness and dignity that I like,' I said. 'But don't run it into the ground. What would you expect me to think? Do I pull the hankie out from under the pillow and sniff it and hold it out and say, 'Well, well, Miss Adrienne Fromsett's initials and all. Miss Fromsett must have known Lavery, perhaps very intimately. Let's say, just for the book, as intimately as my nasty little mind can conceive. And that would be pretty damn intimately. But this is cheap synthetic sandalwood and Miss Fromsett wouldn't use cheap scent. And this was under Lavery's pillow and Miss Fromsett just never keeps her hankies under a man's pillow. Therefore this has absolutely nothing to do with Miss Fromsett. It's just an optical delusion.'

'Oh, shut up,' she said.

I grinned.

'What kind of girl do you think I am?' she snapped.

'I came in too late to tell you.'

She flushed, but delicately and all over her face this time. Then, 'Have you any idea who did it?'

'Ideas, but that's all they are. I'm afraid the police are going to find it simple. Some of Mrs Kingsley's clothes are hanging in Lavery's closet. And when they know the whole story – including what happened at Little Fawn Lake yesterday – I'm afraid they'll just reach for the handcuffs. They have to find her first. But that won't be so hard for them.'

'Crystal Kingsley,' she said emptily. 'So he couldn't be spared even that.'

I said: 'It doesn't have to be. It could be an entirely different motivation, something we know nothing about. It could have been somebody like Dr Almore.'

She looked up quickly, then shook her head. 'It could be,' I insisted. 'We don't know anything against it. He was pretty nervous yesterday, for a man who has nothing to be afraid of. But, of course, it isn't only the guilty who are afraid.'

I stood up and tapped on the edge of the desk looking down at her. She had a lovely neck. She pointed to the handkerchief.

'What about that?' she asked dully.

'If it was mine, I'd wash that cheap scent out of it.'

'It has to mean something, doesn't it? It might mean a lot.'

I laughed. 'I don't think it means anything at all. Women are always leaving their handkerchiefs around. A fellow like Lavery would collect them and keep them in a drawer with a sandalwood sachet. Somebody would find the stock and take one out to use. Or he would lend them, enjoying the reactions to the other girl's initials. I'd say he was that kind of a heel. Good-bye, Miss Fromsett, and thanks for talking to me.'

I started to go, then I stopped and asked her: 'Did you hear the name of the reporter down there who gave Brownwell all his information?'

She shook her head.

'Or the name of Mrs Almore's parents?'

'Not that either. But I could probably find that out for you. I'd be glad to try.'

'How?'

'Those things are usually printed in death notices, aren't they? There is pretty sure to have been a death notice in the Los Angeles papers.'

'That would be very nice of you,' I said. I ran a finger along the edge of the desk and looked at her sideways. Pale ivory skin, dark and lovely eyes, hair as light as hair can be and eyes as dark as night can be.

I walked back down the room and out. The little blonde at the P.B.X. looked at me expectantly, her small red lips parted, waiting for more fun.

I didn't have any more. I went out.

20

No police cars stood in front of Lavery's house, nobody hung around on the sidewalk and when I pushed the front door open there was no smell of cigar or cigarette smoke inside. The sun had gone away from the windows and a fly buzzed softly over one of the liquor glasses. I went down to the end and hung over the railing that led downstairs. Nothing moved in Mr Lavery's house. Nothing made sound except very faintly down below in the bathroom the quiet trickle of water dripping on a dead man's shoulder.

I went to the telephone and looked up the number of the police department in the directory. I dialled and while I was waiting for an answer, I took the little automatic out of my pocket and laid it on the table beside the telephone.

When the male voice said: 'Bay City police – Smoot talking,' I said: 'There's been a shooting at 623 Altair Street. Man named Lavery lives there. He's dead.'

'Six-two-three Altair. Who are you?'

'The name is Marlowe.'

'You there in the house?'

'Right.'

'Don't touch anything at all.'

I hung up, sat down on the davenport and waited.

Not very long. A siren whined far off, growing louder with great surges of sound. Tyres screamed at a corner, and the siren wail died to a metallic growl, then the silence, and the tyres screamed again in front of the house. The Bay City police conserving rubber. Steps hit the sidewalk and I went over to the front door and opened it.

Two uniformed cops barged into the room. They were the usual large size and they had the usual weathered faces and suspicious eyes. One of them had a carnation tucked under his cap, behind his right ear. The other one was older, a little grey and grim. They stood and looked at me warily, then the older one said briefly:

'All right, where is it?'

'Downstairs in the bathroom, behind the shower curtain.'

'You stay here with him, Eddie.'

He went rapidly along the room and disappeared. The other one looked at me steadily and said out of the corner of his mouth:

'Don't make any false moves, buddy.'

I sat down on the davenport again. The cop ranged the room with his eyes. There were sounds below stairs, feet walking. The cop with me suddenly spotted the gun lying on the telephone table. He charged at it violently, like a downfield blocker.

'This the death gun?' he almost shouted.

'I should imagine so. It's been fired.'

'Ha!' He leaned over the gun, baring his teeth at me, and put his hand to his holster. His finger tickled the flap off the stud and he grasped the butt of the black revolver.

'You should what?' he barked.

'I should imagine so.'

'That's very good,' he sneered. 'That's very good indeed.'

'It's not that good,' I said.

He reeled back a little. His eyes were being careful of me. 'What you shoot him for?' he growled.

'I've wondered and wondered.'

'Oh, a wisenheimer.'

'Let's just sit down and wait for the homicide boys,' I said. 'I'm reserving my defence.'

'Don't give me none of that,' he said.

'I'm not giving you any of anything. If I had shot him, I wouldn't be here. I wouldn't have called up. You wouldn't have found the gun. Don't work so hard on the case. You won't be on it more than ten minutes.'

His eyes looked hurt. He took his cap off and the carnation dropped to the floor. He bent and picked it up and twirled it between his fingers, then dropped it behind the fire screen.

'Better not do that,' I told him. 'They might think it's a clue and waste a lot of time on it.'

'Aw hell.' He bent over the screen and retrieved the carnation and put it in his pocket. 'You know all the answers, don't you, buddy?'

The other cop came back up the stairs, looking grave. He stood in the middle of the floor and looked at his wristwatch and made a note in a notebook and then looked out of the front windows, holding the venetian blinds to one side to do it.

The one who had stayed with me said: 'Can I look now?'

'Let it lie, Eddie. Nothing in it for us. You call the coroner?'

'I thought Homicide would do that.'

'Yeah, that's right. Captain Webber will be on it and he likes to do everything himself.' He looked at me and said: 'You're a man named Marlowe?'

I said I was a man named Marlowe.

'He's a wise guy, knows all the answers,' Eddie said.

The older one looked at me absently, looked at Eddie absently, spotted the gun lying on the telephone table and looked at that not at all absently.

'Yeah, that's the death gun,' Eddie said. 'I ain't touched it.'

The other nodded. 'The boys are not so fast to-day. What's your line, mister? Friend of his?' He made a thumb towards the floor.

'Saw him yesterday for the first time. I'm a private operative from L. A.'

'Oh.' He looked at me very sharply. The other cop looked at me with deep suspicion.

'Cripes, that means everything will be all balled up,' he said.

That was the first sensible remark he had made. I grinned at him affectionately.

The older cop looked out of the front window again. 'That's the Almore place across the street, Eddie,' he said.

Eddie went and looked with him. 'Sure is,' he said. 'You can read the plate. Say, this guy downstairs might be the guy –'

'Shut up,' the other one said and dropped the venetian blind. They both turned around and stared at me woodenly.

A car came down the block and stopped and a door

slammed and more steps came down the walk. The older of the prowl-car boys opened the door to two men in plain clothes, one of whom I already knew.

21

The one who came first was a small man for a cop, middle-aged, thin-faced, with a permanently tired expression. His nose was sharp and bent a little to one side, as if somebody had given it the elbow one time when it was into something. His blue pork-pie hat was set very square on his head and chalk-white hair showed under it. He wore a dull brown suit and his hands were in the side pockets of the jacket, with the thumbs outside the seam.

The man behind him was Degarmo, the big cop with the dusty blond hair and the metallic blue eyes and the savage, lined face who had not liked my being in front of Dr Almore's house.

The two uniformed men looked at the small man and touched their caps.

'The body's in the basement, Captain Webber. Been shot twice after a couple of misses, looks like. Dead quite some time. This party's name is Marlowe. He's a private eye from Los Angeles. I didn't question him beyond that.'

'Quite right,' Webber said sharply. He had a suspicious voice. He passed a suspicious eye over my face and nodded briefly. 'I'm Captain Webber,' he said. 'This is Lieutenant Degarmo. We'll look at the body first.'

He went along the room. Degarmo looked at me as if he had never seen me before and followed him. They went downstairs, the older of the two prowl men with them. The cop called Eddie and I stared each other down for a while.

I said: 'This is right across the street from Dr Almore's place, isn't it?'

All the expression went out of his face. There hadn't been much to go. 'Yeah. So what?'

'So nothing,' I said.

He was silent. The voices came up from below, blurred and indistinct. The cop cocked his ear and said in a more friendly tone: 'You remember that one?'

'A little.'

He laughed. 'They killed that one pretty,' he said. 'They wrapped it up and hid it in back of the shelf. The top shelf in the bathroom closet. The one you can't reach without standing on a chair.'

'So they did,' I said. 'I wonder why.'

The cop looked at me sternly. 'There was good reasons, pal. Don't think there wasn't. You know this Lavery well?'

'Not well.'

'On to him for something?'

'Working on him a little,' I said. 'You knew him?'

The cop called Eddie shook his head. 'Nope, I just remembered it was a guy from this house found Almore's wife in the garage that night.'

'Lavery may not have been here then,' I said.

'How long's he been here?'

'I don't know,' I said.

'Would be about a year and a half,' the cop said, musingly. 'The L.A. papers give it any play?'

'Paragraph on the Home Counties page,' I said, just to be moving my mouth.

He scratched his ear and listened. Steps were coming back up the stairs. The cop's face went blank and he moved away from me and straightened up.

Captain Webber hurried over to the telephone and dialled the number and spoke, then held the phone away from his ear and looked back over his shoulder.

'Who's deputy coroner this week, Al?'

'Ed Garland,' the big lieutenant said woodenly.

'Call Ed Garland,' Webber said into the phone. 'Have him come over right away. And tell the flash squad to step on it.'

He put the phone down and barked sharply: 'Who handled this gun?'

I said: 'I did.'

He came over and teetered on his heels in front of me and pushed his small sharp chin up at me. He held the gun delicately on a handkerchief in his hand.

'Don't you know enough not to handle a weapon found at the scene of a crime?'

'Certainly,' I said. 'But when I handled it I didn't know there had been a crime. I didn't know the gun had been fired. It was lying on the stairs and I thought it had been dropped.'

'A likely story,' Webber said bitterly. 'You get a lot of that sort of thing in your business?'

'A lot of what sort of thing?'

He kept his hard stare on me and didn't answer.

I said: 'How would it be for me to tell you my story as it happened?'

He bridled at me like a cockerel. 'Suppose you answer my questions exactly as I choose to put them.'

I didn't say anything to that. Webber swivelled sharply

and said to the two uniformed men: 'You boys can get back to your car and check in with the despatcher.'

They saluted and went out, closing the door softly until it stuck, then getting as mad at it as anybody else. Webber listened until their car went away. Then he put the bleak and callous eye on me once more.

'Let me see your identification.'

I handed him my wallet and he rooted in it. Degarmo sat in a chair and crossed his legs and stared up blankly at the ceiling. He got a match out of his pocket and chewed the end of it. Webber gave me back my wallet. I put it away.

'People in your line make a lot of trouble,' he said.

'Not necessarily,' I said.

He raised his voice. It had been sharp enough before. 'I said they make a lot of trouble, and a lot of trouble is what I meant. But get this straight. You're not going to make any in Bay City.'

I didn't answer him. He jabbed a forefinger at me.

'You're from the big town,' he said. 'You think you're tough and you think you're wise. Don't worry. We can handle you. We're a small place, but we're very compact. We don't have any political tug-of-war down here. We work on the straight line and we work fast. Don't worry about us, mister.'

'I'm not worrying,' I said. 'I don't have anything to worry about. I'm just trying to make a nice clean dollar.'

'And don't give me any of the flip talk,' Webber said. 'I don't like it.'

Degarmo brought his eyes down from the ceiling and curled a forefinger to stare at the nail. He spoke in a heavy bored voice.

'Look, chief, the fellow downstairs is called Lavery. He's dead. I knew him a little. He was a chaser.'

'What of it?' Webber snapped, not looking away from me.

'The whole set-up indicates a dame,' Degarmo said. 'You know what these private eyes work at. Divorce stuff. Suppose we'd let him tie into it, instead of just trying to scare him dumb.'

'If I'm scaring him,' Webber said, 'I'd like to know it. I don't see any signs of it.'

He walked over to the front window and yanked the venetian blind up. Light poured into the room almost dazzlingly, after the long dimness. He came back bouncing on his heels and poked a thin hard finger at me and said:

'Talk.'

I said, 'I'm working for a Los Angeles business man who can't take a lot of loud publicity. That's why he hired me. A month ago his wife ran off and later a telegram came which indicated she had gone with Lavery. But my client met Lavery in town a couple of days ago and he denied it. The client believed him enough to get worried. It seems the lady is pretty reckless. She might have taken up with some bad company and got into a jam. I came down to see Lavery and he denied to me that he had gone with her. I half believed him but later I got reasonable proof that he had been with her in a San Bernardino hotel the night she was believed to have left the mountain cabin where she had been staying. With that in my pocket I came down to tackle Lavery again. No answer to the bell, the door was slightly open. I came inside, looked around, found the gun and searched the house. I found him. Just the way he is now.'

'You had no right to search the house,' Webber said coldly.

'Of course not,' I agreed. 'But I wouldn't be likely to pass up the chance either.'

'The name of this man you're working for?'

'Kingsley.' I gave him the Beverly Hills address. 'He manages a cosmetic company in the Treloar Building on Olive. The Gillerlain Company.'

Webber looked at Degarmo. Degarmo wrote lazily on an envelope. Webber looked back at me and said: 'What else?'

'I went up to this mountain cabin where the lady had been staying. It's at a place called Little Fawn Lake, near Puma Point, forty-six miles into the mountains from San Bernardino.'

I looked at Degarmo. He was writing slowly. His hand stopped a moment and seemed to hang in the air stiffly, then it dropped to the envelope and wrote again. I went on:

'About a month ago the wife of the caretaker at Kingsley's place up there had a fight with him and left, as everybody thought. Yesterday she was found drowned in the lake.'

Webber almost closed his eyes and rocked on his heels. Almost softly he asked: 'Why are you telling me this? Are you implying a connexion?'

'There's a connexion in time. Lavery had been up there. I don't know of any other connexion, but I thought I'd better mention it.'

Degarmo was sitting very still, looking at the floor in

front of him. His face was tight and he looked even more savage than usual. Webber said:

'This woman that was drowned? Suicide?'

'Suicide or murder. She left a good-bye note. But her husband has been arrested on suspicion. The name is Chess. Bill and Muriel Chess, his wife.'

'I don't want any part of that,' Webber said sharply. 'Let's confine ourselves to what went on here.'

'Nothing went on here,' I said, looking at Degarmo. 'I've been down here twice. The first time I talked to Lavery and didn't get anywhere. The second time I didn't talk to him and didn't get anywhere.'

Webber said slowly: 'I'm going to ask you a question and I want an honest answer. You won't want to give it, but now will be as good a time as later. You know I'll get it eventually. The question is this. You have looked through the house and I imagine pretty thoroughly. Have you seen anything that suggests to you that this Kingsley woman has been here?'

'That's not a fair question,' I said. 'It calls for a conclusion of the witness.'

'I want an answer to it,' he said grimly. 'This isn't a court of law.'

'The answer is yes,' I said. 'There are women's clothes hanging in a closet downstairs that have been described to me as being worn by Mrs Kingsley at San Bernardino the night she met Lavery there. The description was not exact though. A black and white suit, mostly white, and a panama hat with a rolled black and white band.'

Degarmo snapped a finger against the envelope he was holding. 'You must be a great guy for a client to have working for him,' he said. 'That puts the woman right in this house where a murder has been committed and she is the woman he's supposed to have gone away with. I don't think we'll have to look far for the killer, chief.'

Webber was staring at me fixedly, with little or no expression on his face but a kind of tight watchfulness. He nodded absently to what Degarmo had said.

I said: 'I'm assuming you fellows are not a pack of damn fools. The clothes are tailored and easy to trace. I've saved you an hour by telling you, perhaps even no more than a phone call.'

'Anything else?' Webber asked quietly.

Before I could answer, a car stopped outside the house, and then another. Webber skipped over to open the door. Three men came in, a short, curly-haired man and a large ox-like man, both carrying heavy black leather cases. Behind them a tall thin man in a dark-grey suit and black tie. He had very bright eyes and a poker face.

Webber pointed a finger at the curly-haired man and said: 'Downstairs in the bathroom, Busoni. I want a lot of prints from all over the house, particularly any that seem to be made by a woman. It will be a long job.'

'I do all the work,' Busoni grunted. He and the ox-like man went along the room and down the stairs.

'We have a corpse for you, Garland,' Webber said to the third man. 'Let's go down and look at him. You've ordered the wagon?'

The bright-eyed man nodded briefly and he and Webber went downstairs after the other two.

Degarmo put the envelope and pencil away. He stared at me woodenly.

I said: 'Am I supposed to talk about our conversation yesterday – or is that a private transaction?'

'Talk about it all you like,' he said. 'It's our job to protect the citizen.'

'You talk about it,' I said. 'I'd like to know more about the Almore case.'

He flushed slowly and his eyes got mean. 'You said you didn't know Almore.'

'I didn't yesterday, or know anything about him. Since then I've learned that Lavery knew Mrs Almore, that she committed suicide, that Lavery found her dead, and that Lavery has at least been suspected of blackmailing him – or of being in a position to blackmail him. Also both your prowl-car boys seemed interested in the fact that Almore's house was across the street from here. And one of them remarked that the case had been killed pretty, or words to that effect.'

Degarmo said in a slow deadly tone: 'I'll have the badge off the son of a bitch. All they do is flap their mouths. God damn empty-headed bastards.'

'Then there's nothing in it,' I said.

He looked at his cigarette. 'Nothing in what?'

'Nothing in the idea that Almore murdered his wife, and had enough pull to get it fixed.'

Degarmo came to his feet and walked over to lean down at me. 'Say that again,' he said softly.

I said it again.

He hit me across the face with his open hand. It jerked my head around hard. My face felt hot and large.

'Say it again,' he said softly.

I said it again. His hand swept and knocked my head to one side again.

'Say it again.'

'Nope. Third time lucky. You might miss.' I put a hand up and rubbed my cheek.

He stood leaning down, his lips drawn back over his teeth, a hard animal glare in his very blue eyes.

'Any time you talk like that to a cop,' he said, 'you know what you got coming. Try it on again and it won't be the flat of a hand I'll use on you.'

I bit hard on my lips and rubbed my cheek.

'Poke your big nose into our business and you'll wake up in an alley with the cats looking at you,' he said.

I didn't say anything. He went and sat down again, breathing hard. I stopped rubbing my face and held my hand out and worked the fingers slowly, to get the hard clench out of them.

'I'll remember that,' I said. 'Both ways.'

22

It was early evening when I got back to Hollywood and up to the office. The building had emptied out and the corridors were silent. Doors were open and the cleaning women were inside with their vacuum cleaners and their dry mops and dusters.

I unlocked the door to mine and picked up an envelope that lay in front of the mail slot and dropped it on the desk without looking at it. I ran the windows up and leaned out, looking at the early neon lights glowing, smelling the warm, foody air that drifted up from the alley ventilator of the coffee shop next door.

I peeled off my coat and tie and sat down at the desk and got the office bottle out of the deep drawer and bought myself a drink. It didn't do any good. I had another, with the same result.

By now Webber would have seen Kingsley. There would be a general alarm out for his wife, already, or very soon. The thing looked cut and dried to them. A nasty affair between two rather nasty people, too much loving, too much drinking, too much proximity ending in a savage hatred and a murderous impulse and death.

I thought this was all a little too simple.

I reached for the envelope and tore it open. It had no stamp. It read: 'Mr Marlowe: Florence Almore's parents are a Mr and Mrs Eustace Grayson, at present residing at the Rossmore Arms, 640 South Oxford Avenue. I

checked this by calling the listed phone number. Yrs
ADRIENNE FROMSETT.'

An elegant handwriting, like the elegant hand that
wrote it. I pushed it to one side and had another drink.
I began to feel a little less savage. I pushed things around
on the desk. My hands felt thick and hot and awkward.
I ran a finger across the corner of the desk and looked at
the streak made by the wiping off of the dust. I looked
at the dust on my finger and wiped that off. I looked at
my watch. I looked at the wall. I looked at nothing.

I put the liquor bottle away and went over to the
wash-bowl to rinse the glass out. When I had done that
I washed my hands and bathed my face in cold water
and looked at it. The flush was gone from the left cheek,
but it looked a little swollen. Not very much, but enough
to make me tighten up again. I brushed my hair and
looked at the grey in it. There was getting to be plenty
of grey in it. The face under the hair had a sick look. I
didn't like the face at all.

I went back to the desk and read Miss Fromsett's note
again. I smoothed it out on the glass and sniffed it and
smoothed it out some more and folded it and put it in
my coat pocket.

I sat very still and listened to the evening grow quiet
outside the open windows. And very slowly I grew quiet
with it.

23

The Rossmore Arms was a gloomy pile of dark red brick built around a huge forecourt. It had a plush-lined lobby containing silence, tubbed plants, a bored canary in a cage as big as a dog-house, a smell of old carpet dust and the cloying fragrance of gardenias long ago.

The Graysons were on the fifth floor in front, in the north wing. They were sitting together in a room which seemed to be deliberately twenty years out of date. It had fat overstuffed furniture and brass doorknobs, shaped like eggs, a huge wall mirror in a gilt frame, a marble-topped table in the window and dark red plush side drapes by the windows. It smelled of tobacco smoke and behind that the air was telling me they had had lamb chops and broccoli for dinner.

Grayson's wife was a plump woman who might once have had big baby-blue eyes. They were faded out now and dimmed by glasses and slightly protuberant. She had kinky white hair. She sat darning socks with her thick ankles crossed, her feet just reaching the floor, and a big wicker sewing basket in her lap.

Grayson was a long, stooped, yellow-faced man with high shoulders, bristly eyebrows and almost no chin. The upper part of his face meant business. The lower part was just saying good-bye. He wore bifocals and he had been gnawing fretfully at the evening paper. I had looked him up in the city directory. He was a C.P.A. and looked it every inch. He even had ink on his fingers and there were four pencils in the pocket of his open vest.

He read my card carefully for the seventh time and looked me up and down and said slowly:

'What is it you want to see us about, Mr Marlowe?'

'I'm interested in a man named Lavery. He lives across the street from Dr Almore. Your daughter was the wife of Dr Almore. Lavery is the man who found your daughter the night she – died.'

They both pointed like bird dogs when I deliberately hesitated on the last word. Grayson looked at his wife and she shook her head.

'We don't care to talk about that,' Grayson said promptly. 'It is much too painful to us.'

I waited a moment and looked gloomy with them. Then I said: 'I don't blame you. I don't want to make you. I'd like to get in touch with the man you hired to look into it, though.'

They looked at each other again. Mrs Grayson didn't shake her head this time.

Grayson asked: 'Why?'

'I'd better tell you a little of my story.' I told them what I had been hired to do, not mentioning Kingsley by name. I told them the incident with Degarmo outside Almore's house the day before. They pointed again on that.

Grayson said sharply: 'Am I to understand that you were unknown to Dr Almore, had not approached him in any way, and that he nevertheless called a police officer because you were outside his house?'

I said: 'That's right. Had been outside for at least an hour though. That is, my car had.'

'That's very queer,' Grayson said.

'I'd say that was one very nervous man,' I said. 'And Degarmo asked me if her folks – meaning your daughter's folks – had hired me. Looks as if he didn't feel safe yet, wouldn't you say?'

'Safe about what?' He didn't look at me saying this. He re-lit his pipe, slowly, then tamped the tobacco down with the end of a big metal pencil and lit it again.

I shrugged and didn't answer. He looked at me quickly and looked away. Mrs Grayson didn't look at me, but her nostrils quivered.

'How did he know who you were?' Grayson asked suddenly.

'Made a note of the car licence, called the Auto Club, looked up the name in the directory. At least that's what I'd have done and I saw him through his window making some of the motions.'

'So he has the police working for him,' Grayson said.

'Not necessarily. If they made a mistake that time, they wouldn't want it found out now.'

'Mistake!' He laughed almost shrilly.

'Okay,' I said. 'The subject is painful but a little fresh air won't hurt it. You've always thought he murdered her, haven't you? That's why you hired this dick – detective.'

Mrs Grayson looked up with quick eyes and ducked her head down and rolled up another pair of mended socks.

Grayson said nothing.

I said: 'Was there any evidence, or was it just that you didn't like him?'

'There was evidence,' Grayson said bitterly, and with

a sudden clearness of voice, as if he had decided to talk about it after all. 'There must have been. We were told there was. But we never got it. The police took care of that.'

'I heard they had this fellow arrested and sent up for drunk driving.'

'You heard right.'

'But he never told you what he had to go on?'

'No.'

'I don't like that,' I said. 'That sounds a little as if this fellow hadn't made up his mind whether to use his information for your benefit or keep it and put a squeeze on the doctor.'

Grayson looked at his wife again. She said quietly: 'Mr Talley didn't impress me that way. He was a quiet unassuming little man. But you can't always judge, I know.'

I said: 'So Talley was his name. That was one of the things I hoped you would tell me.'

'And what were the others?' Grayson asked.

'How can I find Talley – and what it was that laid the groundwork of suspicion in your minds. It must have been there, or you wouldn't have hired Talley without a better showing from him that *he* had grounds.'

Grayson smiled very thinly and primly. He reached for his little chin and rubbed it with one long yellow finger.

Mrs Grayson said: 'Dope.'

'She means that literally,' Grayson said at once, as if the single word had been a green light. 'Almore was, and no doubt is, a dope doctor. Our daughter made that clear to us. In his hearing too. He didn't like it.'

'Just what do you mean by a dope doctor, Mr Grayson?'

'I mean a doctor whose practice is largely with people who are living on the raw edge of nervous collapse, from drink and dissipation. People who have to be given sedatives and narcotics all the time. The stage comes when an ethical physician refuses to treat them any more, outside a sanatorium. But not the Dr Almores. *They* will keep on as long as the money comes in, as long as the patient remains alive and reasonably sane, even if he or she becomes a hopeless addict in the process. A lucrative practice,' he said primly, 'and I imagine a dangerous one to the doctor.'

'No doubt of that,' I said. 'But there's a lot of money in it. Do you know a man named Condy?'

'No. We know who he was. Florence suspected he was a source of Almore's narcotic supply.'

I said: 'Could be. He probably wouldn't want to write himself too many prescriptions. Did you know Lavery?'

'We never saw him. We knew who he was.'

'Ever occur to you that Lavery might have been blackmailing Almore?'

It was a new idea to him. He ran his hand over the top of his head and brought it down over his face and dropped it to his bony knee. He shook his head.

'No. Why should it?'

'He was first to the body,' I said. 'Whatever looked wrong to Talley must have been equally visible to Lavery.'

'Is Lavery that kind of man?'

'I don't know. He has no visible means of support, no job. He gets around a lot, especially with women.'

'It's an idea,' Grayson said. 'And those things can be handled very discreetly.' He smiled wryly. 'I have come across traces of them in my work. Unsecured loans, long outstanding. Investments on the face of them worthless made by men who would not be likely to make worthless investments. Bad debts that should obviously be charged off and have not been, for fear of inviting scrutiny from the income-tax people. Oh yes, those things can easily be arranged.'

I looked at Mrs Grayson. Her hands had never stopped working. She had a dozen pairs of darned socks finished. Grayson's long bony feet would be hard on socks.

'What's happened to Talley? Was he framed?'

'I don't think there's any doubt about it. His wife was very bitter. She said he had been given a doped drink in a bar and he had been drinking with a policeman. She said a police car was waiting across the street for him to start driving and that he was picked up at once. Also that he was given only the most perfunctory examination at the jail.'

'That doesn't mean too much. That's what he told her after he was arrested. He'd tell her something like that automatically.'

'Well, I hate to think the police are not honest,' Grayson said. 'But these things are done, and everybody knows it.'

I said: 'If they made an honest mistake about your daughter's death, they would hate to have Talley show them up. It might mean several lost jobs. If they thought what he was really after was blackmail, they wouldn't be too fussy about how they took care of him. Where is Talley now? What it all boils down to is that if there was any solid clue, he either had it or was on the track of it and knew what he was looking for.'

Grayson said: 'We don't know where he is. He got six months, but that expired long ago.'

'How about his wife?'

He looked at his own wife. She said briefly: '1618½ Westmore Street, Bay City. Eustace and I sent her a little money. She was badly off.'

I made a note of the address and leaned back in my chair and said:

'Somebody shot Lavery this morning in his bathroom.'

Mrs Grayson's pudgy hands became still on the edges of the basket. Grayson sat with his mouth open, holding his pipe in front of it. He made a noise of clearing his throat softly, as if in the presence of the dead. Nothing ever moved slower than his old black pipe going back between his teeth.

'Of course it would be too much to expect,' he said and let it hang in the air and blew a little pale smoke at it, and then added, 'that Dr Almore had any connexion with that.'

'I'd like to think he had,' I said. 'He certainly lives at a handy distance. The police think my client's wife shot him. They have a good case too, when they find her. But if Almore had anything to do with it, it must surely arise out of your daughter's death. That's why I'm trying to find out something about that.'

Grayson said: 'A man who has done one murder wouldn't have more than twenty-five per cent of the hesitation in doing another.' He spoke as if he had given the matter considerable study.

I said: 'Yeah, maybe. What was supposed to be the motive for the first one?'

'Florence was wild,' he said sadly. 'A wild and difficult girl. She was wasteful and extravagant, always picking up new and rather doubtful friends, talking too much and too loudly, and generally acting the fool. A wife like that can be very dangerous to a man like Albert S. Almore. But I don't believe that was the prime motive, was it, Lettie?'

He looked at his wife, but she didn't look at him. She jabbed a darning-needle into a round ball of wool and said nothing.

Grayson sighed and went on: 'We had reason to believe he was carrying on with his office nurse and that Florence had threatened him with a public scandal. He couldn't have anything like that, could he? One kind of scandal might too easily lead to another.'

I said: 'How did he do the murder?'

'With morphine, of course. He always had it, he always used it. He was an expert in the use of it. Then when she was in a deep coma he would have placed her in the garage and started the car motor. There was no autopsy, you know. But if there had been, it was known that she had been given a hypodermic injection that night.'

I nodded and he leaned back satisfied and ran his hand over his head and down his face and let it fall slowly to his bony knee. He seemed to have given a lot of study to this angle too.

I looked at them. A couple of elderly people sitting there quietly, poisoning their minds with hate, a year and a half after it had happened. They would like it if

Almore had shot Lavery. They would love it. It would warm them clear down to their ankles.

After a pause I said: 'You're believing a lot of this because you want to. It's always possible that she committed suicide, and that the cover-up was partly to protect Condy's gambling club and partly to prevent Almore having to be questioned at a public hearing.'

'Rubbish,' Grayson said sharply. 'He murdered her all right. She was in bed, asleep.'

'You don't know that. She might have been taking dope herself. She might have established a tolerance for it. The effect wouldn't last long in that case. She might have got up in the middle of the night and looked at herself in the glass and seen devils pointing at her. These things happen.'

'I think you have taken up enough of our time,' Grayson said.

I stood up. I thanked them both and made a yard towards the door and said: 'You didn't do anything more about it after Talley was arrested?'

'Saw an assistant district attorney named Leach,' Grayson grunted. 'Got exactly nowhere. He saw nothing to justify his office in interfering. Wasn't even interested in the narcotic angle. But Condy's place was closed up about a month later. That might have come out of it somehow.'

'That was probably the Bay City cops throwing a little smoke. You'd find Condy somewhere else, if you knew where to look. With all his original equipment intact.'

I started for the door again and Grayson hoisted himself out of his chair and dragged across the room after me. There was a flush on his yellow face.

'I didn't mean to be rude,' he said. 'I guess Lettie and I oughtn't to brood about this business the way we do.'

'I think you've both been very patient,' I said. 'Was there anybody else involved in all this that we haven't mentioned by name?'

He shook his head, then looked back at his wife. Her hands were motionless holding the current sock on the darning-egg. Her head was tilted a little to one side. Her attitude was of listening, but not to us.

I said: 'The way I got the story, Dr Almore's office nurse put Mrs Almore to bed that night. Would that be the one he was supposed to be playing around with?'

Mrs Grayson said sharply: 'Wait a minute. We never saw the girl. But she had a pretty name. Just give me a minute.'

We gave her a minute. 'Mildred something,' she said, and snapped her teeth.

I took a deep breath. 'Would it be Mildred Haviland, Mrs Grayson?'

She smiled brightly and nodded. 'Of course, Mildred Haviland. Don't you remember, Eustace?'

He didn't remember. He looked at us like a horse that has got into the wrong stable. He opened the door and said: 'What does it matter?'

'And you said Talley was a small man,' I bored on. 'He wouldn't for instance be a big loud bruiser with an overbearing manner?'

'Oh no,' Mrs Grayson said. 'Mr Talley is a man of not more than medium height, middle-aged, with brownish hair and a very quiet voice. He had a sort of worried expression. I mean, he looked as if he always had it.'

'Looks as if he needed it,' I said.

Grayson put his bony hand out and I shook it. It felt like shaking hands with a towel-rack.

'If you get him,' he said and clamped his mouth hard on his pipe stem, 'call back with a bill. If you get Almore, I mean, of course.'

I said I knew he meant Almore, but that there wouldn't be any bill.

I went back along the silent hallway. The self-operating elevator was carpeted in red plush. It had an elderly perfume in it, like three widows drinking tea.

24

The house on Westmore Street was a small frame bunga-
low behind a larger house. There was no number visible
on the smaller house, but the one in front showed a
stencilled 1618 beside the door, with a dim light behind
the stencil. A narrow concrete path led along under
windows to the house at the back. It had a tiny porch
with a single chair on it. I stepped up on the porch and
rang the bell.

It buzzed not very far off. The front door was open
behind the screen but there was no light. From the
darkness a querulous voice said:

'What is it?'

I spoke into the darkness. 'Mr Talley in?'

The voice became flat and without tone. 'Who wants
him?'

'A friend.'

The woman sitting inside in the darkness made a
vague sound in her throat which might have been amusement. Or she might just have been clearing her throat.

'All right,' she said. 'How much is this one?'

'It's not a bill, Mrs Talley. I suppose you are Mrs
Talley?'

'Oh, go away and let me alone,' the voice said. 'Mr
Talley isn't here. He hasn't been here. He won't be here.'

I put my nose against the screen and tried to peer into
the room. I could see the vague outlines of its furniture.

From where the voice came from also showed the shape of a couch. A woman was lying on it. She seemed to be lying on her back and looking up at the ceiling. She was quite motionless.

'I'm sick,' the voice said. 'I've had enough trouble. Go away and leave me be.'

I said: 'I've just come from talking to the Graysons.'

There was a little silence, but no movement, then a sigh. 'I never heard of them.'

I leaned against the frame of the screen door and looked back along the narrow walk to the street. There was a car across the way with parking lights burning. There were other cars along the block.

I said: 'Yes, you have, Mrs Talley. I'm working for them. They're still in there pitching. How about you? Don't you want something back?'

The voice said: 'I want to be let alone.'

'I want information,' I said. 'I'm going to get it. Quietly, if I can. Loud, if it can't be quiet.'

The voice said: 'Another copper, eh?'

'You know I'm not a copper, Mrs Talley. The Graysons wouldn't talk to a copper. Call them up and ask them.'

'I never heard of them,' the voice said. 'I don't have a phone, if I knew them. Go away, copper. I'm sick. I've been sick for a month.'

'My name is Marlowe,' I said. 'Philip Marlowe. I'm a private eye in Los Angeles. I've been talking to the Graysons. I've got something, but I want to talk to your husband.'

The woman on the couch let out a dim laugh which barely reached across the room. 'You've got something,' she said. 'That sounds familiar. My God it does! You've got something. George Talley had something too – once.'

'He can have it again,' I said, 'if he plays his cards right.'

'If that's what it takes,' she said, 'you can scratch him off right now.'

I leaned against the door-frame and scratched my chin instead. Somebody back on the street had clicked a flashlight on. I didn't know why. It went off again. It seemed to be near my car.

The pale blur of face on the couch moved and disappeared. Hair took its place. The woman had turned her face to the wall.

'I'm tired,' she said, her voice now muffled by talking at the wall. 'I'm so damn tired. Beat it, mister. Be nice and go away.'

'Would a little money help any?'

'Can't you smell the cigar smoke?'

I sniffed. I didn't smell any cigar smoke. I said, 'No.'

'They've been here. They were here two hours. God, I'm tired of it all. Go away.'

'Look, Mrs Talley –'

She rolled on the couch and the blur of her face showed again. I could almost see her eyes, not quite.

'Look yourself,' she said. 'I don't know you. I don't want to know you. I have nothing to tell you. I wouldn't tell it, if I had. I live here, mister, if you call it living. Anyway, it's the nearest I can get to living. I want a little peace and quiet. Now you get out and leave me alone.'

'Let me in the house,' I said. 'We can talk this over. I think I can show you –'

She rolled suddenly on the couch again and feet struck the floor. A tight anger came into her voice.

'If you don't get out,' she said, 'I'm going to start yelling my head off. Right now. Now!'

'Okay!' I said quickly. 'I'll stick my card in the door. So you won't forget my name. You might change your mind.'

I got the card out and wedged it into the crack of the screen door. I said: 'Well, good night, Mrs Talley.'

No answer. Her eyes were looking across the room at me, faintly luminous in the dark. I went down off the porch and back along the narrow walk to the street.

Across the way a motor purled gently in the car with the parking lights on. Motors purl gently in thousands of cars on thousands of streets, everywhere.

I got into the Chrysler and started it up.

25

Westmore was a north and south street on the wrong side of town. I drove north. At the next corner I bumped over disused interurban tracks and on into a block of junk yards. Behind wooden fences the decomposing carcases of old automobiles lay in grotesque designs, like a modern battlefield. Piles of rusted parts looked lumpy under the moon. Roof-high piles, with alleys between them.

Headlights glowed in my rear view mirror. They got larger. I stepped on the gas and reached keys out of my pocket and unlocked the glove compartment. I took a ·38 out and laid it on the car seat close to my leg.

Beyond the junk yards there was a brickfield. The tall chimney of the kiln was smokeless, far off over waste land. Piles of dark bricks, a low wooden building with a sign on it, emptiness, no one moving, no light.

The car behind me gained. The low whine of a lightly touched siren growled through the night. The sound loafed over the fringes of a neglected golf course to the east, across the brickyard to the west. I speeded up a bit more, but it wasn't any use. The car behind me came up fast and a huge red spotlight suddenly glared all over the road.

The car came up level and started to cut in. I stood the Chrysler on its nose, swung out behind the police car, and made a U turn with half an inch to spare. I gunned the motor the other way. Behind me sounded the rough clashing of gears, the howl of an infuriated motor, and the red spotlight swept for what seemed miles over the brickyard.

It wasn't any use. They were behind me and coming fast again. I didn't have any idea of getting away. I wanted to get back where there were houses and people to come out and watch and perhaps to remember.

I didn't make it. The police car heaved up alongside again and a hard voice yelled:

'Pull over, or we'll blast a hole in you!'

I pulled over to the kerb and set the brake. I put the gun back in the glove compartment and snapped it shut. The police car jumped on its springs just in front of my left front fender. A fat man slammed out of it roaring.

'Don't you know a police siren when you hear one? Get out of that car!'

I got out of the car and stood beside it in the moonlight. The fat man had a gun in his hand.

'Gimme your licence!' he barked in a voice as hard as the blade of a shovel.

I took it out and held it out. The other cop in the car slid out from under the wheel and came around beside me and took what I was holding out. He put a flash on it and read.

'Name of Marlowe,' he said. 'Hell, the guy's a shamus. Just think of that, Cooney.'

Cooney said: 'Is that all? Guess I won't need this.' He tucked the gun back in his holster and buttoned the leader flap down over it. 'Guess I can handle this with my little flippers,' he said. 'Guess I can at that.'

The other one said: 'Doing fifty-five. Been drinking, I wouldn't wonder.'

'Smell the bastard's breath,' Cooney said.

The other one leaned forward with a polite leer. 'Could I smell the breath, shamus?'

I let him smell the breath.

'Well,' he said judiciously, 'he ain't staggering. I got to admit that.'

''S a cold night for summer. Buy the boy a drink, Officer Dobbs.'

'Now that's a sweet idea,' Dobbs said. He went to the car and got a half-pint bottle out of it. He held it up. It was a third full. 'No really solid drinking here,' he said. He held the bottle out. 'With our compliments, pal.'

'Suppose I don't want a drink,' I said.

'Don't say that,' Cooney whined. 'We might get the idea you wanted feet-prints on your stomach.'

I took the bottle and unscrewed the cap and sniffed. The liquor in the bottle smelled like whisky. Just whisky.

'You can't work the same gag all the time,' I said.

Cooney said: 'Time is eight twenty-seven. Write it down, Officer Dobbs.'

Dobbs went to the car and leaned in to make a note on his report. I held the bottle up and said to Cooney: 'You insist that I drink this?'

'Naw. You could have me jump on your belly instead.'

I tilted the bottle, locked my throat, and filled my mouth with whisky. Cooney lunged forward and sank a fist in my stomach. I sprayed the whisky and bent over choking. I dropped the bottle.

I bent to get it and saw Cooney's fat knee rising at my face. I stepped to one side and straightened and slammed him on the nose with everything I had. His left hand went to his face and his voice howled and his right hand jumped to his gun holster. Dobbs ran at me from the side and his arm swung low. The blackjack hit me behind the left knee, the leg went dead and I sat down hard on the ground, gritting my teeth and spitting whisky.

Cooney took his hand away from his face full of blood.

'Jesus,' he cracked in a thick horrible voice. 'This is blood, my blood.' He let out a wild roar and swung his foot at my face.

I rolled far enough to catch it on my shoulder. It was bad enough taking it there.

Dobbs pushed between us and said: 'We got enough, Charlie. Better not get it all gummed up.'

Cooney stepped backwards three shuffling steps and sat down on the running-board of the police car and held his face. He groped for a handkerchief and used it gently on his nose.

'Just gimme a minute,' he said through the handkerchief. 'Just a minute, pal. Just one little minute.'

Dobbs said, 'Pipe down. We got enough. That's the way it's going to be.' He swung the blackjack slowly beside his leg. Cooney got up off the running-board and staggered forward. Dobbs put a hand against his chest and pushed him gently. Cooney tried to knock the hand out of his way.

'I gotta see blood,' he croaked. 'I gotta see more blood.'

Dobbs said sharply, 'Nothing doing. Pipe down. We got all we wanted.'

Cooney turned and moved heavily away to the other side of the police car. He leaned against it, muttering through his handkerchief. Dobbs said to me:

'Up on the feet, boy friend.'

I got up and rubbed behind my knee. The nerve of the leg was jumping like an angry monkey.

'Get in the car,' Dobbs said. 'Our car.'

I went over and climbed into the police car.

Dobbs said: 'You drive the other heap, Charlie.'

'I'll tear every god-damn fender off 'n it,' Cooney roared.

Dobbs picked the whisky bottle off the ground, threw it over the fence, and slid into the car beside me. He pressed the starter.

'This is going to cost you,' he said. 'You hadn't ought to have socked him.'

I said: 'Just why not?'

'He's a good guy,' Dobbs said. 'A little loud.'

'But not funny,' I said. 'Not at all funny.'

'Don't tell him,' Dobbs said. The police car began to move. 'You'd hurt his feelings.'

Cooney slammed into the Chrysler and started it and clashed the gears as if he was trying to strip them. Dobbs tooled the police car smoothly around and started north again along the brickyard.

'You'll like our new jail,' he said.

'What will the charge be?'

He thought a moment, guiding the car with a gentle hand and watching in the mirror to see that Cooney followed along behind.

'Speeding,' he said. 'Resisting arrest. H.B.D. H.B.D. is police slang for "had been drinking".'

'How about being slammed in the belly, kicked in the shoulder, forced to drink liquor under threat of bodily harm, threatened with a gun and struck with a blackjack while unarmed? Couldn't you make a little something more out of that?'

'Aw, forget it,' he said wearily. 'You think this sort of thing is my idea of a good time?'

'I thought they cleaned this town up,' I said. 'I thought they had it so that a decent man could walk the streets at night without wearing a bullet-proof vest.'

'They cleaned it up some,' he said. 'They wouldn't want it too clean. They might scare away a dirty dollar.'

'Better not talk like that,' I said. 'You'll lose your union card.'

He laughed. 'The hell with them,' he said. 'I'll be in the army in two weeks.'

The incident was over for him. It meant nothing. He took it as a matter of course. He wasn't even bitter about it.

26

The cell block was almost brand-new. The battleship-grey paint on the steel walls and door still had the fresh gloss of newness disfigured in two or three places by squirted tobacco juice. The overhead light was sunk in the ceiling behind a heavy frosted panel. There were two bunks on one side of the cell and a man snored in the top bunk, with a dark-grey blanket wrapped around him. Since he was asleep that early and didn't smell of whisky or gin and had chosen the top berth where he would be out of the way, I judged he was an old lodger.

I sat on the lower bunk. They had tapped me for a gun but they hadn't stripped my pockets. I got out a cigarette and rubbed the hot swelling behind my knee. The pain radiated all the way to the ankle. The whisky I had coughed on my coat front had a rank smell. I held the cloth up and breathed smoke into it. The smoke floated up around the flat square of lighted glass in the ceiling. The jail seemed very quiet. A woman was making a shrill racket somewhere very far off in another part of the jail. My part was as peaceful as a church.

The woman was screaming, wherever she was. The screaming had a thin, sharp, unreal sound, something like the screaming of coyotes in the moonlight, but it didn't have the rising keening note of the coyote. After a while the sound stopped.

I smoked two cigarettes through and dropped the

butts into the small toilet in the corner. The man in the upper berth still snored. All I could see of him was damp greasy hair sticking out over the edge of the blanket. He slept on his stomach. He slept well. He was one of the best.

I sat down on the bunk again. It was made of flat steel slats with a thin hard mattress over them. Two dark-grey blankets were folded on it quite neatly. It was a very nice jail. It was on the twelfth floor of the new city hall. It was a very nice city hall. Bay City was a very nice place. People lived there and thought so. If I lived there, I would probably think so. I would see the nice blue bay and the cliffs and the yacht harbour and the quiet streets of houses, old houses brooding under old trees and new houses with sharp green lawns and wire fences and staked saplings set into the parkway in front of them. I knew a girl who lived on Twenty-fifth Street. It was a nice street. She was a nice girl. She liked Bay City.

She wouldn't think about the Mexican and Negro slums stretched out on the dismal flats south of the old interurban tracks. Nor of the waterfront dives along the flat shore south of the cliffs, the sweaty little dance halls on the pike, the marijuana joints, the narrow fox faces watching over the tops of newspapers in far too quiet hotel lobbies, nor the pickpockets and grifters and con men and drunk rollers and pimps and queans on the board walk.

I went over to stand by the door. There was nobody stirring across the way. The lights in the cell block were bleak and silent. Business in the jail was rotten.

I looked at my watch. Nine fifty-four. Time to go home and get your slippers on and play over a game of chess. Time for a tall cool drink and a long quiet pipe. Time to sit with your feet up and think of nothing. Time to start yawning over your magazine. Time to be a human being, a householder, a man with nothing to do but rest and suck in the night air and rebuild the brain for to-morrow.

A man in the blue-grey jail uniform came along between the cells reading numbers. He stopped in front of mine and unlocked the door and gave me the hard stare they think they have to wear on their pans for ever and for ever and for ever. I'm a cop, brother, I'm tough, watch your step, brother, or we'll fix you up so you'll crawl on your hands and knees, brother, snap out of it, brother, let's get a load of the truth, brother, let's go, and let's not forget we're tough guys, we're cops, and we do what we like with punks like you.

'Out,' he said.

I stepped out of the cell and he relocked the door and jerked his thumb and we went along to a wide steel gate and he unlocked that and we went through and he relocked it and the keys tinkled pleasantly on the big steel ring, and after a while we went through a steel door that was painted like wood on the outside and battleship-grey on the inside.

Degarmo was standing there by the counter talking to the desk sergeant.

He turned his metallic blue eyes on me and said: 'How you doing?'

'Fine.'

'Like our jail?'

'I like your jail fine.'

'Captain Webber wants to talk to you.'

'That's fine,' I said.

'Don't you know any words but fine?'

'Not right now,' I said. 'Not in here.'

'You're limping a little,' he said. 'You trip over something?'

'Yeah,' I said. 'I tripped over a blackjack. It jumped up and bit me behind the left knee.'

'That's too bad,' Degarmo said, blank-eyed. 'Get your stuff from the property clerk.'

'I've got it,' I said. 'It wasn't taken away from me.'

'Well, that's fine,' he said.

'It sure is,' I said. 'It's fine.'

The desk sergeant lifted his shaggy head and gave us both a long stare. 'You ought to see Cooney's little Irish nose,' he said. 'If you want to see something fine. It's spread over his face like syrup on a waffle.'

Degarmo said absently: 'What's the matter? He get in a fight?'

'I wouldn't know,' the desk sergeant said. 'Maybe it was the same blackjack that jumped up and bit him.'

'For a desk sergeant you talk too damn much,' Degarmo said.

'A desk sergeant always talks too god-damn much,' the desk sergeant said. 'Maybe that's why he isn't a lieutenant on homicide.'

'You see how we are here,' Degarmo said. 'Just one great big happy family.'

'With beaming smiles on our faces,' the desk sergeant said, 'and our arms spread wide in welcome, and a rock in each hand.'

Degarmo jerked his head at me and we went out.

27

Captain Webber pushed his sharp bent nose across the desk at me and said: 'Sit down.'

I sat down in a round-backed wooden armchair and eased my left leg away from the sharp edge of the seat. It was a large neat corner office. Degarmo sat at the end of the desk and crossed his legs and rubbed his ankle thoughtfully, and looked out of a window.

Webber went on: 'You asked for trouble, and you got it. You were doing fifty-five miles an hour in a residential zone and you attempted to get away from a police car that signalled you to stop with its siren and red spotlight. You were abusive when stopped and you struck an officer in the face.'

I said nothing. Webber picked a match off his desk and broke it in half and threw the pieces over his shoulder.

'Or are they lying – as usual?' he asked.

'I didn't see their report,' I said. 'I was probably doing fifty-five in a residential district, or anyhow within city limits. The police car was parked outside a house I visited. It followed me when I drove away and I didn't at that time know it was a police car. It had no good reason to follow me and I didn't like the look of it. I went a little fast, but all I was trying to do was get to a better-lighted part of town.'

Degarmo moved his eyes to give a bleak meaningless stare. Webber snapped his teeth impatiently.

He said: 'After you knew it was a police car you made a half-turn in the middle of the block and still tried to get away. Is that right?'

I said: 'Yes. It's going to take a little frank talk to explain that.'

'I'm not afraid of a little frank talk,' Webber said. 'I tend to kind of specialize in frank talk.'

I said: 'These cops that picked me up were parked in front of the house where George Talley's wife lives. They were there before I got there. George Talley is the man who used to be a private detective down here. I wanted to see him. Degarmo knows why I wanted to see him.'

Degarmo picked a match out of his pocket and chewed on the soft end of it quietly. He nodded, without expression. Webber didn't look at him.

I said: 'You are a stupid man, Degarmo. Everything you do is stupid, and done in a stupid way. When you went up against me yesterday in front of Almore's house you had to get tough when there was nothing to get tough about. You had to make me curious when I had nothing to be curious about. You even had to drop hints which showed me how I could satisfy that curiosity, if it became important. All you had to do to protect your friends was to keep your mouth shut until I made a move. I never would have made one, and you would have saved all this.'

Webber said: 'What the devil has all this got to do with your being arrested in the twelve hundred block on Westmore Street?'

'It has to do with the Almore case,' I said. 'George Talley worked on the Almore case – until he was pinched for drunk-driving.'

'Well, I never worked on the Almore case,' Webber snapped. 'I don't know who stuck the first knife into Julius Caesar either. Stick to the point, can't you?'

'I am sticking to the point. Degarmo knows about the Almore case and he doesn't like it talked about. Even your prowl-car boys know about it. Cooney and Dobbs had no reason to follow me unless it was because I visited the wife of a man who had worked on the Almore case. I wasn't doing fifty-five miles an hour when they started to follow me. I tried to get away from them because I had a good idea I might get beaten up for going there. Degarmo had given me that idea.'

Webber looked quickly at Degarmo. Degarmo's hard blue eyes looked across the room at the wall in front of him.

I said: 'And I didn't bust Cooney in the nose until after he had forced me to drink whisky and then hit me in the stomach when I drank it, so that I would spill it down my coat front and smell of it. This can't be the first time you have heard of that trick, captain.'

Webber broke another match. He learned back and looked at his small tight knuckles. He looked again at Degarmo and said: 'If you got made chief of police to-day, you might let me in on it.'

Degarmo said: 'Hell, the shamus just got a couple of playful taps. Kind of kidding. If a guy can't take a joke –'

Webber said: 'You put Cooney and Dobbs over there?'

'Well – yes, I did,' Degarmo said. 'I don't see why we have to put up with these snoopers coming into our town and stirring up a lot of dead leaves just to promote themselves a job and work a couple of old suckers for a big fee. Guys like that need a good sharp lesson.'

'Is that how it looks to you?' Webber asked.

'That's exactly how it looks to me,' Degarmo said.

'I wonder what fellows like you need,' Webber said. 'Right now I think you need a little air. Would you please take it, lieutenant?'

Degarmo opened his mouth slowly. 'You mean you want me to breeze on out?'

Webber leaned forward suddenly and his sharp little chin seemed to cut the air like the forefoot of a cruiser. 'Would you be so kind?'

Degarmo stood up slowly, a dark flush staining his cheekbones. He leaned a hard hand flat on the desk and looked at Webber. There was a little charged silence. He said:

'Okay, captain. But you're playing this wrong.'

Webber didn't answer him. Degarmo walked to the door and out. Webber waited for the door to close before he spoke.

'Is it your line that you can tie this Almore business a year and a half ago to the shooting in Lavery's place today? Or is it just a smoke-screen you're lying down because you know damn well Kingsley's wife shot Lavery?'

I said: 'It was tied to Lavery before he was shot. In a rough sort of way, perhaps only with a granny knot. But enough to make a man think.'

'I've been into this matter a little more thoroughly than you might think,' Webber said coldly. 'Although I never had anything personally to do with the death of Almore's wife and I wasn't chief of detectives at that time. If you didn't even know Almore yesterday morning, you must have heard a lot about him since.'

I told him exactly what I had heard, both from Miss Fromsett and from the Graysons.

'Then it's your theory that Lavery may have black-mailed Dr Almore?' he asked at the end. 'And that that may have something to do with the murder?'

'It's not a theory. It's no more than a possibility. I wouldn't be doing a job if I ignored it. The relations, if any, between Lavery and Almore might have been deep and dangerous or just the merest acquaintance, or not even that. For all I positively know they may never even have spoken to each other. But if there was nothing funny about the Almore case, why get so tough with anybody who shows an interest in it? It could be coincidence that George Talley was hooked for drunk-driving just when he was working on it. It could be coincidence that Almore called a cop because I stared at his house, and that Lavery was shot before I could talk to him a second time. But it's no coincidence that two of your men were watching Talley's home to-night, ready, willing and able to make trouble for me, if I went there.'

'I grant you that,' Webber said. 'And I'm not done with that incident. Do you want to file charges?'

'Life's too short for me to be filing charges of assault against police officers,' I said.

He winced a little. 'Then we'll wash all that out and charge it to experience,' he said. 'And as I understand you were not even booked, you're free to go home any time you want to. And if I were you, I'd leave Captain Webber to deal with the Lavery case and with any remote connexion it might turn out to have with the Almore case.'

I said: 'And with any remote connexion it might

have with a woman named Muriel Chess being found drowned in a mountain lake near Puma Point yesterday?'

He raised his little eyebrows. 'You think that?'

'Only you might not know her as Muriel Chess. Supposing that you knew her at all you might have known her as Mildred Haviland, who used to be Dr Almore's office nurse. Who put Mrs Almore to bed the night she was found dead in the garage, and who, if there was any hanky-panky about that, might know who it was, and be bribed or scared into leaving town shortly thereafter.'

Webber picked up two matches and broke them. His small bleak eyes were fixed on my face. He said nothing.

'And at that point,' I said, 'you run into a real basic coincidence, the only one I'm willing to admit in the whole picture. For this Mildred Haviland met a man named Bill Chess in a Riverside beer parlour and for reasons of her own married him and went to live with him at Little Fawn Lake. And Little Fawn Lake was the property of a man whose wife was intimate with Lavery, who had found Mrs Almore's body. That's what I call a real coincidence. It can't be anything else, but it's basic, fundamental. Everything else flows from it.'

Webber got up from his desk and went over to the water-cooler and drank two paper cups of water. He crushed the cups slowly in his hand and twisted them into a ball and dropped the ball into a brown metal basket under the cooler. He walked to the windows and stood looking out over the bay. This was before the dim-out went into effect, and there were many lights in the yacht harbour.

He came slowly back to the desk and sat down. He

reached up and pinched his nose. He was making up his mind about something.

He said slowly: 'I can't see what the hell sense there is in trying to mix that up with something that happened a year and a half later.'

'Okay,' I said, 'and thanks for giving me so much of your time.' I got up to go.

'Your leg feel pretty bad?' he asked, as I leaned down to rub it.

'Bad enough, but it's getting better.'

'Police business,' he said almost gently, 'is a hell of a problem. It's a good deal like politics. It asks for the highest type of men, and there's nothing in it to attract the highest type of men. So we have to work with what we get – and we get things like this.'

'I know,' I said. 'I've always known that. I'm not bitter about it. Good night, Captain Webber.'

'Wait a minute,' he said. 'Sit down a minute. If we've got to have the Almore case in this, let's drag it out into the open and look at it.'

'It's about time somebody did that,' I said. I sat down again.

28

Webber said quietly: 'I suppose some people think we're just a bunch of crooks down here. I suppose they think a fellow kills his wife and then calls me up on the phone and says: "Hi, Cap, I got a little murder down here cluttering up the front-room. And I've got five hundred iron men that are not working." And then I say: "Fine. Hold everything and I'll be right down with a blanket."'

'Not quite that bad,' I said.

'What did you want to see Talley about when you went to his house to-night?'

'He had some line on Florence Almore's death. Her parents hired him to follow it up, but he never told them what it was.'

'And you thought he would tell you?' Webber asked sarcastically.

'All I could do was try.'

'Or was it just that Degarmo getting tough with you made you feel like getting tough right back at him?'

'There might be a little of that in it too,' I said.

'Talley was a petty blackmailer,' Webber said contemptuously. 'On more than one occasion. Anyway, to get rid of him was good enough. So I'll tell you what it was he had. He had a slipper he had stolen from Florence Almore's foot.'

'A slipper?'

He smiled faintly. 'Just a slipper. It was later found

hidden in his house. It was a green velvet dancing-pump with some little stones set into the heel. It was custom-made, by a man in Hollywood who makes theatrical foot-wear and such. Now ask me what was important about this slipper.'

'What was important about it, captain?'

'She had two pair of them, exactly alike, made on the same order. It seems that is not unusual. In case one of them gets scuffed or some drunken ox tries to walk up a lady's leg.' He paused and smiled thinly. 'It seems that one pair had never been worn.'

'I think I'm beginning to get it,' I said.

He leaned back and tapped the arms of his chair. He waited.

'The walk from the side door of the house to the garage is rough concrete,' I said. 'Fairly rough. Suppose she didn't walk it, but was carried. And suppose whoever carried her put her slippers on – and got one that had not been worn.'

'Yes?'

'And suppose Talley noticed this while Lavery was telephoning to the doctor, who was out on his rounds. So he took the unworn slipper, regarding it as evidence that Florence Almore had been murdered.'

Webber nodded his head. 'It was evidence if he left it where it was, for the police to find it. After he took it, it was just evidence that he was a rat.'

'Was a monoxide test made of her blood?'

He put his hands flat on his desk and looked down at them. 'Yes,' he said. 'And there was monoxide all right. Also the investigating officers were satisfied with appearances. There was no sign of violence. They were satisfied that Dr Almore had not murdered his wife. Perhaps they were wrong. I think the investigation was a little superficial.'

'And who was in charge of it?' I asked.

'I think you know the answer to that.'

'When the police came, didn't they notice that a slipper was missing?'

'When the police came there was no slipper missing. You must remember that Dr Almore was back at his home, in response to Lavery's call, before the police were called. All we know about the missing shoe is from Talley himself. He might have taken the unworn shoe from the house. The side door was unlocked. The maids were asleep. The objection to that is that he wouldn't have been likely to know there was an unworn slipper to take. I wouldn't put it past him to think of it. He's a sharp sneaky little devil. But I can't fix the necessary knowledge on him.'

We sat there and looked at each other, thinking about it.

'Unless,' Webber said slowly, 'we can suppose that this nurse of Almore's was involved with Talley in a scheme to put the bite on Almore. It's possible. There are things in favour of it. There are more things against it. What reasons have you for claiming that the girl drowned up in the mountains was this nurse?'

'Two reasons, neither one conclusive separately, but pretty powerful taken together. A tough guy who looked and acted like Degarmo was up there a few weeks ago showing a photograph of Mildred Haviland that looked something like Muriel Chess. Different hair and eyebrows and so on, but a fair resemblance. Nobody helped him much. He called himself De Soto and said he was a Los Angeles cop. There isn't any Los Angeles cop named De Soto. When Muriel Chess heard about it, she looked scared. If it was Degarmo, that's easily established. The other reason is that a golden anklet with a heart on it was hidden in a box of powdered sugar in the Chess cabin. It was found after her death, after her husband had been arrested. On the back of the heart was engraved: "*Al to Mildred. June 28th. 1938. With all my love.*"'

'It could have been some other Al and some other Mildred,' Webber said.

'You don't really believe that, captain.'

He leaned forward and made a hole in the air with his forefinger. 'What do you want to make of all this exactly?'

'I want to make it that Kingsley's wife didn't shoot Lavery. That his death had something to do with the Almore business. And with Mildred Haviland. And possibly with Dr Almore. I want to make it that Kingsley's wife disappeared because something happened that gave her a bad fright, that she may or may not have guilty knowledge, but that she hasn't murdered anybody. There's five hundred dollars in it for me, if I can determine that. It's legitimate to try.'

He nodded. 'Certainly it is. And I'm the man that would help you, if I could see any grounds for it. We haven't found the woman, but the time has been very short. But I can't help you put something on one of my boys.'

I said: 'I heard you call Degarmo Al. But I was thinking of Almore. His name's Albert.'

Webber looked at his thumb. 'But he was never married to the girl,' he said quietly. 'Degarmo was. I can tell you she led him a pretty dance. A lot of what seems bad in him is the result of it.'

I sat very still. After a moment I said: 'I'm beginning to see things I didn't know existed. What kind of a girl was she?'

'Smart, smooth and no good. She had a way with men. She could make them crawl over her shoes. The big boob would tear your head off right now, if you said anything against her. She divorced him, but that didn't end it for him.'

'Does he know she is dead?'

Webber sat quiet for a long moment before he said: 'Not from anything he has said. But how could he help it, if it's the same girl?'

'He never found her in the mountains – so far as we know.' I stood up and leaned down on the desk. 'Look, captain, you're not kidding me, are you?'

'No. Not one damn bit. Some men are like that and some women can make them like it. If you think Degarmo went up there looking for her because he wanted to hurt her, you're as wet as a bar towel.'

'I never quite thought that,' I said. 'It would be possible, provided Degarmo knew the country up there pretty well. Whoever murdered the girl did.'

'This is all between us,' he said. 'I'd like you to keep it that way.'

I nodded, but I didn't promise him. I said good night again and left. He looked after me as I went down the room. He looked hurt and sad.

The Chrysler was in the police lot at the side of the building with the keys in the ignition and none of the fenders smashed. Cooney hadn't made good on his threat. I drove back to Hollywood and went up to my apartment in the Bristol. It was late, almost midnight.

The green and ivory hallway was empty of all sound except that a telephone bell was ringing in one of the apartments. It rang insistently and got louder as I came near to my door. I unlocked the door. It was my telephone.

I walked across the room in darkness to where the phone stood on the ledge of an oak desk against the side wall. It must have rung at least ten times before I got to it.

I lifted it out of the cradle and answered, and it was Derace Kingsley on the line.

His voice sounded tight and brittle and strained. 'Good Lord, where in hell have you been?' he snapped. 'I've been trying to reach you for hours.'

'All right. I'm here now,' I said. 'What is it?'

'I've heard from her.'

I held the telephone very tight and drew my breath in slowly and let it out slowly. 'Go ahead,' I said.

'I'm not far away. I'll be over there in five or six minutes. Be prepared to move.'

He hung up.

I stood there holding the telephone half-way between my ear and the cradle. Then I put it down very slowly and looked at the hand that had held it. It was half-open and clenched stiff, as if it was still holding the instrument.

29

The discreet midnight tapping sounded on the door and I went over and opened it. Kingsley looked as big as a horse in a creamy Shetland sports coat with a green and yellow scarf around the neck inside the loosely turned-up collar. A dark reddish-brown snapbrim hat was pulled low on his forehead and under its brim his eyes looked like the eyes of a sick animal.

Miss Fromsett was with him. She was wearing slacks and sandals and a dark-green coat and no hat and her hair had a wicked lustre. In her ears hung ear-drops made of a pair of tiny artificial gardenia blooms, hanging one above the other, two on each ear. Gillerlain Regal, the Champagne of Perfumes, came in at the door with her.

I shut the door and indicated the furniture and said: 'A drink will probably help.'

Miss Fromsett sat in an armchair and crossed her legs and looked around for cigarettes. She found one and lit it with a long casual flourish and smiled bleakly at a corner of the ceiling.

Kingsley stood in the middle of the floor trying to bite his chin. I went out to the dinette and mixed three drinks and brought them in and handed them. I went over to the chair by the chess table with mine.

Kingsley said: 'What have you been doing and what's the matter with the leg?'

I said: 'A cop kicked me. A present from the Bay City

police department. It's a regular service they give down there. As to where I've been – in jail for drunk-driving. And from the expression on your face, I think I may be right back there soon.'

'I don't know what you're talking about,' he said shortly. 'I haven't the foggiest idea. This is no time to kid around.'

'All right, don't,' I said. 'What did you hear and where is she?'

He sat down with his drink and flexed the fingers of his right hand and put it inside his coat. It came out with an envelope, a long one.

'You have to take this to her,' he said. 'Five hundred dollars. She wanted more, but this is all I could raise. I cashed a cheque at a night-club. It wasn't easy. She has to get out of town.'

I said: 'Out of what town?'

'Bay City somewhere. I don't know where. She'll meet you at a place called the Peacock Lounge, on Arguello Boulevard, at Eighth Street, or near it.'

I looked at Miss Fromsett. She was still looking at the corner of the ceiling as if she had just come along for the ride.

Kingsley tossed the envelope across and it fell on the chess table. I looked inside it. It was money all right. That much of his story made sense. I let it lie on the small polished table with its inlaid squares of brown and pale gold.

I said: 'What's the matter with her drawing her own money? Any hotel would clear a cheque for her. Most of them would cash one. Has her bank account got lockjaw or something?'

'That's no way to talk,' Kingsley said heavily. 'She's in trouble. I don't know how she knows she's in trouble. Unless a pick-up order has been broadcast. Has it?'

I said I didn't know. I hadn't had much time to listen to police calls. I had been too busy listening to live policemen. Kingsley said: 'Well, she won't risk cashing a cheque now. It was all right before. But not now.' He lifted his eyes slowly and gave me one of the emptiest stares I had ever seen.

'All right, we can't make sense where there isn't any,' I said. 'So she's in Bay City. Did you talk to her?'

'No. Miss Fromsett talked to her. She called the office. It was just after hours but that cop from the beach, Captain Webber, was with me. Miss Fromsett naturally didn't want her to talk at all then. She told her to call back. She wouldn't give any number we could call.'

I looked at Miss Fromsett. She brought her glance down from the ceiling and pointed it at the top of my head. There was nothing in her eyes at all. They were like drawn curtains.

Kingsley went on: 'I didn't want to talk to her. She didn't want to talk to me. I don't want to see her. I guess there's no doubt she shot Lavery. Webber seemed quite sure of it.'

'That doesn't mean anything,' I said. 'What he says and what he thinks don't even have to be on the same map. I don't like her knowing the cops were after her. It's a long time since anybody listened to the police short-wave for amusement. So she called back later. And then?'

'It was almost half-past six,' Kingsley said. 'We had to sit there in the office and wait for her to call. You tell him.' He turned his head to the girl.

Miss Fromsett said: 'I took the call in Mr Kingsley's office. He was sitting right beside me, but he didn't speak. She said to send the money down to the Peacock place and asked who would bring it.'

'Did she sound scared?'

'Not in the least. Completely calm. I might say, icily calm. She had it all worked out. She realized somebody would have to bring the money she might not know. She seemed to know Derry – Mr Kingsley wouldn't bring it.'

'Call him Derry,' I said. 'I'll be able to guess who you mean.'

She smiled faintly. 'She will go into this Peacock Lounge every hour about fifteen minutes past the hour. I – I guess I assumed you would be the one to go. I described you to her. And you're to wear Derry's scarf. I described that. He keeps some clothes at the office and this was among them. It's distinctive enough.'

It was all of that. It was an affair of fat green kidneys laid down on an egg-yolk background. It would be almost as distinctive as if I went in there wheeling a red, white and blue wheelbarrow.

'For a blimp brain she's doing all right,' I said.

'This is no time to fool around,' Kingsley put in sharply.

'You said that before,' I told him. 'You've got a hell of a crust assuming I'll go down there and take a getaway stake to somebody I know the police are looking for.'

He twisted a hand on his knee and his face twisted into a crooked grin.

'I admit it's a bit thick,' he said. 'Well, how about it?'

'It makes accessories after the fact out of all three of us. That might not be too tough for her husband and his confidential secretary to talk out of, but what they would do to me would be nobody's dream of a vacation.'

'I'm going to make it worth your while,' he said. 'And we wouldn't be accessories if she hasn't done anything.'

'I'm willing to suppose it,' I said. 'Otherwise I wouldn't be talking to you. And in addition to that, if I decide she did do any murder, I'm going to turn her over to the police.'

'She won't talk to you,' he said.

I reached for the envelope and put it in my pocket. 'She will, if she wants this.' I looked at my strap watch. 'If I start right away, I might make the one-fifteen deadline. They must know her by heart in that bar after all these hours. That makes it nice too.'

'She's dyed her hair dark brown,' Miss Fromsett said. 'That ought to help a little.'

I said: 'It doesn't help me to think she is just an innocent wayfarer.' I finished my drink and stood up. Kingsley swallowed his at a gulp and stood up and got the scarf off his neck and handed it to me.

'What did you do to get the police on your neck down there?' he asked.

'I was using some information Miss Fromsett very kindly got for me. And that led to my looking for a man named Talley who worked on the Almore case. And that led to the clink. They had the house staked. Talley was the dick the Graysons hired,' I added, looking at the tall dark girl. 'You'll probably be able to explain to him what it's all about. It doesn't matter anyway. I haven't time to go into it now. You two want to wait here?'

Kingsley shook his head. 'We'll go to my place and wait for a call from you.'

Miss Fromsett stood up and yawned. 'No. I'm tired, Derry. I'm going home and going to bed.'

'You'll come with me,' he said sharply. 'You've got to keep me from going nuts.'

'Where do you live, Miss Fromsett?' I asked.

'Bryson Tower on Sunset Place. Apartment 716. Why?' She gave me a speculative look.

'I might want to reach you some time.'

Kingsley's face looked bleakly irritated, but his eyes still were the eyes of a sick animal. I wound his scarf around my neck and went out to the dinette to switch off the light. When I came back they were both standing by the door. Kingsley had his arm around her shoulders. She looked very tired and rather bored.

'Well, I certainly hope –' he started to stay, then took a quick step and put his hand out. 'You're a pretty level guy, Marlowe.'

'Go on, beat it,' I said. 'Go away. Go far away.'

He gave a queer look and they went out.

I waited until I heard the elevator come up and stop, and the doors open and close again, and the elevator start down. Then I went out myself and took the stairs down to the basement garage and got the Chrysler awake again.

30

The Peacock Lounge was a narrow front next to a gift shop in whose window a tray of small crystal animals shimmered in the street light. The Peacock had a glass brick front and soft light glowed out around the stained-glass peacock that was set into the brick. I went in around a Chinese screen and looked along the bar and then sat at the outer edge of a small booth. The light was amber, the leather was Chinese red and the booths had polished plastic tables. In one booth four soldiers were drinking beer moodily, a little glassy in the eyes and obviously bored even with drinking beer. Across from them a party of two girls and two flashy-looking men were making the only noise in the place. I saw nobody that looked like my idea of Crystal Kingsley.

A wizened waiter with evil eyes and a face like a gnawed bone put a napkin with a printed peacock on it down on the table in front of me and gave me a bacardi cocktail. I sipped it and looked at the amber face of the bar clock. It was just past one-fifteen.

One of the men with the two girls got up suddenly and stalked along to the door and went out. The voice of the other man said:

'What did you have to insult the guy for?'

A girl's tinny voice said: 'Insult him? I like that. He propositioned me.'

The man's voice said complainingly: 'Well, you didn't have to insult him, did you?'

One of the soldiers suddenly laughed deep in his chest and then wiped the laugh off his face with a brown hand and drank a little more beer. I rubbed the back of my knee. It was hot and swollen still but the paralysed feeling had gone away.

A tiny, white-faced Mexican boy with enormous black eyes came in with morning papers and scuttled along the booths trying to make a few sales before the barman threw him out. I bought a paper and looked through it to see if there were any interesting murders. There were not.

I folded it and looked up as a slim, brown-haired girl in coal-black slacks and a yellow shirt and a long grey coat came out of somewhere and passed the booth without looking at me. I tried to make up my mind whether her face was familiar or just such a standard type of lean, rather hard, prettiness that I must have seen it ten thousand times. She went out of the street door around the screen. Two minutes later the little Mexican boy came back in, shot a quick look at the barman, and scuttled over to stand in front of me.

'Mister,' he said, his great big eyes shining with mischief. Then he made a beckoning sign and scuttled out again.

I finished my drink and went after him. The girl in the grey coat and yellow shirt and black slacks was standing in front of the gift shop, looking in at the window. Her eyes moved as I went out. I went and stood beside her.

She looked at me again. Her face was white and tired.

Her hair looked darker than dark brown. She looked away and spoke to the window.

'Give me the money, please.' A little mist formed on the plate-glass from her breath.

I said: 'I'd have to know who you are.'

'You know who I am,' she said softly. 'How much did you bring?'

'Five hundred.'

'It's not enough,' she said. 'Not nearly enough. Give it to me quickly. I've been waiting half of eternity for somebody to get here.'

'Where can we talk?'

'We don't have to talk. Just give me the money and go the other way.'

'It's not that simple. I'm doing this at quite a risk. I'm at least going to have the satisfaction of knowing what goes on and where I stand.'

'Damn you,' she said acidly. 'Why couldn't he come himself? I don't want to talk. I want to get away as soon as I can.'

'You didn't want him to come himself. He understood that you didn't even want to talk to him on the phone.'

'That's right,' she said quickly and tossed her head.

'But you've got to talk to me,' I said. 'I'm not as easy as he is. Either to me or to the law. There's no way out of it. I'm a private detective and I have to have some protection too.'

'Well, isn't he charming,' she said. 'Private detective and all.' Her voice held a low sneer.

'He did the best he knew how. It wasn't easy for him to know what to do.'

'What do you want to talk about?'

'You, and what you've been doing and where you've been and what you expect to do. Things like that. Little things, but important.'

She breathed on the glass of the shop window and waited while the mist of her breath disappeared.

'I think it would be much better,' she said in the same cool empty voice, 'for you to give me the money and let me work things out for myself.'

'No.'

She gave me another sharp sideways glance. She shrugged the shoulders of the grey coat impatiently.

'Very well, if it has to be that way. I'm at the Granada, two blocks north on Eighth. Apartment 618. Give me ten minutes. I'd rather go in alone.'

'I have a car.'

'I'd rather go alone.' She turned quickly and walked away.

She walked back to the corner and crossed the boulevard and disappeared along the block under a line of pepper trees. I went and sat in the Chrysler and gave her the ten minutes before I started it.

The Granada was an ugly grey building on a corner. The plate-glass entrance-door was level with the street. I drove around the corner and saw a milky globe with 'Garage' painted on it. The entrance to the garage was down a ramp into the hard rubber-smelling silence of parked cars in rows. A lanky Negro came out of a glassed-in office and looked the Chrysler over.

'How much to leave this here a short time? I'm going upstairs.'

He gave me a shady leer. 'Kinda late, boss. She needs a good dustin' too. Be a dollar.'

'What goes on here?'

'Be a dollar,' he said woodenly.

I got out. He gave me a ticket. I gave him the dollar. Without my asking him he said the elevator was in back of the office, by the men's room.

I rode up to the sixth floor and looked at numbers on doors and listened to stillness and smelled beach air coming in at the ends of corridors. The place seemed decent enough. There would be a few happy ladies in any apartment house. That would explain the lanky Negro's dollar. A great judge of character, that boy.

I came to the door of Apartment 618 and stood outside it a moment and then knocked softly.

31

She still had the grey coat on. She stood back from the door and I went past her into a square room with twin wall beds and a minimum of uninteresting furniture. A small lamp on a window-table made a dim yellowish light. The window behind it was open.

The girl said: 'Sit down and talk then.'

She closed the door and went to sit in a gloomy Boston rocker across the room. I sat down on a thick davenport. There was a dull-green curtain hanging across an open door space at one end of the davenport. That would lead to dressing-room and bathroom. There was a closed door at the other end. That would be the kitchenette. That would be all there was.

The girl crossed her ankles and leaned her head back against the chair and looked at me under long beaded lashes. Her eyebrows were thin and arched and as brown as her hair. It was a quiet, secret face. It didn't look like the face of a woman who would waste a lot of motion.

'I got a rather different idea of you,' I said, 'from Kingsley.'

Her lips twisted a little. She said nothing.

'From Lavery too,' I said. 'It just goes to show that we talk different languages to different people.'

'I haven't time for this sort of talk,' she said. 'What is it you have to know?'

'He hired me to find you. I've been working on it. I supposed you would know that.'

'Yes. His office sweetie told me that over the phone. She told me you would be a man named Marlowe. She told me about the scarf.'

I took the scarf off my neck and folded it up and slipped it into a pocket. I said:

'So I know a little about your movements. Not very much. I know you left your car at the Prescott Hotel in San Bernardino and that you met Lavery there. I know you sent a wire from El Paso. What did you do then?'

'All I want from you is the money he sent. I don't see that my movements are any of your business.'

'I don't have to argue about that,' I said. 'It's a question of whether you want the money.'

'Well, we went to El Paso,' she said, in a tired voice. 'I thought of marrying him then. So I sent that wire. You saw the wire?'

'Yes.'

'Well, I changed my mind. I asked him to go home and leave me. He made a scene.'

'Did he go home and leave you?'

'Yes. Why not?'

'What did you do then?'

'I went to Santa Barbara and stayed there a few days. Over a week, in fact. Then to Pasadena. Same thing. Then to Hollywood. Then I came down here. That's all.'

'You were alone all this time?'

She hesitated a little and then said: 'Yes.'

'Not with Lavery – any part of it?'

'Not after he went home.'

'What was the idea?'

'Idea of what?' Her voice was a little sharp.

'Idea of going these places and not sending any word. Didn't you know he would be very anxious?'

'Oh, you mean my husband,' she said coolly. 'I don't think I worried much about him. He'd think I was in Mexico, wouldn't he? As for the idea of it all – well, I just had to think things out. My life had got to be a hopeless tangle. I had to be somewhere quite alone and try to straighten myself out.'

'Before that,' I said, 'you spent a month at Little Fawn Lake trying to straighten it out and not getting anywhere. Is that it?'

She looked down at her shoes and then up at me and nodded earnestly. The wavy brown hair surged forward along her cheeks. She put her left hand up and pushed it back and then rubbed her temple with one finger.

'I seemed to need a new place,' she said. 'Not necessarily an interesting place. Just a strange place. Without associations. A place where I would be very much alone. Like an hotel.'

'How are you getting on with it?'

'Not very well. But I'm not going back to Derace Kingsley. Does he want me to?'

'I don't know. Why did you come down here to the town where Lavery was?'

She bit a knuckle and looked at me over her hand.

'I wanted to see him again. He's all mixed up in my mind. I'm in love with him and yet – well, I suppose in a way I am. But I don't think I want to marry him. Does that make sense?'

'That part of it makes sense. But staying away from

home in a lot of crummy hotels doesn't. You've lived your own life for years, as I understand it.'

'I had to be alone to – to think things out,' she said a little desperately and bit the knuckle again, hard. 'Won't you please give me the money and go away?'

'Sure. Right away. But wasn't there any other reason for your going away from Little Fawn Lake just then? Anything connected with Muriel Chess, for instance?'

She looked surprised. But anyone can look surprised. 'Good heavens, what would there be? That frozen-faced little drip – what is she to me?'

'I thought you might have had a fight with her – about Bill.'

'Bill? Bill Chess?' She seemed even more surprised. Almost too surprised.

'Bill claims you made a pass at him.'

She put her head back and let out a tinny and unreal laugh. 'Good heavens, that muddy-faced boozer?' Her face sobered suddenly. 'What's happened? Why all the mystery?'

'He might be a muddy-faced boozer,' I said. 'The police think he's a murderer too. Of his wife. She's been found drowned in the lake. After a month.'

She moistened her lips and held her head on one side, staring at me fixedly. There was a quiet little silence. The damp breath of the Pacific slid into the room around us.

'I'm not too surprised,' she said slowly. 'So it came to that in the end. They fought terribly at times. Did you think that had something to do with my leaving?'

I nodded. 'There was a chance of it.'

'It didn't have anything to do with it at all,' she said

seriously, and shook her head back and forth. 'It was just the way I told you. Nothing else.'

'Muriel's dead,' I said. 'Drowned in the lake. You don't get much of a boot out of that, do you?'

'I hardly knew the girl,' she said. 'Really. She kept to herself. After all –'

'I don't suppose you knew she had once worked in Dr Almore's office?'

She looked completely puzzled now. 'I was never in Dr Almore's office,' she said slowly. 'He made a few house calls a long time ago. I – what are you talking about?'

'Muriel Chess was really a girl called Mildred Haviland, who had been Dr Almore's office nurse.'

'That's a queer coincidence,' she said wonderingly. 'I knew Bill met her in Riverside. I didn't know how or under what circumstances or where she came from. Dr Almore's office, eh? It doesn't have to mean anything, does it?'

I said, 'No. I guess it's a genuine coincidence. They do happen. But you see why I had to talk to you. Muriel being found drowned and you having gone away and Muriel being Mildred Haviland who was connected with Dr Almore at one time – as Lavery was also, in a different way. And, of course, Lavery lives across the street from Dr Almore. Did he, Lavery, seem to know Muriel from somewhere else?'

She thought about it, biting her lower lip gently. 'He saw her up there,' she said finally. 'He didn't act as if he had ever seen her before.'

'And he would have,' I said. 'Being the kind of guy he was.'

'I don't think Chris had anything to do with Dr Almore,' she said. 'He knew Dr Almore's wife. I don't think he knew the doctor at all. So he probably wouldn't know Dr Almore's office nurse.'

'Well, I guess there's nothing in all this to help me,' I said. 'But you can see why I had to talk to you. I guess I can give you the money now.'

I got the envelope out and stood up to drop it on her knee. She let it lie there. I sat down again.

'You do this character very well,' I said. 'This confused innocence with an undertone of hardness and bitterness. People have made a bad mistake about you. They have been thinking of you as a reckless little idiot with no brains and no control. They have been very wrong.'

She stared at me, lifting her eyebrows. She said nothing. Then a small smile lifted the corners of her mouth. She reached for the envelope, tapped it on her knee, and laid it aside on the table. She stared at me all the time.

'You did the Fallbrook character very well too,' I said. 'Looking back on it, I think it was a shade overdone. But at the time it had me going all right. That purple hat that would have been all right on blonde hair but looked like hell on straggly brown, that messed-up make-up that looked as if it had been put on in the dark by somebody with a sprained wrist, the jittery screwball manner. All very good. And when you put the gun in my hand like that – I fell like a brick.'

She snickered and put her hands in the deep pockets of her coat. Her heels tapped on the floor.

'But why did you go back at all?' I asked. 'Why take such a risk in broad daylight, in the middle of the morning?'

'So you think I shot Chris Lavery?' she said quietly.

'I don't think it. I know it.'

'Why did I go back? Is that what you want to know?'

'I don't really care,' I said.

She laughed. A sharp cold laugh. 'He had all my money,' she said. 'He had stripped my purse. He had it all, even silver. That's why I went back. There wasn't any risk at all. I know how he lived. It was really safer to go back. To take in the milk and the newspaper, for instance. People lose their heads in these situations. I don't, I didn't see why I should. It's so very much safer not to.'

'I see,' I said. 'Then, of course, you shot him the night before. I ought to have thought of that, not that it matters. He had been shaving. But guys with dark beards and lady friends sometimes shave the last thing at night, don't they?'

'It has been heard of,' she said almost gaily. 'And just what are you going to do about it?'

'You're a cold-blooded little bitch if ever I saw one,' I said. 'Do about it? Turn you over to the police, naturally. It will be a pleasure.'

'I don't think so.' She threw the words out, almost with a lilt. 'You wondered why I gave you the empty gun. Why not? I had another one in my bag. Like this.'

Her right hand came up from her coat pocket and she pointed it at me.

I grinned. It may not have been the heartiest grin in the world, but it was a grin.

'I've never liked this scene,' I said. 'Detective confronts murderer. Murderer produces gun, points same at detective. Murderer tells detective the whole sad story, with the idea of shooting him at the end of it. Thus wasting a lot of valuable time, even if in the end murderer did shoot detective. Only murderer never does. Something always happens to prevent it. The gods don't like this scene either. They always manage to spoil it.'

'But this time,' she said softly and got up and moved towards me softly across the carpet, 'suppose we make it a little different. Suppose I don't tell you anything and nothing happens and I do shoot you?'

'I still wouldn't like the scene,' I said.

'You don't seem to be afraid,' she said, and slowly licked her lips, coming towards me very gently without any sound of footfalls on the carpet.

'I'm not afraid,' I lied. 'It's too late at night, too still, and the window is open and the gun would make too much noise. It's too long a journey down to the street and you're not good with guns. You would probably miss me. You missed Lavery three times.'

'Stand up,' she said.

I stood up.

'I'm going to be too close to miss,' she said. She pushed the gun against my chest. 'Like this. I really can't miss now, can I? Now be very still. Hold your hands up by your shoulders and then don't move at all. If you move at all, the gun will go off.'

I put my hands up beside my shoulders. I looked down at the gun. My tongue felt a little thick, but I could still wave it.

Her probing left hand didn't find a gun on me. It dropped and she bit her lip, staring at me. The gun bored into my chest. 'You'll have to turn around now,' she said, polite as a tailor at a fitting.

'There's something a little off key about everything you do,' I said. 'You're definitely not good with guns. You're much too close to me, and I hate to bring this up – but there's that old business of the safety-catch not being off. You've overlooked that too.'

So she started to do two things at once. To take a long step backwards and to feel with her thumb for the safety-catch, without taking her eyes off my face. Two very simple things, needing only a second to do. But she didn't like my telling her. She didn't like my thought riding over hers. The minute confusion of it jarred her.

She let out a small choked sound and I dropped my right hand and yanked her face hard against my chest. My left hand smashed down on her right wrist, the heel of my hand against the base of her thumb. The gun jerked out of her hand to the floor. Her face writhed against my chest and I think she was trying to scream.

Then she tried to kick me and lost what little balance she had left. Her hands came up to claw at me. I caught her wrist and began to twist it behind her back. She was very strong, but I was very much stronger. So she decided to go limp and let her whole weight sag against the hand that was holding her head. I couldn't hold her up with one hand. She started to go down and I had to bend down with her.

There were vague sounds of our scuffling on the floor by the davenport, and hard breathing, and if a floorboard creaked I didn't hear it. I thought a curtain-ring checked sharply on a rod. I wasn't sure and I had no time to consider the question. A figure loomed up suddenly on my left, just behind, and out of range of clear vision. I knew there was a man there and that he was a big man.

That was all I knew. The scene exploded into fire and darkness. I didn't even remember being slugged. Fire and darkness and just before the darkness a sharp flash of nausea.

32

I smelled of gin. Not just casually, as if I had taken four or five drinks of a winter morning to get out of bed on, but as if the Pacific Ocean was pure gin and I had nose-dived off the boat deck. The gin was in my hair and eyebrows, on my chin and under my chin. It was on my shirt. I smelled like dead toads.

My coat was off and I was lying flat on my back beside the davenport on somebody's carpet and I was looking at a framed picture. The frame was of cheap soft wood varnished and the picture showed part of an enormously high pale-yellow viaduct across which a shiny black locomotive was dragging a Prussian-blue train. Through one lofty arch of the viaduct a wide yellow beach showed and was dotted with sprawled bathers and striped beach umbrellas. Three girls walked close up, with paper parasols, one girl in cerise, one in pale blue, one in green. Beyond the beach a curving bay was bluer than any bay has any right to be. It was drenched with sunshine and flecked and dotted with aching white sails. Beyond the inland curve of the bay three ranges of hills rose in three precisely opposed colours, gold and terra-cotta and lavender.

Across the bottom of the picture was printed in large capitals, SEE THE FRENCH RIVIERA BY THE BLUE TRAIN.

It was a fine time to bring that up.

I reached up wearily and felt the back of my head. It felt pulpy. A shoot of pain from the touch went clear to the soles of my feet. I groaned, and made a grunt out of the groan, from professional pride – what was left of it. I rolled over slowly and carefully and looked at the foot of a pulled-down wall-bed; one twin, the other being still up in the wall. The flourish of design on the painted wood was familiar. The picture had hung over the davenport and I hadn't even looked at it.

When I rolled a square gin bottle rolled off my chest and hit the floor. It was water white, and empty. It didn't seem possible there could be so much gin in just one bottle.

I got my knees under me and stayed on all fours for a while, sniffing like a dog who can't finish his dinner, but hates to leave it. I moved my head around on my neck. It hurt. I moved it around some more and it still hurt, so I climbed up on my feet and discovered I didn't have any shoes on.

The shoes were lying against the baseboard, looking as dissipated as shoes ever looked. I put them on wearily. I was an old man now. I was going down the last long hill. I still had a tooth left though. I felt it with my tongue. It didn't seem to taste of gin.

'It will all come back to you,' I said. 'Some day it will all come back to you. And you won't like it.'

There was the lamp on the table by the open window. There was the fat green davenport. There was the doorway with the green curtain across it. Never sit with your back to a green curtain. It always turns out badly. Something always happens. Who had I said that to? A girl with a gun. A girl with a clear, empty face and dark-brown hair that had been blonde.

I looked around for her. She was still there. She was lying on the pulled-down twin bed.

She was wearing a pair of tan stockings and nothing else. Her hair was tumbled. There were dark bruises on her throat. Her mouth was open and a swollen tongue filled it to overflowing. Her eyes bulged and the whites of them were not white.

Across her naked belly four angry scratches leered crimson red against the whiteness of flesh. Deep angry scratches, gouged out by four bitter finger-nails.

On the davenport there were tumbled clothes, mostly hers. My coat was there also. I disentangled it and put it on. Something crackled under my hand in the tumbled clothes. I drew out a long envelope with money still in it. I put it in my pocket. Marlowe, five hundred dollars. I hoped it was all there. There didn't seem much else to hope for.

I stepped on the balls of my feet softly, as if walking on very thin ice. I bent down to rub behind my knee and wondered which hurt most, my knee, or my head when I bent down to rub the knee.

Heavy feet came along the hallway and there was a hard mutter of voices. The feet stopped. A hard fist knocked on the door.

I stood there leering at the door, with my lips drawn back tight against my teeth. I waited for somebody to open the door and walk in. The knob was tried, but nobody walked in. The knocking began again, stopped, the voices muttered again. The steps went away. I wondered how long it would take to get the manager with a passkey. Not very long.

Not nearly long enough for Marlowe to get home from the French Riviera.

I went to the green curtain and brushed it aside and looked down a short dark hallway into a bathroom. I went in there and put the light on. Two wash rugs on the floor, a bath mat folded over the edge of the tub, a pebbled glass window at the corner of the tub. I shut the bathroom door and stood on the edge of the tub and eased the window up. This was the sixth floor. There was no screen. I put my head out and looked into darkness and a narrow glimpse of a street with trees. I looked sideways and saw that the bathroom window of the next apartment was not more than three feet away. A well-nourished mountain goat could make it without any trouble at all.

The question was whether a battered private detective could make it, and if so, what the harvest would be.

Behind me a rather remote and muffled voice seemed to be chanting the policeman's litany: 'Open it up or we'll kick it in.' I sneered back at the voice. They wouldn't kick it in because kicking in a door is hard on the feet. Policemen are kind to their feet. Their feet are about all they are kind to.

I grabbed a towel off the rack and pulled the two halves of the window down and eased out on the sill. I swung half of me over to the next sill, holding on to the frame of the open window. I could just reach to push the next window down, if it was unlocked. It wasn't unlocked. I got my foot over there and kicked the glass over the catch. It made a noise that ought to have been heard in Reno. I wrapped the towel around my left hand and reached in to turn the catch. Down on the street a car went by, but nobody yelled at me.

I pushed the broken window down and climbed across to the other sill. The towel fell out of my hand and fluttered down into the darkness to a strip of grass far below, between the two wings of the building.

I climbed in at the window of the other bathroom.

33

I climbed down into darkness and groped through darkness to a door and opened it and listened. Filtered moonlight coming through north windows showed a bedroom with twin beds, made up and empty. Not wall beds. This was a larger apartment. I moved past the beds to another door and into a living-room. Both rooms were closed up and smelled musty. I felt my way to a lamp and switched it on. I ran a finger along the wood of a table edge. There was a light film of dust, such as accumulates in the cleanest room when it is left shut up.

The room contained a library dining-table, an armchair radio, a book-rack built like a hod, a big bookcase full of novels with their jackets still on them, a dark wood high-boy with a siphon and a cut-glass bottle of liquor and four striped glasses upside down on an Indian brass tray. Beside this paired photographs in a double silver frame, a youngish middle-aged man and woman, with round healthy faces and cheerful eyes. They looked out at me as if they didn't mind my being there at all.

I sniffed the liquor, which was Scotch, and used some of it. It made my head feel worse but it made the rest of me feel better. I put a light on in the bedroom and poked into closets. One of them had a man's clothes, tailor-made, plenty of them. The tailor's label inside a coat pocket declared the owner's name to be H. G.

Talbot. I went to the bureau and poked around and found a soft blue shirt that looked a little small for me. I carried it into the bathroom and stripped mine off and washed my face and chest and wiped my hair off with a wet towel and put the blue shirt on. I used plenty of Mr Talbot's rather insistent hair tonic on my hair and used his brush and comb to tidy it up. By that time I smelled of gin only remotely, if at all.

The top button of the shirt wouldn't meet its button-hole, so I poked into the bureau again and found a dark-blue crêpe tie and strung it around my neck. I got my coat back on and looked at myself in the mirror. I looked slightly too neat for that hour of the night, even for as careful a man as Mr Talbot's clothes indicated him to be. Too neat and too sober.

I rumpled my hair a little and pulled the tie loose, and went back to the whisky decanter and did what I could about being too sober. I lit one of Mr Talbot's cigarettes and hoped that Mr and Mrs Talbot, wherever they were, were having a much better time than I was. I hoped I would live long enough to come and visit them.

I went to the living-room door, the one giving on the hallway, and opened it and leaned in the opening smoking. I didn't think it was going to work. But I didn't think waiting there for them to follow my trail through the window was going to work any better.

A man coughed a little way down the hall and I poked my head out farther and he was looking at me. He came towards me briskly, a small sharp man in a neatly pressed police uniform. He had reddish hair and red-gold eyes.

I yawned and said languidly: 'What goes on, officer?'

He stared at me thoughtfully. 'Little trouble next door to you. Hear anything?'

'I thought I heard knocking. I just got home a little while ago.'

'Little late,' he said.

'That's a matter of opinion,' I said. 'Trouble next door, eh?'

'A dame,' he said. 'Know her?'

'I think I've seen her.'

'Yeah,' he said. 'You ought to see her now –' He put his hands to his throat and bulged his eyes out and gurgled unpleasantly. 'Like that,' he said. 'You didn't hear nothing, huh?'

'Nothing I noticed – except the knocking.'

'Yeah. What was the name?'

'Talbot.'

'Just a minute, Mr Talbot. Wait there just a minute.'

He went along the hallway and leaned into an open doorway through which light streamed out. 'Oh, Lieutenant,' he said. 'The man next door is on deck.'

A tall man came out of the doorway and stood looking along the hall straight at me. A tall man with rusty hair and very blue, blue eyes. Degarmo. That made it perfect.

'Here's the guy lives next door,' the small neat cop said helpfully. 'His name's Talbot.'

Degarmo looked straight at me, but nothing in his acid blue eyes showed that he had ever seen me before. He came quietly along the hall and put a hard hand against my chest and pushed me back into the room. When he had me half a dozen feet from the door he said over his shoulder:

'Come in here and shut the door, Shorty.'

The small cop came in and shut the door.

'Quite a gag,' Degarmo said lazily. 'Put a gun on him, Shorty.'

Shorty flicked his black belt holster open and had his ·38 in his hand like a flash. He licked his lips.

'Oh boy,' he said softly, whistling a little. 'Oh boy. How'd you know, Lieutenant?'

'Know what?' Degarmo asked, keeping his eyes fixed on mine. 'What were you thinking of doing, pal – going down to get a paper – to find out if she was dead?'

'Oh boy,' Shorty said. 'A sex-killer. He pulled the girl's clothes off and choked her with his hands, Lieutenant. How'd you know?'

Degarmo didn't answer him. He just stood there, rocking a little on his heels, his face empty and granite-hard.

'Yah, he's the killer, sure,' Shorty said suddenly. 'Sniff the air in here, Lieutenant. The place ain't been aired out for days. And look at the dust on those bookshelves. And the clock on the mantel's stopped, Lieutenant. He come in through the – lemme look a minute, can I, Lieutenant?'

He ran out of the room into the bedroom. I heard him fumbling around. Degarmo stood woodenly.

Shorty came back. 'Come in at the bathroom window. There's broken glass in the tub. And something stinks of gin in there something awful. You remember how that apartment smelled of gin when we went in? Here's a shirt, Lieutenant. Smells like it was washed in gin.'

He held the shirt up. It perfumed the air rapidly. Degarmo looked at it vaguely and then stepped forward and yanked my coat open and looked at the shirt I was wearing.

'I know what he done,' Shorty said. 'He stole one of the guy's shirts that lives here. You see what he done, Lieutenant?'

'Yeah.' Degarmo held his hand against my chest and let it fall slowly. They were talking about me as if I was a piece of wood.

'Frisk him, Shorty.'

Shorty ran around me feeling here and there for a gun. 'Nothing on him,' he said.

'Let's get him out the back way,' Degarmo said. 'It's our pinch, if we make it before Webber gets here. That lug Reed couldn't find a moth in a shoe-box.'

'You ain't even detailed on the case,' Shorty said doubtfully. 'Didn't I hear you was suspended or something?'

'What can I lose,' Degarmo asked, 'if I'm suspended?'

'I can lose this here uniform,' Shorty said.

Degarmo looked at him wearily. The small cop blushed and his bright red-gold eyes were anxious.

'Okay, Shorty. Go and tell Reed.'

The small cop licked his lip. 'You say the word, Lieutenant, and I'm with you. I don't have to know you got suspended.'

'We'll take him down ourselves, just the two of us,' Degarmo said.

'Yeah, sure.'

Degarmo put his finger against my chin. 'A sex-killer,' he said quietly. 'Well, I'll be damned.' He smiled at me thinly, moving only the extreme corners of his wide brutal mouth.

34

We went out of the apartment and along the hall the other way from Apartment 618. Light streamed from the still open door. Two men in plain clothes now stood outside it smoking cigarettes inside their cupped hands, as if a wind was blowing. There was a sound of wrangling voices from the apartment.

We went around the bend of the hall and came to the elevator. Degarmo opened the fire door beyond the elevator shaft and we went down echoing concrete steps, floor after floor. At the lobby floor Degarmo stopped and held his hand on the doorknob and listened. He looked back over his shoulder.

'You got a car?' he asked me.

'In the basement garage.'

'That's an idea.'

We went on down the steps and came out into the shadowy basement. The lanky Negro came out of the little office and I gave him my car check. He looked furtively at the police uniform on Shorty. He said nothing. He pointed to the Chrysler.

Degarmo climbed under the wheel of the Chrysler. I got in beside him and Shorty got into the back seat. We went up the ramp and out into the damp cool night air. A big car with twin red spotlights was charging towards us from a couple of blocks away.

Degarmo spat out of the car window and yanked the

Chrysler the other way. 'That will be Webber,' he said. 'Late for the funeral again. We sure skinned his nose on that one, Shorty.'

'I don't like it too well, Lieutenant. I don't, honest.'

'Keep the chin up, kid. You might get back on homicide.'

'I'd rather wear buttons and eat,' Shorty said. The courage was oozing out of him fast.

Degarmo drove the car hard for ten blocks and then slowed a little. Shorty said uneasily:

'I guess you know what you're doing, Lieutenant, but this ain't the way to the Hall.'

'That's right,' Degarmo said. 'It never was, was it?'

He let the car slow down to a crawl and then turned into a residential street of small exact houses squatting behind small exact lawns. He braked the car gently and coasted over to the kerb and stopped about the middle of the block. He threw an arm over the back of the seat and turned his head to look back at Shorty.

'You think this guy killed her, Shorty?'

'I'm listening,' Shorty said in a tight voice.

'Got a flash?'

'No.'

I said: 'There's one in the car pocket on the left side.'

Shorty fumbled around and metal clicked and the white beam of the flashlight came on. Degarmo said:

'Take a look at the back of this guy's head.'

The beam moved and settled. I heard the small man's breathing behind me and felt it on my neck. Something felt for and touched the bump on my head. I grunted. The light went off and the darkness of the street rushed in again.

Shorty said: 'I guess maybe he was sapped, Lieutenant. I don't get it.'

'So was the girl,' Degarmo said. 'It didn't show much but it's there. She was sapped so she could have her clothes pulled off and be clawed up before she was killed. So the scratches would bleed. Then she was throttled. And none of this made any noise. Why would it? And there's no telephone in that apartment. Who reported it, Shorty?'

'How the hell would I know? A guy called up and said a woman had been murdered in 618 Granada Apartments on Eighth. Reed was still looking for a cameraman when you come in. The desk said a guy with a thick voice, likely disguised. Didn't give any name at all.'

'All right then,' Degarmo said. 'If you had murdered the girl, how would you get out of there?'

'I'd walk out,' Shorty said. 'Why not? Hey,' he barked at me suddenly, 'why didn't you?'

I didn't answer him. Degarmo said tonelessly: 'You wouldn't climb out of a bathroom window six floors up and then bust in another bathroom window into a strange apartment where people would likely be sleeping, would you? You wouldn't pretend to be the guy that lived there and you wouldn't throw away a lot of your time by calling the police, would you? Hell, that girl could have laid there for a week. You wouldn't throw away the chance of a start like that, would you, Shorty?'

'I don't guess I would,' Shorty said cautiously. 'I don't guess I would call up at all. But you know these sex fiends do funny things, Lieutenant. They ain't normal like us. And this guy could have had help and the other guy could have knocked him out to put him in the middle.'

'Don't tell me you thought that last bit up all by yourself,' Degarmo grunted. 'So here we sit, and the fellow that knows all the answers is sitting here with us and not saying a word.' He turned his big head and stared at me. 'What were you doing there?'

'I can't remember,' I said. 'The crack on the head seems to have blanked me out.'

'We'll help you to remember,' Degarmo said. 'We'll take you up back in the hills a few miles where you can be quiet and look at the stars and remember. You'll remember all right.'

Shorty said: 'That ain't no way to talk, Lieutenant. Why don't we just go back to the Hall and play this the way it says in the rule book?'

'To hell with the rule book,' Degarmo said. 'I like this guy. I want to have one long sweet talk with him. He just needs a little coaxing, Shorty. He's just bashful.'

'I don't want any part of it,' Shorty said.

'What you want to do, Shorty?'

'I want to go back to the Hall.'

'Nobody's stopping you, kid. You want to walk?'

Shorty was silent for a moment. 'That's right,' he said at last, quietly. 'I want to walk.' He opened the car door and stepped out on to the kerbing. 'And I guess you know I have to report all this, Lieutenant?'

'Right,' Degarmo said. 'Tell Webber I was asking for him. Next time he buys a hamburger, tell him to turn down an empty plate for me.'

'That don't make any sense to me,' the small cop said. He slammed the car door shut. Degarmo let the clutch in and gunned the motor and hit forty in the first block and a half. In the third block he hit fifty. He slowed down at the boulevard and turned east and began to cruise along at a legal speed. A few late cars drifted by both ways, but for the most part the world lay in the cold silence of early morning.

After a little while we passed the city limits and Degarmo spoke. 'Let's hear you talk,' he said quietly. 'Maybe we can work this out.'

The car topped a long rise and dipped down to where the boulevard wound through the park-like grounds of the veterans' hospital. The tall triple electroliers had haloes from the beach fog that had drifted in during the night. I began to talk.

'Kingsley came over to my apartment to-night and said he had heard from his wife over the phone. She wanted some money quick. The idea was I was to take it to her and get her out of whatever trouble she was in. My idea was a little different. She was told how to identify me and I was to be at the Peacock Lounge at Eighth and Arguello at fifteen minutes past the hour. Any hour.'

Degarmo said slowly: 'She had to breeze and that meant she had something to breeze from, such as murder.' He lifted his hands lightly and let them fall on the wheel again.

'I went down there, hours after she had called. I had been told her hair was dyed brown. She passed me going out of the bar, but I didn't know her. I had never seen her in the flesh. All I had seen was what looked like a pretty good snapshot, but could be that and still not a very good likeness. She sent a Mexican kid in to call me out. She wanted the money and no conversation. I wanted her story. Finally she saw she would have to talk a little and told me she was at the Granada. She made me wait ten minutes before I followed her over.'

Degarmo said: 'Time to fix up a plant.'

'There was a plant all right, but I'm not sure she was in on it. She didn't want me to come up there, didn't want to talk. Yet she ought to have known I would insist on some explanation before I gave up the money, so her reluctance could have been just an act, to make me feel that I was controlling the situation. She could act all right. I found that out. Anyhow I went and we talked. Nothing she said made very much sense until we talked about Lavery getting shot. Then she made too much sense too quick. I told her I was going to turn her over to the police.'

Westwood Village, dark except for one all-night service station and a few distant windows in apartment houses, slid away to the north of us.

'So she pulled a gun,' I said. 'I think she meant to use it, but she got too close to me and I got a headlock on her. While we were wrestling around, somebody came out from behind a green curtain and slugged me. When I came out of that the murder was done.'

Degarmo said slowly: 'You get any kind of a look at who slugged you?'

'No. I felt or half-saw he was a man and a big one. And this lying on the davenport, mixed in with clothes.' I reached Kingsley's yellow-and-green scarf out of my pocket and draped it over his knee. 'I saw Kingsley wearing this earlier this evening,' I said.

Degarmo looked down at the scarf. He lifted it under

the dashlight. 'You wouldn't forget that too quick,' he said. 'It steps right up and smacks you in the eye. Kingsley, huh? Well, I'm damned. What happened then?'

'Knocking on the door. Me still woozy in the head, not too bright and a bit panicked. I had been flooded with gin and my shoes and coat stripped off and maybe I looked and smelled a little like somebody who would yank a woman's clothes off and strangle her. So I got out through the bathroom window, cleaned myself up as well as I could, and the rest you know.'

Degarmo said: 'Why didn't you lie dormy in the place you climbed into?'

'What was the use? I guess even a Bay City cop would have found the way I had gone in a little while. If I had any chance at all, it was to walk out before that was discovered. If nobody was there who knew me, I had a fair chance of getting out of the building.'

'I don't think so,' Degarmo said. 'But I can see where you didn't lose much trying. What's your idea of the motivation here?'

'Why did Kingsley kill her – if he did? That's not hard. She had been cheating on him, making him a lot of trouble, endangering his job and now she had killed a man. Also, she had money and Kingsley wanted to marry another woman. He might have been afraid that with money to spend she could beat the rap and be left laughing at him. If she didn't beat the rap, and got sent up, her money would be just as thoroughly beyond his reach. He'd have to divorce her to get rid of her. There's plenty of motive for murder in all that. Also he saw a chance to make me the goat. It wouldn't stick, but it would make confusion and delay. If murderers didn't

241

think they could get away with their murders, very few would be committed.'

Degarmo said: 'All the same it could be somebody else, somebody who isn't in the picture at all. Even if he went down there to see her, it could still be somebody else. Somebody else could have killed Lavery too.'

'If you like it that way.'

He turned his head. 'I don't like it any way at all. But if I crack the case, I'll get by with a reprimand from the police board. If I don't crack it, I'll be thumbing a ride out of town. You said I was dumb. Okay, I'm dumb. Where does Kingsley live? One thing I know is how to make people talk.'

'Nine-six-five Carson Drive, Beverly Hills. About five blocks on you turn north to the foothills. It's on the left side, just below Sunset. I've never been there, but I know how the block numbers run.'

He handed me the green-and-yellow scarf. 'Tuck that back into your pocket until we want to spring it on him.'

35

It was a two-storeyed white house with a dark roof. Bright moonlight lay against its wall like a fresh coat of paint. There were wrought-iron grilles against the lower halves of the front windows. A level lawn swept up to the front door which was set diagonally into the angle of a jutting wall. All the visible windows were dark.

Degarmo got out of the car and walked along the parkway and looked back along the drive to the garage. He moved down the driveway and the corner of the house hid him. I heard the sound of a garage door going up, then the thud as it was lowered again. He reappeared at the corner of the house, shook his head at me, and walked across the grass to the front door. He leaned his thumb on the bell and juggled a cigarette out of his pocket with one hand and put it between his lips.

He turned away from the door to light it and the flare of the match cut deep lines into his face. After a while there was light on the fan over the door. The peephole in the door swung back. I saw Degarmo holding up his shield. Slowly and as if unwillingly the door was opened. He went in.

He was gone four or five minutes. Light went on behind various windows, then off again. Then he came out of the house and while he was walking back to the car the light went off in the fan and the whole house was again as dark as we had found it.

He stood beside the car smoking and looking off down the curve of the street.

'One small car in the garage,' he said. 'The cook says it's hers. No sign of Kingsley. They say they haven't seen him since this morning. I looked in all the rooms. I guess they told the truth. Webber and a print man were there late this afternoon and the dusting-powder is still all over the main bedroom. Webber would be getting prints to check against what we found in Lavery's house. He didn't tell me what he got. Where would he be – Kingsley?'

'Anywhere,' I said. 'On the road, in an hotel, in a Turkish bath getting the kinks out of his nerves. But we'll have to try his girl-friend first. Her name is Fromsett and she lives at the Bryson Tower on Sunset Place. That's away downtown, near Bullock's Wilshire.'

'She does what?' Degarmo asked, getting in under the wheel.

'She holds the fort in his office and holds his hand out of office hours. She's no office cutie, though. She has brains and style.'

'This situation is going to use all she has,' Degarmo said. He drove down to Wilshire and we turned east again.

Twenty-five minutes brought us to the Bryson Tower, a white stucco palace with fretted lanterns in the fore-court and tall date-palms. The entrance was in an L, up marble steps, through a Moorish archway, and over a lobby that was too big and a carpet that was too blue. Blue Ali Baba oil jars were dotted around, big enough to keep tigers in. There was a desk and a night clerk with one of those moustaches that get stuck under your finger-nail.

Degarmo lunged past the desk towards an open

elevator beside which a tired old man sat on a stool waiting for a customer. The clerk snapped at Degarmo's back like a terrier.

'One moment, please. Whom did you wish to see?'

Degarmo spun on his heel and looked at me wonderingly. 'Did he say "whom"?'

'Yeah, but don't hit him,' I said. 'There is such a word.'

Degarmo licked his lips. 'I knew there was,' he said. 'I often wondered where they kept it. Look, buddy,' he said to the clerk, 'we want up seven-sixteen. Any objections?'

'Certainly I have,' the clerk said coldly. 'We don't announce guests at' – he lifted his arm and turned it neatly to look at the narrow oblong watch on the inside of his wrist – 'at twenty-three minutes past four in the morning.'

'That's what I thought,' Degarmo said. 'So I wasn't going to bother you. You get the idea?' He took his shield out of his pocket and held it so that the light glinted on the gold and the blue enamel. 'I'm a police lieutenant.'

The clerk shrugged. 'Very well. I hope there isn't going to be any trouble. I'd better announce you then. What names?'

'Lieutenant Degarmo and Mr Marlowe.'

'Apartment 716. That will be Miss Fromsett. One moment.'

He went behind a glass screen and we heard him talking on the phone after a longish pause. He came back and nodded.

'Miss Fromsett is in. She will receive you.'

'That's certainly a load off my mind,' Degarmo said. 'And don't bother to call your house-peeper and send him up to the scatter. I'm allergic to house-peepers.'

The clerk gave a small cold smile and we got into the elevator.

The seventh floor was cool and quiet. The corridor seemed a mile long. We came at last to a door with 716 on it in gilt numbers in a circle of gilt leaves. There was an ivory button beside the door. Degarmo pushed it and chimes rang inside the door and it was opened.

Miss Fromsett wore a quilted blue robe over her pyjamas. On her feet were small tufted slippers with high heels. Her dark hair was fluffed out engagingly and the cold cream had been wiped from her face and just enough make-up applied.

We went past her into a rather narrow room with several handsome oval mirrors and grey period furniture upholstered in blue damask. It didn't look like apartment-house furniture. She sat down on a slender love seat and leaned back and waited calmly for somebody to say something.

I said: 'This is Lieutenant Degarmo of the Bay City police. We're looking for Kingsley. He's not at his house. We thought you might be able to give us an idea where to find him.'

She spoke to me without looking at me. 'Is it that urgent?'

'Yes. Something has happened.'

'What has happened?'

Degarmo said bluntly: 'We just want to know where Kingsley is, sister. We don't have time to build up a scene.'

The girl looked at him with complete absence of expression. She looked back at me and said:

'I think you had better tell me, Mr Marlowe.'

'I went down there with the money,' I said. 'I met her as arranged. I went to her apartment to talk to her. While there I was slugged by a man who was hidden behind a curtain. I didn't see the man. When I came out of it she had been murdered.'

'Murdered?'

I said: 'Murdered.'

She closed her fine eyes and the corners of her lovely mouth drew in. Then she stood up with a quick shrug and went over to a small, marble-topped table with spindly legs. She took a cigarette out of a small embossed silver box and lit it, staring emptily down at the table. The match in her hand was waved more and more slowly until it stopped, still burning, and she dropped it into a tray. She turned and put her back to the table.

'I suppose I ought to scream or something,' she said. 'I don't seem to have any feeling about it at all.'

Degarmo said: 'We don't feel so interested in your feelings right now. What we want to know is where Kingsley is. You can tell us or not tell us. Either way you can skip the attitudes. Just make your mind up.'

She said to me quietly: 'The lieutenant here is a Bay City officer?'

I nodded. She turned at him slowly, with a lovely contemptuous dignity. 'In that case,' she said, 'he has no more right in my apartment than any other loud-mouthed bum that might try to toss his weight around.'

Degarmo looked at her bleakly. He grinned and walked across the room and stretched his long legs from a deep downy chair. He waved his hand at me.

'Okay, you work on her. I can get all the co-operation I need from the L.A. boys, but by the time I had things explained to them, it would be a week from next Tuesday.'

I said: 'Miss Fromsett, if you know where he is, or where he started to go, please tell us. You can understand that he has to be found.'

She said calmly, 'Why?'

Degarmo put his head back and laughed. 'This babe is good,' he said. 'Maybe she thinks we should keep it a secret from him that his wife has been knocked off.'

'She's better than you think,' I told him. His face sobered and he bit his thumb. He looked her up and down insolently.

She said: 'Is it just because he has to be told?'

I took the yellow-and-green scarf out of my pocket and shook it out loose and held it in front of her.

'This was found in the apartment where she was murdered. I think you have seen it.'

She looked at the scarf and she looked at me, and in neither of the glances was there any meaning. She said: 'You ask for a great deal of confidence, Mr Marlowe. Considering that you haven't been such a very smart detective after all.'

'I ask for it,' I said, 'and I expect to get it. And how smart I've been is something you don't really know anything about.'

'This is cute,' Degarmo put in. 'You two make a nice team. All you need is acrobats to follow you. But right now –'

She cut through his voice as if he didn't exist. 'How was she murdered?'

'She was strangled and stripped naked and scratched up.'

'Derry wouldn't have done anything like that,' she said quietly.

Degarmo made a noise with his lips. 'Nobody ever knows what anybody else will do, sister. A cop knows that much.'

She still didn't look at him. In the same level tone she asked: 'Do you want to know where we went after we left your apartment and whether he brought me home – things like that?'

'Yes.'

'Because if he did, he wouldn't have had time to go down to the beach and kill her? Is that it?'

I said, 'That's a good part of it.'

'He didn't bring me home,' she said slowly. 'I took a taxi on Hollywood Boulevard, not more than five minutes after we left your place. I didn't see him again. I supposed he went home.'

Degarmo said: 'Usually the bim tries to give her boyfriend a bit more alibi than that. But it takes all kinds, don't it?'

Miss Fromsett said to me: 'He wanted to bring me home, but it was a long way out of his way and we were both tired. The reason I was telling you this is because I know it doesn't matter in the least. If I thought it did, I wouldn't tell you.'

'So he did have time,' I said.

She shook her head. 'I don't know. I don't know how much time was needed. I don't know how he could have known where to go. Not from me, not from her through me. She didn't tell me.' Her dark eyes were on mine, searching, probing. 'Is this the kind of confidence you ask for?'

I folded the scarf up and put it back in my pocket. 'We want to know where he is now.'

'I can't tell you because I have no idea.' Her eyes had followed the scarf down to my pocket. They stayed there. 'You say you were slugged. You mean knocked unconscious?'

'Yes. By somebody who was hidden out behind a curtain. We still fall for it. She pulled a gun on me and I was busy trying to take it away from her. There's no doubt she shot Lavery.'

Degarmo stood up suddenly: 'You're making yourself a nice smooth scene, fellow,' he growled. 'But you're not getting anywhere. Let's blow.'

I said: 'Wait a minute. I'm not finished. Suppose he had something on his mind, Miss Fromsett, something that was eating pretty deep into him. That was how he looked tonight. Suppose he knew more about all this than we realized – or than I realized – and knew things were coming to a head. He would want to go somewhere quietly and try to figure out what to do. Don't you think he might?'

I stopped and waited, looking sideways at Degarmo's impatience. After a moment the girl said tonelessly: 'He wouldn't run away or hide, because it wasn't anything he could run away and hide from. But he might want a time to himself to think.'

'In a strange place, in an hotel,' I said, thinking of the story that had been told me in the Granada. 'Or in a much quieter place than that.'

I looked around for the telephone.

'It's in my bedroom,' Miss Fromsett said, knowing at once what I was looking for.

I went down the room and through the door at the end. Degarmo was right behind me. The bedroom was ivory and ashes of roses. There was a big bed with no footboard and a pillow with the rounded hollow of a head. Toilet articles glistened on a built-in dresser with panelled mirrors on the wall above it. An open door showed mulberry bathroom tiles. The phone was on a night table by the bed.

I sat down on the edge of the bed and patted the place where Miss Fromsett's head had been and lifted the phone and dialled long distance. When the operator answered I asked for Constable Jim Patton at Puma Point, person to person, very urgent. I put the phone back in the cradle and lit a cigarette. Degarmo glowered down at me, standing with his legs apart, tough and tireless and ready to be nasty. 'What now?' he grunted.

'Wait and see.'

'Who's running this show?'

'Your asking me shows that. I am – unless you want the Los Angeles police to run it.'

He scratched a match on his thumb-nail and watched it burn and tried to blow it out with a long steady breath that just bent the flame over. He got rid of that match and put another between his teeth and chewed on it. The phone rang in a moment.

'Ready with your Puma Point call.'

Patton's sleepy voice came on the line. 'Yes? This is Patton at Puma Point.'

'This is Marlowe in Los Angeles,' I said. 'Remember me?'

'Sure I remember you, son. I ain't only half awake though.'

'Do me a favour,' I said. 'Although I don't know why you should. Go or send over to Little Fawn Lake and see if Kingsley is there. Don't let him see you. You can spot his car outside the cabin or maybe see lights. And see that he stays put. Call me back as soon as you know. I'm coming up. Can you do that?'

Patton said: 'I got no reason to stop him if he wants to leave.'

'I'll have a Bay City police officer with me who wants to question him about a murder. Not your murder, another one.'

There was a drumming silence along the wire. Patton said: 'You ain't just bein' tricky, are you, son?'

'No. Call me back at Tunbridge 2722.'

'Should likely take me half an hour,' he said.

I hung up. Degarmo was grinning now. 'This babe flash you a signal I couldn't read?'

I stood up off the bed. 'No. I'm just trying to read his mind. He's no cold killer. Whatever fire there was is all burned out of him by now. I thought he might go to the quietest and most remote place he knows – just to get a grip of himself. In a few hours he'll probably turn himself in. It would look better for you if you got to him before he did that.'

'Unless he puts a slug in his head,' Degarmo said coldly. 'Guys like him are very apt to do that.'

'You can't stop him until you find him.'

'That's right.'

We went back into the living-room. Miss Fromsett poked her head out of her kitchenette and said she was making coffee, and did we want any. We had some coffee and sat around looking like people seeing friends off at the railroad station.

The call from Patton came through in about twenty-five minutes. There was light in the Kingsley cabin and a car was parked beside it.

36

We ate some breakfast at Alhambra and I had the tank filled. We drove out Highway 70 and started moving past the trucks into the rolling ranch country. I was driving. Degarmo sat moodily in the corner, his hands deep in his pockets.

I watched the fat straight rows of orange trees spin by like the spokes of a wheel. I listened to the whine of the tyres on the pavement and I felt tired and stale from lack of sleep and too much emotion.

We reached the long slope south of San Dimas that goes up to a ridge and drops down into Pomona. This is the ultimate end of the fog belt, and the beginning of that semi-desert region where the sun is as light and dry as old sherry in the morning, as hot as a blast furnace at noon, and drops like an angry brick at nightfall.

Degarmo stuck a match in the corner of his mouth and said almost sneeringly:

'Webber gave me hell last night. He said he was talking to you and what about.'

I said nothing. He looked at me and looked away again. He waved a hand outwards. 'I wouldn't live in this damn country if they gave it to me. The air's stale before it gets up in the morning.'

'We'll be coming to Ontario in a minute. We'll switch over to Foothill Boulevard and you'll see five miles of the finest grevillea trees in the world.'

'I wouldn't know one from a fireplug,' Degarmo said.

We came to the centre of town and turned north on Euclid, along the splendid parkway. Degarmo sneered at the grevillea trees.

After a while he said: 'That was my girl that drowned in the lake up there. I haven't been right in the head since I heard about it. All I can see is red. If I could get my hands on that guy Chess –'

'You made enough trouble,' I said, 'letting her get away with murdering Almore's wife.'

I stared straight ahead through the windshield. I knew his head moved and his eyes froze on me. I didn't know what his hands were doing. I didn't know what expression was on his face. After a long time his words came. They came through tight teeth and edgeways, and they scraped a little as they came out.

'You a little crazy or something?'

'No,' I said. 'Neither are you. You know as well as anybody could know anything that Florence Almore didn't get up out of bed and walk down to that garage. You know she was carried. You know that was why Talley stole her slipper, the slipper that had never walked on a concrete path. You knew that Almore gave his wife a shot in the arm at Condy's place and that it was just enough and not any too much. He knew his shots in the arm the way you know how to rough up a bum that hasn't any money or any place to sleep. You know that Almore didn't murder his wife with morphine and that if he wanted to murder her, morphine would be the last thing in the world he would use. But you know that somebody else did, and that Almore carried her down to the garage and put here there – technically still alive to breathe in some monoxide, but medically just as dead as though she had stopped breathing. You know all that.'

Degarmo said softly: 'Brother, how did you ever manage to live so long?'

I said: 'By not falling for too many gags and not getting too much afraid of professional hard guys. Only a heel would have done what Almore did, only a heel and a badly scared man who had things on his soul that wouldn't stand daylight. Technically he may even have been guilty of murder. I don't think the point has ever been settled. Certainly he would have a hell of a time proving that she was in such a deep coma that she was beyond any possibility of help. But as a practical matter of who killed her, you know the girl killed her.'

Degarmo laughed. It was a grating unpleasant laugh, not only mirthless, but meaningless.

We reached Foothill Boulevard and turned east again. I thought it was still cool, but Degarmo was sweating. He couldn't take his coat off because of the gun under his arm.

I said: 'The girl, Mildred Haviland, was playing house with Almore and his wife knew it. She had threatened him. I got that from her parents. The girl, Mildred Haviland, knew all about morphine and where to get all of it she needed and how much to use. She was alone in the house with Florence Almore, after she put her to bed. She was in a perfect spot to load a needle with four or five grains and shoot it into an unconscious woman through the same puncture Almore had already made. She would die, perhaps while Almore was still out of the house, and he would come home and find her dead. The problem would be his. He would have to solve it.

Nobody would believe anybody else had doped his wife to death. Nobody that didn't know all the circumstances. But you knew. I'd have to think you much more of a damn fool than I think you are to believe you didn't know. You covered the girl up. You were in love with her still. You scared her out of town, out of danger, out of reach, but you covered up for her. You let the murder ride. She had you that way. Why did you go up to the mountains looking for her?'

'And how did I know where to look?' he said harshly. 'It wouldn't bother you to add an explanation of that, would it?'

'Not at all,' I said. 'She got sick of Bill Chess and his boozing and his tempers and his down-at-heels living. But she had to have money to make a break. She thought she was safe now, that she had something on Almore that was safe to use. So she wrote him for money. He sent you up to talk to her. She didn't tell Almore what her present name was or any details or where or how she was living. A letter addressed to Mildred Haviland at Puma Point would reach her. All she had to do was ask for it. But no letter came and nobody connected her with Mildred Haviland. All you had was an old photo and your usual bad manners, and they didn't get you anywhere with those people.'

Degarmo said gratingly: 'Who told you she tried to get money from Almore?'

'Nobody. I had to think of something to fit what happened. If Lavery or Mrs Kingsley had known who Muriel Chess had been, and had tipped it off, you would have known where to find her and what name she was using. You didn't know those things. Therefore the lead

257

had to come from the only person up there who knew who she was, and that was herself. So I assume she wrote to Almore.'

'Okay,' he said at last. 'Let's forget it. It doesn't make any difference any more now. If I'm in a jam, that's my business. I'd do it again, in the same circumstances.'

'That's all right,' I said. 'I'm not planning to put the bite on anybody myself. Not even on you. I'm telling you this mostly so you won't try to hang any murders on Kingsley that don't belong to him. If there is one that does, let it hang.'

'Is that why you're telling me?' he asked.

'Yeah.'

'I thought maybe it was because you hated my guts,' he said.

'I'm all done with hating you,' I said. 'It's all washed out of me. I hate people hard, but I don't hate them very long.'

We were going through the grape country now, the open sandy grape country along the scarred flanks of the foot-hills. We came in a little while to San Bernardino and I kept on through it without stopping.

37

At Crestline, elevation 5,000 feet, it had not yet started to warm up. We stopped for a beer. When we got back into the car, Degarmo took the gun from his under-arm holster and looked it over. It was a ·38 Smith and Wesson on a ·44 frame, a wicked weapon with a kick like a ·45 and a much greater effective range.

'You won't need that,' I said. 'He's big and strong, but he's not that kind of tough.'

He put the gun back under his arm and grunted. We didn't talk any more now. We had no more to talk about. We rolled around the curves and along the sharp sheer edges walled with white guard rails and in some places with walls of field stone and heavy iron chains. We climbed through the tall oaks and on to the altitudes where the oaks are not so tall and the pines are taller and taller. We came at last to the dam at the end of Puma Lake.

I stopped the car and the sentry threw his piece across his body and stepped up to the window.

'Close all the windows of your car before proceeding across the dam, please.'

I reached back to wind up the rear window on my side. Degarmo held his shield up. 'Forget it, buddy. I'm a police officer,' he said with his usual tact.

The sentry gave him a solid expressionless stare. 'Close all windows, please,' he said in the same tone he had used before.

'Nuts to you,' Degarmo said. 'Nuts to you, soldier boy.'

'It's an order,' the sentry said. His jaw muscles bulged very slightly. His dull greyish eyes stared at Degarmo. 'And I didn't write the order, mister. Up with the windows.'

'Suppose I told you to go jump in the lake,' Degarmo sneered.

The sentry said: 'I might do it. I scare easily.' He patted the breech of his rifle with a leathery hand.

Degarmo turned and closed the windows on his side. We drove across the dam. There was a sentry in the middle and one at the far end. The first one must have flashed them some kind of signal. They looked at us with steady watchful eyes, without friendliness.

I drove on through the piled masses of granite and down through the meadows of coarse grass where cows grazed. The same gaudy slacks and short shorts and peasant handkerchiefs as yesterday, the same light breeze and golden sun and clear blue sky, the same smell of pine needles, the same cool softness of a mountain summer. But yesterday was a hundred years ago, something crystallized in time, like a fly in amber.

I turned off on the road to Little Fawn Lake and wound around the huge rocks and past the little gurgling waterfall. The gate into Kingsley's property was open and Patton's car was standing in the road pointing towards the lake, which was invisible from that point. There was nobody in it. The card sign on the windshield still read, '*Keep Jim Patton Constable. He Is Too Old To Go To Work.*'

Close to it and pointed the other way was a small

battered coupé. Inside the coupé a lion-hunter's hat. I stopped my car behind Patton's and locked it and got out. Andy got out of the coupé and stood staring at us woodenly.

I said: 'This is Lieutenant Degarmo of the Bay City police.'

Andy said: 'Jim's just over the ridge. He's waiting for you. He ain't had any breakfast.'

We walked up the road to the ridge as Andy got back into his coupé. Beyond it the road dropped to the tiny blue lake. Kingsley's cabin across the water seemed to be without life.

'That's the lake,' I said.

Degarmo looked down at it silently. His shoulders moved in a heavy shrug. 'Let's go get the bastard,' was all he said.

We went on and Patton stood up from behind a rock. He was wearing the same old Stetson and khaki pants and shirt buttoned to his thick neck. The star on his left breast still had a bent point. His jaws moved slowly, munching.

'Nice to see you again,' he said, not looking at me, but at Degarmo.

He put his hand out and shook Degarmo's hard paw. 'Last time I seen you, Lieutenant, you was wearing another name. Kind of undercover, I guess you'd call it. I guess I didn't treat you right neither. I apologize. Guess I know who that photo of yours was all the time.'

Degarmo nodded and said nothing.

'Likely if I'd of been on my toes and played the game right, a lot of trouble would have been saved,' Patton said. 'Maybe a life would have been saved. I feel kind of bad about it, but then again I ain't a fellow that feels too bad about anything very long. Suppose we sit down here and you tell me what it is we're supposed to be doing now.'

Degarmo said: 'Kingsley's wife was murdered in Bay City last night. I have to talk to him about it.'

'You mean you suspect him?' Patton asked.

'And how,' Degarmo grunted.

Patton rubbed his neck and looked across the lake. 'He ain't showed outside the cabin at all. Likely he's still asleep. Early this morning I snuck around the cabin. There was a radio goin' then and I heard sounds like a man would make playing with a bottle and a glass. I stayed away from him. Was that right?'

'We'll go over there now,' Degarmo said.

'You got a gun, Lieutenant?'

Degarmo patted under his left arm. Patton looked at me. I shook my head, no gun.

'Kingsley might have one, too,' Patton said. 'I don't hanker after no fast shooting around here, Lieutenant. It wouldn't do me no good to have a gun-fight. We don't have that kind of community up here. You look to me like a fellow who would jack his gun out kind of fast.'

'I've got plenty of swift, if that's what you mean,' Degarmo said: 'But I want this guy talking.'

Patton looked at Degarmo, looked at me, looked back at Degarmo and spat tobacco juice in a long stream to one side.

'I ain't heard enough to even approach him,' he said stubbornly.

So we sat down on the ground and told him the story. He listened silently, not blinking an eye. At the end he said to me: 'You got a funny way of working for people, seems to me. Personally I think you boys are plumb misinformed. We'll go over and see. I'll go in first – in case you would know what you are talking about and Kingsley would have a gun and would be a little desperate. I got a big belly. Makes a nice target.'

We stood up off the ground and started around the lake the long way. When we came to the little pier I said:

'Did they autopsy her yet, sheriff ?'

Patton nodded. 'She drowned all right. They say they're satisfied that's how she died. She wasn't knifed or shot or had her head cracked in or anything. There's marks on the body, but too many to mean anything. And it ain't a very nice body to work with.'

Degarmo looked white and angry.

'I guess I oughtn't to have said that, Lieutenant,' Patton added mildly. 'Kind of tough to take. Seeing you knew the lady pretty well.'

Degarmo said: 'Let's get it over and do what we have to do.'

We went on along the shore of the lake and came to Kingsley's cabin. We went up the heavy steps. Patton went quietly across the porch to the door. He tried the screen. It was not hooked. He opened it and tried the door. That was unlocked also. He held the door shut, with the knob turned in his hand, and Degarmo took hold of the screen and pulled it wide. Patton opened the door and we walked into the room.

Derace Kingsley lay back in a deep chair by the cold fireplace with his eyes closed. There was an empty glass and an almost empty whisky bottle on the table beside him. The room smelled of whisky. A dish near the bottle was choked with cigarette-stubs. Two crushed empty packs lay on top of the stubs.

All the windows in the room were shut. It was already close and hot in there. Kingsley was wearing a sweater and his face was flushed and heavy. He snored and his hands hung lax outside the arms of the chair, the finger-tips touching the floor.

Patton moved to within a few feet of him and stood looking silently down at him for a long moment before he spoke.

'Mr Kingsley,' he said then, in a calm, steady voice, 'we got to talk to you a little.'

38

Kingsley moved with a kind of jerk, and opened his eyes and moved them without moving his head. He looked at Patton, then at Degarmo, lastly at me. His eyes were heavy, but the light sharpened in them. He sat up slowly in the chair and rubbed his hands up and down the sides of his face.

'I was asleep,' he said. 'Fell asleep a couple of hours ago. I was as drunk as a skunk, I guess. Anyway, much drunker than I like to be.' He dropped his hands and let them hang.

Patton said: 'This is Lieutenant Degarmo of the Bay City police. He has to talk to you.'

Kingsley looked briefly at Degarmo and his eyes came around to stare at me. His voice when he spoke again sounded sober and quiet and tired to death.

'So you let them get her?' he said.

I said: 'I would have, but I didn't.'

Kingsley thought about that, looking at Degarmo. Patton had left the front door open. He pulled the brown venetian blinds up at two front windows and pulled the windows up. He sat in a chair near one of them and clasped his hands over his stomach. Degarmo stood glowering down at Kingsley.

'Your wife is dead, Kingsley,' he said brutally. 'If it's any news to you.'

Kingsley stared at him and moistened his lips.

'Takes it easy, don't he?' Degarmo said. 'Show him the scarf.'

I took the green-and-yellow scarf out and dangled it. Degarmo jerked a thumb. 'Yours?'

Kingsley nodded. He moistened his lips again.

'Careless of you to leave it behind you,' Degarmo said. He was breathing a little hard. His nose was pinched and deep lines ran from his nostrils to the corners of his mouth.

Kingsley said very quietly: 'Leave it behind me where?' He had barely glanced at the scarf. He hadn't looked at all at me.

'In the Granada Apartments, on Eighth Street, in Bay City. Apartment 618. Am I telling you something?'

Kingsley now very slowly lifted his eyes to meet mine. 'Is that where she was?' he breathed.

I nodded. 'She didn't want me to go there. I wouldn't give her the money until she talked to me. She admitted she killed Lavery. She pulled a gun and planned to give me the same treatment. Somebody came from behind the curtain and knocked me out without letting me see him. When I came to she was dead.' I told him how she was dead and how she looked. I told him what I had done and what had been done to me.

He listened without moving a muscle of his face. When I had done talking he made a vague gesture towards the scarf. 'What has that got to do with it?'

'The lieutenant regards it as evidence that you were the party hidden out in the apartment.'

Kingsley thought that over. He didn't seem to get the implications of it very quickly. He leaned back in the chair and rested his head against the back. 'Go on,' he said at length. 'I suppose you know what you're talking about. I'm quite sure I don't.'

Degarmo said: 'All right, play dumb. See what it gets you. You could begin by accounting for your time last night after you dropped your biddy at her apartment house.'

Kingsley said evenly: 'If you mean Miss Fromsett, I didn't. She went home in a taxi. I was going home myself, but I didn't. I came up here instead. I thought the trip and the night air and the quiet might help me to get straightened out.'

'Just think of that,' Degarmo jeered. 'Straightened out from what, if I might ask?'

'Straightened out from all the worry I had been having.'

'Hell,' Degarmo said, 'a little thing like strangling your wife and clawing her belly wouldn't worry you that much, would it?'

'Son, you hadn't ought to say things like that,' Patton put in from the background. 'That ain't no way to talk. You ain't produced anything yet that sounds like evidence.'

'No?' Degarmo swung his hard head at him. 'What about this scarf, fatty? Isn't that evidence?'

'You didn't fit it in to anything – not that I heard,' Patton said peacefully. 'And I ain't fat, either, just well covered.'

Degarmo swung away from him disgustedly. He jabbed his finger at Kingsley.

'I suppose you didn't go down to Bay City at all?' he said harshly.

'No. Why should I? Marlowe was taking care of that.

267

And I don't see why you are making a point of the scarf. Marlowe was wearing it.'

Degarmo stood rooted and savage. He turned very slowly and gave me his bleak angry stare.

'I don't get this,' he said. 'Honest, I don't. It wouldn't be that somebody is kidding me, would it? Somebody like you?'

I said: 'All I told about the scarf was that it was in the apartment and that I had seen Kingsley wearing it earlier in the evening. That seemed to be all you wanted. I might have added that I had later worn the scarf myself, so the girl I was to meet could identify me that much easier.'

Degarmo backed away from Kingsley and leaned against the wall at the end of the fireplace. He pulled his lower lip out with thumb and forefinger of his left hand. His right hand hung lax at his side, the fingers slightly curved.

I said: 'I told you all I had ever seen of Mrs Kingsley was a snapshot. One of us had to be sure of being able to identify the other. The scarf seemed obvious enough for identification. As a matter of fact I had seen her once before, although I didn't know it when I went to meet her. But I didn't recognize her at once.' I turned to Kingsley. 'Mrs Fallbrook,' I said.

'I thought you said Mrs Fallbrook was the owner of the house,' he answered slowly.

'That's what she said at the time. That's what I believed at the time. Why wouldn't I?'

Degarmo made a sound in his throat. His eyes were a little crazy. I told him about Mrs Fallbrook and her purple hat and her fluttery manner and the empty gun she had been holding and how she gave it to me.

When I stopped, he said very carefully: 'I didn't hear you tell Webber any of that.'

'I didn't tell him. I didn't want to admit I had already been in the house three hours before. That I had gone to talk it over with Kingsley before I reported it to the police.'

'That's something we're going to love you for,' Degarmo said with a cold grin. 'Jesus, what a sucker I've been. How much you paying this shamus to cover up your murders for you, Kingsley?'

'His usual rates,' Kingsley told him emptily. 'And a five hundred dollar bonus if he can prove my wife didn't murder Lavery.'

'Too bad he can't earn that,' Degarmo sneered.

'Don't be silly,' I said. 'I've already earned it.'

There was a silence in the room. One of those charged silences which seem about to split apart with a peal of thunder. It didn't. It remained, hung heavy and solid, like a wall. Kingsley moved a little in his chair, and after a long moment, he nodded his head.

'Nobody could possibly know that better than you know it, Degarmo,' I said.

Patton had as much expression on his face as a chunk of wood. He watched Degarmo quietly. He didn't look at Kingsley at all. Degarmo looked at a point between my eyes, but not as if that was anything in the room with him. Rather as if he was looking at something very far away, like a mountain across a valley.

After what seemed a very long time, Degarmo said quietly: 'I don't see why. I don't know anything about Kingsley's wife. To the best of my knowledge I never laid eyes on her – until last night.'

He lowered his eyelids a little and watched me broodingly. He knew perfectly well what I was going to say. I said it anyway.

'And you never saw her last night. Because she had already been dead for over a month. Because she had been drowned in Little Fawn Lake. Because the woman you saw dead in the Granada Apartments was Mildred Haviland, and Mildred Haviland was Muriel Chess. And since Mrs Kingsley was dead long before Lavery was shot, it follows that Mrs Kingsley did not shoot him.'

Kingsley clenched his fists on the arms of his chair, but he made no sound, no sound at all.

39

There was another heavy silence. Patton broke it by saying in his careful slow voice: 'That's kind of a wild statement, ain't it? Don't you kind of think Bill Chess would know his own wife?'

I said: 'After a month in the water? With his wife's clothes on her and some of his wife's trinkets? With water-soaked blonde hair like his wife's hair and almost no recognizable face? Why would he even have a doubt about it? She left a note that might be a suicide note. She was gone away. They had quarrelled. Her clothes and car had gone away. During the month she was gone, he had heard nothing from her. He had no idea where she had gone. And then this corpse comes up out of the water with Muriel's clothes on it. A blonde woman about his wife's size. Of course there would be differences and if any substitution had been suspected, they would have been found and checked. But there was no reason to suspect any such thing. Crystal Kingsley was still alive. She had gone off with Lavery. She had left her car in San Bernardino. She had sent a wire to her husband from El Paso. She was all taken care of, so far as Bill Chess was concerned. He had no thoughts about her at all. She didn't enter the picture anywhere for him. Why should she?'

Patton said: 'I ought to of thought of it myself. But if I had, it would be one of those ideas a fellow would throw away almost as quick as he thought of it. It would look too kind of far-fetched.'

'Superficially, yes,' I said. 'But only superficially. Suppose the body had not come up out of the lake for a year, or not at all, unless the lake was dragged for it. Muriel Chess was gone and nobody was going to spend much time looking for her. We might never have heard of her again. Mrs Kingsley was a different proposition. She had money and connexions and an anxious husband. She would be searched for, as she was, eventually. But not very soon, unless something happened to start suspicion. It might have been a matter of months before anything was found out. The lake might have been dragged, but if a search along her trail seemed to indicate that she had actually left the lake and gone down the hill, even as far as San Bernardino, and the train from there east, then the lake might never have been dragged. And even if it was and the body was found, there was rather better than an even chance that the body would not be correctly identified. Bill Chess was arrested for his wife's murder. For all I know he might even have been convicted of it, and that would have been that, as far as the body in the lake was concerned. Crystal Kingsley would still be missing, and it would be an unsolved mystery. Eventually it would be assumed that something had happened to her and that she was no longer alive. But nobody would know where or when or how it had happened. If it hadn't been for Lavery, we might not be here talking about it now. Lavery is the key to the whole thing. He was in the Prescott Hotel in San Bernardino the night Crystal Kingsley was supposed to have left here. He saw a woman there who had Crystal Kingsley's car, who was wearing Crystal Kingsley's clothes, and of course he knew who she was. But he didn't have to know there was anything wrong. He didn't have to know they were Crystal Kingsley's clothes or that the woman had put Crystal Kingsley's car in the hotel garage. All he had to know was that he met Muriel Chess. Muriel took care of the rest.'

I stopped and waited for somebody to say anything. Nobody did. Patton sat immovable in his chair, his plump, hairless hands clasped comfortably across his stomach. Kingsley leaned his head back and he had his eyes half-closed and he was not moving. Degarmo leaned against the wall by the fireplace, taut and white-faced and cold, a big, hard, solemn man whose thoughts were deeply hidden.

I went on talking.

'If Muriel Chess impersonated Crystal Kingsley, she murdered her. That's elementary. All right, let's look at it. We know who she was and what kind of woman she was. She had already murdered before she met and married Bill Chess. She had been Dr Almore's office nurse and his little pal and she had murdered Dr Almore's wife in such a neat way that Almore had to cover up for her. And she had been married to a man in the Bay City police who also was sucker enough to cover up for her. She got the men that way, she could make them jump through hoops. I didn't know her long enough to see why, but her record proves it. What she was able to do with Lavery proves it. Very well, she killed people who got in her way, and Kingsley's wife got in her way too. I hadn't meant to talk about this, but it doesn't matter much now. Crystal Kingsley could make the men do a little jumping through hoops too. She made Bill Chess jump and Bill Chess's wife wasn't the girl to take that and smile. Also, she was sick to death of her life up here – she must have been – and she wanted to get away. But she needed money. She had tried to get it from Almore, and that sent Degarmo up here looking for her. That scared her a little. Degarmo is the sort of fellow you are never quite sure of. She was right not to be sure of him, wasn't she, Degarmo?'

Degarmo moved his foot on the ground. 'The sands are running against you, fellow,' he said grimly. 'Speak your little piece while you can.'

'Mildred didn't positively have to have Crystal Kingsley's car and clothes and credentials and what not, but they helped. What money she had must have helped a great deal, and Kingsley says she liked to have a good deal of money with her. Also she must have had jewellery which could eventually be turned into money. All this made killing her a rational as well as an agreeable thing to do. That disposes of motive, and we come to means and opportunity.

'The opportunity was made to order for her. She had quarrelled with Bill and he had gone off to get drunk. She knew her Bill and how drunk he could get and how long he would stay away. She needed time. Time was of the essence. She had to assume that there was time. Otherwise the whole thing flopped. She had to pack her own clothes and take them in her car to Coon Lake and hide them there, because they had to be gone. She had to walk back. She had to murder Crystal Kingsley and dress her in Muriel's clothes and get her down in the lake. All that took time. As to the murder itself, I imagine she got her drunk or knocked her on the head and drowned her in the bathtub in this cabin. That would be logic and simple too. She was a nurse, she knew how to handle things like bodies. She knew how to swim – we have it from Bill that she was a fine swimmer. And a drowned body will sink. All she had to do was guide it down into the deep water where she wanted it. There is nothing in all this beyond the powers of one woman who could swim. She did it, she dressed in Crystal Kingsley's clothes, packed what else of hers she wanted, got into Crystal Kingsley's car and departed. And at San Bernardino she ran into her first snag – Lavery.

'Lavery knew her as Muriel Chess. We have no evidence and no reason whatever to assume that he knew her as anything else. He had seen her up here and he was probably on his way up here again when he met her. She wouldn't want that. All he would find would be a locked-up cabin, but he might get talking to Bill and it was part of her plan that Bill should not know positively that she had ever left Little Fawn Lake. So that when, and if, the body was found, he would identify it. So she put her hooks into Lavery at once, and that wouldn't be too hard. If there is one thing we know for certain about Lavery, it is that he couldn't keep his hands off the women. The more of them, the better. He would be easy for a smart girl like Mildred Haviland. So she played him and took him away with her. She took him to El Paso and there sent a wire he knew nothing about. Finally she played him back to Bay City. She probably couldn't help that. He wanted to go home and she couldn't let him get too far from her. Because Lavery was dangerous to her. Lavery alone could destroy all the indications that Crystal Kingsley had actually left Little Fawn Lake. When the search for Crystal Kingsley eventually began, it had to come to Lavery, and at that moment Lavery's life wasn't worth a plugged nickel. His first denials might not be believed, as they were not, but when he opened up with the whole story, that would be believed, because it could be checked. So the search began and immediately Lavery was shot dead in his bathroom, the very night after I went down to talk to him. That's about all there is to it, except why she went back to the house the next morning. That's just one of those things that murderers seem to do. She said he had taken her money, but I don't believe it. I think more likely she got to thinking he had some of his own hidden away, or that she had better edit the job with a cool head and make sure it was all in order and pointing the right way; or perhaps it was just what she said, and to take in the paper and the milk. Anything is possible. She went back and I found her there and she put on an act that left me with both feet in my mouth.'

Patton said: 'Who killed her, son? I gather you don't like Kingsley for that little job.'

I looked at Kingsley and said: 'You didn't talk to her on the phone, you said. What about Miss Fromsett? Did she think she was talking to your wife?'

Kingsley shook his head. 'I doubt it. It would be pretty hard to fool her that way. All she said was that she seemed very changed and subdued. I had no suspicion then. I didn't have any until I got up here. When I walked into this cabin last night, I felt there was something wrong. It was too clean and neat and orderly. Crystal didn't leave things that way. There would have been clothes all over the bedroom, cigarette-stubs all over the house, bottles and glasses all over the kitchen. There would have been unwashed dishes and ants and flies. I thought Bill's wife might have cleaned up, and then I remembered that Bill's wife wouldn't have, not on that particular day. She had been too busy quarrelling with Bill and being murdered, or committing suicide, which-ever it was. I thought about all this in a confused sort of way, but I don't claim I actually made anything of it.'

Patton got up from his chair and went out on the porch. He came back wiping his lips with his tan handker-chief. He sat down again, and eased himself over on his left hip, on account of the hip holster on the other side. He looked thoughtfully at Degarmo. Degarmo stood against the wall, hard and rigid, a stone man. His right hand still hung down at his side, with the fingers curled.

Patton said: 'I still ain't heard who killed Muriel. Is that part of the show or is that something that still has to be worked out?'

I said: 'Somebody who thought she needed killing, somebody who had loved her and hated her, somebody who was too much of a cop to let her get away with any more murders, but not enough of a cop to pull her in and let the whole story come out. Somebody like Degarmo.'

40

Degarmo straightened away from the wall and smiled bleakly. His right hand made a hard clean movement and was holding a gun. He held it with a lax wrist, so that it pointed down at the floor in front of him. He spoke to me without looking at me.

'I don't think you have a gun,' he said. 'Patton has a gun but I don't think he can get it out fast enough to do him any good. Maybe you have a little evidence to go with that last guess. Or wouldn't that be important enough for you to bother with?'

'A little evidence,' I said. 'Not very much. But it will grow. Somebody stood behind that green curtain in the Granada for more than half an hour and stood as silently as only a cop on a stake-out knows how to stand. Somebody who had a blackjack. Somebody who knew I had been hit with one without looking at the back of my head. You told Shorty, remember? Somebody who knew the dead girl had been hit with one, too, although it wouldn't have showed and he wouldn't have been likely at that time to have handled the body enough to find out. Somebody who stripped her and raked her body with scratches in the kind of sadistic hate a man like you might feel for a woman who had made a small private hell for him. Somebody who has blood and cuticle under his finger-nails right now, plenty enough for a chemist

278

to work on. I bet you won't let Patton look at the finger-nails of your right hand, Degarmo.'

Degarmo lifted the gun a little and smiled. A wide white smile.

'And just how did I know where to find her?' he asked.

'Almore saw her – coming out of, or going into, Lavery's house. That's what made him so nervous, that's why he called you when he saw me hanging around. As to how exactly you trailed her to the apartment, I don't know. I don't see anything difficult about it. You could have hid out in Almore's house and followed her, or followed Lavery. All that would be routine work for a copper.'

Degarmo nodded and stood silent for a moment, thinking. His face was grim, but his metallic blue eyes held a light that was almost amusement. The room was hot and heavy with a disaster that could no longer be mended. He seemed to feel it less than any of us.

'I want to get out of here,' he said at last. 'Not very far, maybe, but no hick cop is going to put the arm on me. Any objections?'

Patton said quietly: 'Can't be done, son. You know I got to take you. None of this ain't proved, but I can't just let you walk out.'

'You have a nice fat belly, Patton. I'm a good shot. How do you figure to take me?'

'I been trying to figure,' Patton said and rumpled his hair under his pushed-back hat. 'I ain't got very far with it. I don't want no holes in my belly. But I can't let you make a monkey of me in my own territory either.'

'Let him go,' I said. 'He can't get out of these mountains. That's why I brought him up here.'

Patton said soberly: 'Somebody might get hurt taking him. That wouldn't be right. If it's anybody, it's got to be me.'

Degarmo grinned. 'You're a nice boy, Patton,' he said. 'Look, I'll put the gun back under my arm and we'll start from scratch. I'm good enough for that too.'

He tucked the gun under his arm. He stood with his arms hanging, his chin pushed forward a little, watching. Patton chewed softly, with his pale eyes on Degarmo's vivid eyes.

'I'm sitting down,' he complained. 'I ain't as fast as you anyways. I just don't like to look yellow.' He looked at me sadly. 'Why the hell did you have to bring this up here? It ain't any part of my troubles. Now look at the jam I'm in.' He sounded hurt and confused and rather feeble.

Degarmo put his head back a little and laughed. While he was still laughing, his right hand jumped for his gun again.

I didn't see Patton move at all. The room throbbed with the roar of his frontier Colt.

Degarmo's arm shot straight out to one side and the heavy Smith and Wesson was torn out of his hand and thudded against the knotty pine wall behind him. He shook his numbed right hand and looked down at it with wonder in his eyes.

Patton stood up slowly. He walked slowly across the room and kicked the revolver under a chair. He looked at Degarmo sadly. Degarmo was sucking a little blood off his knuckles.

'You give me a break,' Patton said sadly. 'You hadn't ought ever to give a man like me a break. I been a shooter more years than you been alive, son.'

Degarmo nodded to him and straightened his back and started for the door.

'Don't do that,' Patton told him calmly.

Degarmo kept on going. He reached the door and pushed on the screen. He looked back at Patton and his face was very white now.

'I'm going out of here,' he said. 'There's only one way you can stop me. So long, fatty.'

Patton didn't move a muscle.

Degarmo went out through the door. His feet made heavy sounds on the porch and then on the steps. I went to the front window and looked out. Patton still hadn't moved. Degarmo came down off the steps and started across the top of the little dam.

'He's crossing the dam,' I said. 'Has Andy got a gun?'

'I don't figure he'd use one if he had,' Patton said calmly. 'He don't know any reason why he should.'

'Well, I'll be damned,' I said.

Patton sighed. 'He hadn't ought to have given me a break like that,' he said. 'Had me cold. I got to give it back to him. Kind of puny too. Won't do him a lot of good.'

'He's a killer,' I said.

'He ain't that kind of killer,' Patton said. 'You lock your car?'

I nodded. 'Andy's coming down to the other end of the dam,' I said. 'Degarmo has stopped him. He's speaking to him.'

'He'll take Andy's car maybe,' Patton said sadly.

'Well, I'll be damned,' I said again. I looked back at Kingsley. He had his head in his hands and he was staring at the floor. I turned back to the window. Degarmo was out of sight beyond the rise. Andy was half-way across the dam, coming slowly, looking back over his shoulder now and then. The sound of a starting car came distinctly. Andy looked up at the cabin, then turned back and started to run back along the dam.

The sound of the motor died away. When it was quite gone, Patton said: 'Well, I guess we better go back to the office and do some telephoning.'

Kingsley got up suddenly and went out to the kitchen and came back with a bottle of whisky. He poured himself a stiff drink and drank it standing. He waved a hand at it and walked heavily out of the room. I heard bed-springs creak.

Patton and I went quietly out of the cabin.

41

Patton had just finished putting his calls through to block the highways when a call came through from the sergeant in charge of the guard detail at Puma Lake dam. We went out and got into Patton's car and Andy drove very fast along the lake road through the village and along the lake shore back to the big dam at the end. We were waved across the dam to where the sergeant was waiting in a jeep beside the headquarters hut.

The sergeant waved his arm and started the jeep and we followed him a couple of hundred feet along the highway to where a few soldiers stood on the edge of the canyon looking down. Several cars had stopped there and a cluster of people was grouped near the soldiers. The sergeant got out of the jeep and Patton and Andy and I climbed out of the official car and went over by the sergeant.

'Guy didn't stop for the sentry,' the sergeant said, and there was bitterness in his voice. 'Damn near knocked him off the road. The sentry in the middle of the bridge had to jump fast to get missed. The one at this end had enough. He called the guy to halt. Guy kept going.'

The sergeant chewed his gun and looked down into the canyon.

'Orders are to shoot in a case like that,' he said. 'The sentry shot.' He pointed down to the grooves in the shoulder at the edge of the drop. 'This is where he went off.'

A hundred feet down in the canyon a small coupé was smashed against the side of a huge granite boulder. It was almost upside down, leaning a little. There were three men down there. They had moved the car enough to lift something out.

Something that had been a man.

RAYMOND CHANDLER

THE BIG SLEEP

'Neither of the two people in the room paid any attention to the way I came in, although only one of them was dead.'

Los Angeles PI Philip Marlowe is working for the Sternwood family. Old man Sternwood, crippled and wheelchair-bound, is being given the squeeze by a blackmailer and he wants Marlowe to make the problem go away. But with Sternwood's two wild, devil-may-care daughters prowling LA's seedy backstreets, Marlowe's got his work cut out – and that's before he stumbles over the first corpse …

RAYMOND CHANDLER

FAREWELL, MY LOVELY

'Cute little redhead,' she said slowly and thickly. 'Yeah, I remember her. Song and dance. Nice legs and generous with 'em.'

Eight years ago Moose Malloy and cute little redhead Velma were getting married – until someone framed Malloy for armed robbery. Now his stretch is up and he wants Velma back. PI Philip Marlowe meets Malloy one hot day in Hollywood and, out of the generosity of his jaded heart, agrees to help him. Dragged from one smoky bar to another, Marlowe's search for Velma turns up plenty of dangerous gangsters with a nasty habit of shooting first and talking later. And soon what started as a search for a missing person becomes a matter of life and death …

RAYMOND CHANDLER

THE HIGH WINDOW

'He lay crumpled on his back. Very lonely, very dead. The safe door was wide open. A metal drawer was pulled out. It was empty now. There may have been money in it once.'

Philip Marlowe's on a case: his client, a dried-up husk of a woman, wants him to recover a rare gold coin called a Brasher Doubloon, missing from her late husband's collection. That's the simple part. It becomes more complicated when Marlowe finds that everyone who handles the coin suffers a run of very bad luck: they always end up dead. That's also unlucky for a private investigator, because leaving a trail of corpses around LA gets cops' noses out of joint. If Marlowe doesn't wrap this one up fast, he's going to end up in jail – or worse, in a box in the ground …

RAYMOND CHANDLER

THE LITTLE SISTER

'If you hire me,' I said, 'I'm the guy you hire. Me. Just as I am. If you think you're going to find any lay readers in this business, you're crazy. So you need help. What's your name and trouble?'

Her name is Orfamay Quest and she's come all the way from Manhattan, Kansas, to find her missing brother Orrin. Or least ways that's what she tells PI Philip Marlowe, offering him a measly twenty bucks for the privilege. But Marlowe's feeling charitable – though it's not long before he wishes he wasn't so sweet. You see, Orrin's trail leads Marlowe to luscious movie starlets, uppity gangsters, suspicious cops and corpses with ice picks jammed in their necks. When trouble comes calling, sometimes it's best to pretend to be out …

RAYMOND CHANDLER

THE LONG GOOD-BYE

'Alcohol is like love,' he said. 'The first kiss is magic, the second is intimate, the third is routine. After that you just take the girl's clothes off.'

Down-and-out drunk Terry Lennox has a problem: his millionaire wife is dead and he needs to get out of LA fast. So he turns to his only friend in the world: Philip Marlowe, Private Investigator. He's willing to help a man down on his luck, but later, Lennox commits suicide in Mexico and things start to turn nasty. Marlowe finds himself drawn into a sordid crowd of adulterers and alcoholics in LA's Idle Valley, where the rich are suffering one big suntanned hangover. Marlowe is sure Lennox didn't kill his wife, but how many more stiffs will turn up before he gets to the truth?